Mystery
at
Hideaway
House

BOOKS BY CLARE CHASE

EVE MALLOW MYSTERY SERIES
Mystery on Hidden Lane
Mystery at Apple Tree Cottage
Mystery at Seagrave Hall
Mystery at the Old Mill
Mystery at the Abbey Hotel
Mystery at the Church
Mystery at Magpie Lodge
Mystery at Lovelace Manor
Mystery at Southwood School
Mystery at Farfield Castle
Mystery at Saltwater Cottages
Mystery on Meadowsweet Grove
Mystery at Lockley Grange

BELLA WINTER MYSTERY SERIES
The Antique Store Detective
The Antique Store Detective and the May Day Murder
The Antique Store Detective and the Deadly Inheritance

TARA THORPE MYSTERY SERIES
Murder on the Marshes
Death on the River
Death Comes to Call

Murder in the Fens

Mystery at Hideaway House

CLARE CHASE

bookouture

Published by Bookouture in 2025

An imprint of Storyfire Ltd.
Carmelite House
50 Victoria Embankment
London EC4Y 0DZ

www.bookouture.com

The authorised representative in the EEA is Hachette Ireland
8 Castlecourt Centre
Dublin 15 D15 XTP3
Ireland
(email: info@hbgi.ie)

ISBN: 978-1-83618-336-5
eBook ISBN: 978-1-83618-335-8

For the marvellous mum gang!

PROLOGUE

Duncan Blake stumbled along in the dark, cursing the tree root he'd just tripped over. He kicked out in frustration, the blood pounding in his head. This very moment, the masked figure was probably attacking another of his properties, but which? One of the three buildings he owned, or the cottage he rented? They were spread across the Kesham grounds. He couldn't watch all four.

He paused and stood motionless, fists clenched, steadying his breathing. He'd been working on the lodge that night and still had his tool belt on. His hammer felt weighty in its holster. The thought of swinging it at the unknown vandal filled his head – the sweet, temporary satisfaction it would bring.

The dark wood, thick with trees, pressed in close. The entire area was silent, giving no hint of which way to turn. Perhaps the vandal had taken a night off, but Duncan doubted it. After the eggs thrown at his home, they seemed to be upping their game. It was down to him to take action, of course. Calling the police was out of the question after the lines he'd crossed; who knew what the vandal might reveal if they were caught?

As he reached the clearing by Kesham Hall, his anger

pivoted to anxiety. What if the vandal turned their attention to his family? He'd left them alone.

He paused again as an owl hooted. Hadn't there been another sound? A twig cracking?

Isolated in the clearing, Duncan stared into the trees. The noise had come from the direction of his house. Fear gripped him. Angela and Cesca were sleeping there, protected only by a rotten front door and windows which rattled in their frames. Anyone could force their way in.

He strode across the clearing, so distracted that it was a moment before he sensed movement behind him.

Whisking round, he sighed in relief. It wasn't the balaclava-clad vandal. There was a different confrontation in store but no matter. If word had got out, he knew how to stay in control.

It took less than two minutes to realise his mistake. He'd been too confident, too unguarded. Suddenly, his belt was lighter, the hammer gone, but he wasn't the one who'd drawn it.

He barely registered what was happening before the blow came. His hands were raised in a useless form of defence, and he crumpled to the ground, knowing it was all over. To think that it should come to this...

1

ONE DAY EARLIER

It was a warm Friday afternoon in July, and Eve Mallow was striding through the historic Kesham estate with her dachshund Gus and best friend Viv Montague. They were there for what Viv insisted on referring to as 'Operation Angela'.

'Please don't call it that.' Eve felt hot and anxious, her patience wearing thin, thanks to nerves and the heavy luggage. 'I feel like a fraud.'

'Nonsense!' Viv's hair, marigold orange this season, gleamed in the sun. She was loaded up too, carrying a bag of provisions for Eve and her husband Robin's two-night stay on the estate. 'You're doing the right thing, going undercover.'

'You make me sound like a spy.' Eve felt faintly sick, misgivings making her stomach tense. She was visiting Kesham as a journalist, to review the building Angela's husband had just restored, ready to market as a holiday let. Duncan would be hoping for excellent publicity. He'd spent well over a year (and a small fortune, Eve imagined) renovating Hideaway House, an eighteenth-century folly, and needed the rental income to fund a second project on the estate. She'd warned him she'd be honest, but she could tell he hadn't taken her seriously.

Managing expectations wasn't so much of a problem when she stuck to her speciality, obituaries, where the subjects couldn't answer back.

Yet it was Eve who'd suggested the whole thing. All so she could address her and Viv's concerns over Angela.

'You worry too much.' Viv dropped the bottle of lemonade she'd balanced on top of the supplies and it landed near Gus's tail, making him jump. As she leaned forward to retrieve it, a tin of scones and several more items joined the avalanche.

Eve took a deep breath, dumped the overnight bag and the dog bed she was carrying on the ground and crouched to help pick everything up.

Once they were back to walking, Eve spoke again. 'Now that I've offered to write the article, I'm duty-bound to take it seriously.' She'd got a national glossy she often wrote for, *Icon*, interested, thanks to Duncan's reputation. After a stint as chief executive of the Built Heritage Trust, he'd made the switch to TV and presented many seasons of shows on restoration. It was embarrassing to admit, but his good looks, charisma and passion had had Eve hooked. 'I'll make the piece part-review, part human-interest and culture. If I love Hideaway House, it'll shine through and he'll get his good publicity. But only if.'

'It's a bit of a pain that the car park's so far from the house,' Viv said.

Eve cast her a sidelong glance. 'I might suggest Duncan provides a wheelbarrow.' All the same, the journey was beautiful. They were walking along a grassy path, between patches of foxgloves and enchanter's nightshade, the flickering wing beats of butterflies catching the sun. To either side of them, there was dense, dark woodland.

'Anyway, never mind about the article,' Viv said. 'You will follow through on Operation Angela, won't you?'

Eve counted to ten and nodded. 'Of course.' They'd been

through all this. She wasn't running the gauntlet of the review for nothing.

Besides, Eve felt a responsibility for Angela, who'd been working at Viv's teashop, Monty's, for the last few months. Eve worked there part-time too, with special responsibility for chaos avoidance. The regular pay was a godsend, and she'd loved whipping the business into shape.

Angela liked her privacy, which was relatable, but in her case it was extreme. She never talked about herself. She'd earned Eve and Viv's admiration through the qualities she'd displayed at the teashop. There was her patience. (Angela was able to cope with Gwen Harris's complaints without rushing to the kitchen to scream. Eve shared this rare talent, so she felt they were kindred spirits.) She was quick and resourceful too. (When Molly Walker's son managed to break a window, showering his mother in glass, she'd cordoned off the area in an instant, rescuing Molly and keeping her son at bay. No mean feat.) And she was loyal as well. (Viv had overheard her 'singing Monty's praises when a holidaymaker suggested visiting a *different* café, of all things.') So they'd got to feel fond of Angela, despite the lack of casual chat.

What Eve knew of her personal life, she'd discovered on the grapevine, and it led her to wonder if Angela ever slept. She and Duncan had a small child, and on top of Monty's, Angela was working early shifts as a cleaner, as well as on the Kesham projects, thanks to her profession as a stonemason.

Eve and Viv suspected Duncan had brought her to Suffolk as a labourer – mainly in cafés, offices and shops – to support his passion. *He* didn't seem to be compromising by taking on casual work. The fact that Angela never spoke of life's challenges worried Eve. Unless she was superhuman, she must be bottling things up.

This had been borne out when Eve accidentally overheard Angela on a call.

The words came back to her. 'Things have gone so terribly wrong. I feel utterly desperate. I'd resort to anything to have things back the way they were. *Anything.* Sometimes I dream the most terrible things...'

She'd been sobbing, her voice frighteningly intense. Eve had been wondering uneasily about offering a listening ear ever since. If Angela was going to finally lose control, it might happen in a spectacular way. The trouble was, Eve didn't officially *know* anything was wrong. She could hardly confess to listening in. When she'd confided in Viv, Viv had threatened to march straight over to Kesham and 'have it out' with Duncan. It had taken all Eve's powers of persuasion to stop her. They couldn't be sure he was the problem; more subtlety was needed. And that was how Eve had got herself into this messy situation. Duncan, Angela and their daughter Cesca were living on the estate. Now that Eve was on site too, she hoped to 'accidentally' witness whatever was making Angela desperate. It would give her carte blanche to bring it up and offer help.

At last, Eve, Viv and Gus arrived in the clearing that was home to Hideaway House, the old folly where she would spend the next two nights.

Viv seemed overtaken by the moment, her eyes wide. 'Wow! I wish I could stay here! It's like something out of a fairy tale.'

As Eve put down her luggage and stretched her aching arms, she agreed. The house was like a miniature castle: square and apparently single storey (unless you counted the roof garden) with small towers at each of its four corners. It was bathed in sunlight, giving its beautiful brickwork a rosy glow.

Viv bounded up the steps to the front door, provisions still in her arms, though it was Eve who had the key. Meanwhile, Gus investigated the building's boundaries, then turned to look out through the iron railings that surrounded it. Hideaway House was raised on a mound, and Gus looked like the king of the castle.

Eve crossed the grassy clearing. 'If you want to get inside, you're going to have to let me unlock the door.'

Viv stepped back a fraction and Eve did the honours before grabbing the luggage again.

'Double wow.' Viv ran in like a small child entering a new Wendy house, with Gus on her heels, infected by her excitement. Eve felt depressingly mature, trailing in after them, but she'd got the heaviest load to carry.

On first sight, it was perfect, and unlike anything Eve had seen before. The interior was one grand room, with tall arched windows in three of the four walls, reaching almost to the ceiling. Only one of the towers contained a staircase. Now she was indoors, Eve could see two were decorative, curved outside, but flat within. A four-poster bed was set against one and a fireplace was built into the second.

Viv was flitting around the room, examining every detail, and narrowly missed Gus, who was doing the same.

Eve wished Robin was there to appreciate the chaotic energy. He was due to join her as soon as he'd finished work.

Gus was sniffing at a cupboard set into the fourth tower and Eve went to investigate. She found it contained the most charming miniature kitchen, the recessed lights making the oak worktop glow. The cupboard doors held extra shelves housing beautiful glassware and china.

Viv put her hands on Eve's shoulders, making her jump. 'I love it, but it must have cost a fortune. No wonder Angela's working herself into the ground.'

Eve grimaced. 'They probably need her income just to cover living costs.' Because despite Duncan's successful career, he wasn't rich. In a fit of curiosity after pondering Angela's long hours, she'd done some digging and everything had become clear.

Before Duncan came to Kesham, he'd bought a Grade II-listed manor house to restore – very similar in style and period to Kesham Hall – only to uncover multiple problems. The costs had spiralled, and then there'd been a fire... The authorities had required Duncan to rebuild the place, using all the right materials, but whispers online said the substandard insurance he'd skimped on only covered a basic repair. He of all people should have known better. Eve guessed he'd trashed the family finances and Angela was paying for it.

She cast her gaze over the wonderful workmanship in Hideaway House. 'Maybe Duncan got a grant. Or a loan.' Viv was right – this place must have eaten money. It had been almost derelict when he'd bought it.

Eve strode to the remaining tower, Viv and Gus hard on her heels. The stairs went down, as well as up to the roof garden. So, the place wasn't single storey after all. She descended the spiral staircase with its whitewashed brick walls. At the bottom, she found the bathroom. The clawfoot bath and paintings gave it an envy-sparking, luxurious feel.

Viv was already back climbing the staircase, and Eve rushed to catch up. She, Viv and Gus ploughed on, past the ground floor and up to the roof.

'You lucky, lucky things! This place is a dream.' Emerging into the open air, Viv rushed to the tower opposite. At that level, it had been hollowed out to form a small room, open to the elements via a large archway, but with a roof to provide shade or shelter, as required. 'You'll be able to sit up here with tea, scones and a book.'

Things were certainly looking rosy as far as the review went, and that should help Angela as well as Duncan, once the rental money started flowing.

There was a decent-sized balustrade between the towers, and Eve's shoulders relaxed. She wouldn't have to worry about Gus falling. Robin would love it, she was sure, and he deserved a break. He was a gardener now, but he'd once been a detective and still did some freelance projects for his old force. It put him in his element, but the responsibility took its toll.

She wandered around the roof. Four paths radiated from Hideaway House through the woods. Beyond the end of one, in the distance, she could see the mellow red brick of Kesham Hall. In other directions, she saw open countryside, but there were more buildings out there somewhere, including Duncan's second restoration project. Now Eve had seen Hideaway House she could understand what drove him. But to what lengths was he going to to achieve his dreams? If his business couldn't function without exploiting Angela, he shouldn't be running it.

'Target acquired.' Viv interrupted her thoughts, stepping back from the balustrade, and pointing to one of the paths.

Eve crept forward and saw it was Duncan Blake himself, walking hand-in-hand with Angela, her beautiful red hair flowing over her shoulders. Holding Angela's other hand was a little girl of around four who was darker, with rosy cheeks and curls. Cesca. Eve hadn't heard about her from Angela, but from Moira, the village storekeeper.

Duncan looked blissfully happy. His face was open and youthful, though he was in his forties now, around ten years older than Angela. Angela was smiling too, but there was something heartbreakingly wistful in her eyes.

Cesca had just skipped round to show Duncan a daisy when Eve waved to them. Interacting could only help uncover Angela's troubles. Duncan waved back and grinned, his tan contrasting his white vest.

'It goes to show that good muscles don't equal good character,' Viv said, just the wrong side of a stage whisper.

'We don't know the background yet.' Eve was already heading for the staircase and praying Duncan hadn't heard. He'd messed up over the restoration of the mansion, but Eve doubted that had caused Angela's current misery. On the phone, she'd said: 'Things have gone so terribly wrong,' not

'Things went wrong.' Eve had a feeling her desperation had been triggered by something fresh.

On the ground floor, she opened the door to let the Blakes in. Duncan introduced Cesca, who buried her face in her mum's skirt.

Time to take the pressure off. Eve offered them tea and started to ask questions about Hideaway House.

As the kettle boiled, she saw Cesca peer at Gus, who was an excellent oiler of social wheels.

When Eve asked about Angela's work as a stonemason, it felt weird. It was so extraordinary that she'd never mentioned it, despite the shared hours at Monty's.

Angela blushed, and it was Duncan who answered. 'She's one of the most accomplished craftspeople I've known. Just look at the architraves around the doors and windows,' he pointed this way and that, 'and the corbels outside, holding up the canopy above the door.' He held Angela close. It was good to see the pride in his eyes, but lavish praise was easily given. It could be used to cajole and placate. Unless it was backed by support and a fair deal it counted for nothing in Eve's book.

Gus was getting wildly excited, thanks to the attentions of an increasingly confident Cesca. Angela looked at her watch. 'I should get her home and sort out her tea.' She squeezed Duncan's arm. 'You stay here and explain everything.'

However he treated her, Eve was convinced she still loved him. She seemed keen to go, though. Perhaps Eve had been looking at her too intently.

Duncan kissed Angela and hugged his daughter, then Eve and Gus went to see them off. Eve had just given Cesca a last wave and turned back towards the house, when she spotted a small wooden box, lying to the left of the stone steps that led to the front door. Eve and Viv had approached from the other side when they'd arrived; it could have been there all along.

She crouched to open it, gently nudging Gus out of the way with a fond pat.

Inside was a dog-eared Stephen King novel, a notebook with what looked like diary entries, the name 'Tod' scrawled inside the cover, and a navy-blue beanie.

It was only when Eve picked up the last item that she saw the typed note underneath.

Hideaway House has history. If you stay here, you have blood on your hands.

2

Eve paused, crouched next to the doorway, feeling winded. What did it mean? Whose blood? This person called Tod, who'd presumably owned the contents of the box? A former Hideaway House resident, Eve guessed. The hat, scrappy diary and well-thumbed paperback were so personal. Their normality contrasted violently with the message.

As Eve put the lid back on and rose slowly, feeling wobbly, secondary reactions took hold. She'd never considered that problems unrelated to Angela might rear their heads while she was here. If renters at Hideaway House were going to be targeted with notes such as this, it would definitely affect her article. Eve needed to know the background. It might just be a mischief-maker, but it looked like something more. Presumably any former resident would have lived here before Duncan bought the place, and its dark history would reflect badly on the people at the hall, not him. Yet it was Duncan's business that the note writer was threatening.

Eve glanced around, wondering if the person who'd left the box was watching. But if they were hiding in the woods, it was impossible to tell. The trees were too densely packed, the shadows deep.

Whoever had left it might hope she'd dash straight to Duncan, demanding answers, but Eve liked to look before she leaped. Once he left, she'd read the diary to find out more.

She walked back indoors and fought to disguise her fears.

Duncan and Viv had taken seats at the table and Eve encouraged them to stay put. She was glad of the chance to make fresh tea, hiding her expression as she worked.

She made herself focus on transferring scones, cream and jam to the table, where Viv was grilling Duncan on the restoration costs.

'How did you manage it all?' Eve heard her say. 'Rob a bank?'

She wasn't being aggressive exactly, but she could be very partisan when it came to employees. It was time to intervene before Duncan took offence. Eve wouldn't let him off the hook, but a softly-softly approach tended to pay dividends. 'Here we are.' She pushed the plate of scones towards them and poured the tea.

Luckily, Duncan appeared to be taking Viv's robust questions in good part. 'It's been a game, getting the finance together, I can tell you. But where there's a will, there's a way.'

Viv opened her mouth again.

'Someone mentioned you had local connections,' Eve said hastily. 'Did that make you determined to do this particular restoration?'

He nodded. 'I was saying to Viv that I lived on the estate as a child. I used to come here as a teenager.' He nodded at the room they occupied. 'I dated Jojo, the daughter of Mr and Mrs Landers who owned Kesham Hall back then. We were the ones who christened this place Hideaway House. We used to sneak in here and talk all night. It's where I asked her to marry me.'

He shook his head. 'She said yes, and I put the ring pull from a Coke can on her finger. But of course we never got hitched.' He glanced at them. 'It meant a lot at the time. Teenagers, huh?'

'What did her parents think?' Viv managed to sound rather rude, though Eve had been wondering the same thing. If her twins had even hinted at an engagement in their teens, she'd have panicked.

Duncan shrugged. 'They were fine about it, despite me being the son of their stable hand. In fact, when my parents split up, they took me in for six months before they had to sell up. Old man Landers got a job in California.'

So he'd had two upheavals in quick succession at a young age. It was useful to know what made him tick. It might have a bearing on Angela's troubles.

'What did you do when they booted you out?' Viv took another scone and Eve tried not to grimace at her tone. 'Did you go back to your mum or your dad?'

Duncan gave a wry smile. 'Neither. My mum was drying out and my dad was in a single room in a shared house. But that was okay. I was at uni soon after. Went to make my way in the world.'

But it sounded traumatic to Eve. He'd been young to be without a bolthole. And presumably Jojo had gone to the States with her parents. Even if they'd kept in touch, it would have altered their relationship irrevocably. It wasn't surprising they'd never got married.

The change must have been hugely challenging for Duncan, emotionally and practically. He must have learned to think on his feet, given he'd not only survived, but thrived. 'It must have been hard to leave such an amazing place,' Eve said aloud. 'I could see the hall in the distance from the roof. It's very beautiful.'

Duncan's eyes were far away. 'It was,' he said at last, but a moment later, he was grinning again. 'I always had a feeling I'd be back, though. When I heard the current owners weren't maintaining the estate buildings, I thought I'd see if I could buy one or two and make something of them.'

'Well, this place is a triumph.' Eve could tell Viv thought she was being disloyal, but if she wanted to understand Angela and Hideaway House's problems, she needed to build a rapport.

He smiled. 'I'm pleased with what Angela and I have achieved so far. Work on the lodge is at an early stage, but I'm raring to go.'

'Might you buy more buildings, if the current owners are happy to sell?'

He nodded. 'For sure, if I can.'

'The finance must be tricky, as Viv said.' It felt worth mentioning again, delicately. Where *had* he got the money?

'You have to be creative. Work with what you have.'

Eve would have to leave it at that for now. 'As well as writing a straight review, I'd love to talk about the restoration process and your childhood memories too.'

'Of course.'

He was animated as he spoke, gesticulating and laughing often. His stories were engaging, from drinking cider with Jojo Landers on the rooftop of Hideaway House, to being taught how to maintain masonry by the gardener and odd-job man who'd lived at the lodge. He told them about life at Kesham Hall after his parents left too. It sounded as though the Landerses had treated him like a son – except you didn't normally move to America leaving your teenage child behind. As for the hall, moving in must have felt like stepping into a different world. Eve, who'd grown up in a bungalow in Seattle, could barely begin to imagine.

As he described a dining room with a huge fireplace and ancient wall hangings, Eve wondered if the hall's current owners would be able to explain the items in the box. She'd want to talk to them when the time was right. She could work it into a conversation about Hideaway House's transformation. Eve knew them by sight; they'd moved to the hall around two years earlier and she'd seen them shopping at the store in Saxford St Peter, Eve and Viv's home village. Moira the store-keeper had a massive crush on the husband. He was a lord, and she was a sucker for status.

Duncan turned to Eve, pulling her out of her thoughts. 'You must come and talk to my apprentice Hattie and see our work at the lodge. Tomorrow morning at eleven, perhaps? We bring in other experts, naturally, but she and I keep going, even when there's no one else on site.'

Eve had come across Hattie. She was making some extra money just like Angela, in her case pulling pints in Eve's local. Eve thought of her as a watchful presence who didn't chat, but that was understandable. She had what Moira called darkly, 'A past.' The whole village had an opinion on her. If she didn't want to engage, Eve could empathise.

'Eleven sounds good.' She stood up as Duncan did. 'I'll see you then.'

Viv left at the same time as Duncan, though she'd be back the following day for tea with 'the gang' – Eve and Robin's closest Saxford friends who wanted to see inside Hideaway House. Once she was alone, Eve looked at the notebook from the myste-rious box, having brought the whole thing inside.

The diary entries were strange.

Went to have a look at the Tuppington-Hynds. Saw Lord Edward and the boys.

It was the Tuppington-Hynds who lived at Kesham Hall and owned what was left of the estate. Edward was the dad, cooed over by Moira, but what did the entry mean? The writer talked about them as though they were an exhibit.

Another said:

Lady Muck aka Fifi came to complain about the noise (again).

Fifi was Edward's wife, but beyond that, the entry made no sense. Hideaway House was a long way from the hall. Even if this Tod had played music from the roof garden full blast, she doubted the Tuppington-Hynds would have heard. Perhaps they had other tenants who'd complained. Eve would have to check who lived close by.

Ten minutes later, Robin arrived. His eyes lit up at the sight of the room and he pulled her into a hug and kissed her. 'This is amazing.'

She didn't want to rain on his parade. Even if there were problems at Kesham, they still had the weekend ahead, and it *was* romantic. She and Robin had been living together for a while, but being married still felt new, and going on a joint adventure was something to treasure. They were both so busy that it didn't happen often.

But after she'd showed him round, she told him about the box. They read more of Tod's diary together, sitting at the table. The entries didn't reveal his thoughts, except in the way they'd described Fifi – it was more a bald list of problems and events.

The roof leaks now.

Visited the lake. Trespassed.

Tap's broken.

'Weird, isn't it?' Eve said to Robin.
He nodded, still absorbed.

Eve had put the name 'Tod' and 'Hideaway House' into Google, but nothing had come up. Now, she checked her mapping app to see who might have complained about the noise, but the results didn't help. There were several estate buildings but none close enough to suffer from anything that went on at Hideaway House.

When she and Robin had read the entire notebook, they pottered about unpacking their things, then made pasta with mushrooms in a cream and wine sauce which they took to eat on the roof.

Robin poured her some Prosecco. 'If it weren't for your worries over Angela and the weird note, I'd suggest staying here for ever.'

'I hear you.' Even washing up felt fun in the toy kitchen, and when they decided on an evening walk, she couldn't quell a feeling of pleasant anticipation, despite it all.

Holding hands, with Gus at their heels, they set off. The only sounds were a blackbird singing and the faint rustle of leaves in the gentle breeze.

It was dusk before they saw another building: White Cottage, according to the sign. Eve knew it was where Angela, Duncan and Cesca were staying. She'd pictured a fairy-tale place with whitewashed walls and a thatched roof. In fact, the house was a dirty off-white, with peeling paint and jagged patches of exposed brick. Eve had been right about the thatch, but that was in a terrible state too – uneven and bedraggled. It couldn't hold out the rain, surely? As the owners of the rental, the Tuppington-Hynds ought to be maintaining it. Duncan and Angela should complain; it didn't look safe.

Eve suddenly felt bad about staying in luxury when Cesca must be sleeping in a damp room. Come winter it would be a health hazard. She was about to whisper her surprise to Robin when she heard voices.

It sounded as though Duncan and Angela were outside, at the back of their house.

'We've been through all this.' Duncan sounded faintly irritable. 'You know I love you and you say you love me.'

'Of course I do!'

'What about a bit of trust then? I'm doing this for us! I just need you to be patient. This is going to transform our lives – before you know it, you'll see.'

That sounded like massaging the facts. If the latest restoration took as long as the first, Angela was in it for the long haul.

'But we were happy before, weren't we?' She sounded close to tears. 'Downsizing after the fire wasn't *so* bad, and we made ends meet.'

He sighed heavily. 'By watching every penny. But this is the next step. I'm looking to the future, but I'm starting to think you've lost faith in me. Have you, Angela?'

At last, she replied. 'No. No, you know I haven't.'

'Good. I promise it'll be worth it in the end. I must be off now. I'm going to crack on at the lodge.'

He worked long hours too, then. Angela must feel like a single parent and it had to be hard, seeing so little of each other. It looked as though she'd been talking about their current circumstances, that time on the phone. She'd said she wanted to turn back the clock.

Eve didn't want to come face to face with Duncan as he left White Cottage, so she and Robin walked on. She breathed a sigh of relief as he took a different path and failed to see them. She'd hate him to know he'd been overheard.

A moment later, she caught the faint sound of sobbing behind them. Angela must still be outside. Eve felt the urge to offer comfort. But how could she when she'd been eavesdropping again?

She was distracted by Robin, who put a hand on her arm, then nodded in Duncan's direction. Eve looked to see he'd veered onto a different path. She didn't know what he was up to, but she understood Robin's interest.

Duncan had lied to Angela; he was no longer walking towards the lodge.

That night, Eve lay awake in the grand bed in the grand room that made up Hideaway House. She and Robin had drawn the long, green curtains, covering the tall windows, and with only the dark woods outside the room was almost pitch black. Eve could just make out the shadowy armchairs with their high backs. She couldn't sleep for wondering about the 'history' mentioned in the anonymous note, and worrying over Angela's misery.

She wasn't sure what time it was when she heard the sound outside. It was faint, not alarming, though she couldn't guess what it might be. The sound repeated, but it was even quieter the second time. Just a single tap. Eve was almost curious enough to get out of bed, but she was drowsy and desperate to drop off. Then suddenly, the next sound was louder. It separated into a tap and a crack, a fraction of a second apart. Louder taps followed as Gus barked and Eve leaped out of bed, rushing to the window. Something being thrown? Hard, yet wet too? Robin was beside her as she pulled back a curtain.

The egg running down the window meant Eve's view was impaired but beyond the white and yolk, everything looked still. She hadn't been quick enough.

Then the noise came again, from behind them, as Gus wheeled round and continued to bark. She and Robin crossed the room in a flash, dashing round the large armchairs, but when they pulled back those curtains their view was blocked again by spattered eggs. This time, Eve glimpsed movement beyond, but it wasn't any help. The person was already disappearing through the trees, something dark covering their head.

Robin unlocked the door and ran outside, but he returned a couple of minutes later, shaking his head. 'It's like looking for a needle in a haystack. It makes me wonder if they planned where to hide before they started.'

Eve's heart was going like the clappers. The eggs were harmless, but it was horrible to feel someone was wishing them ill. This might all be to do with Duncan, or the Tuppington-Hynds up at the hall, but it was starting to feel personal. Her and Robin's temporary home had come under attack.

3

Robin made them hot chocolates with a dash of brandy and they pooled impressions of what had happened until they had everything written down, including a map showing where the vandal had struck and the escape route they'd taken.

'I'll let the police know,' Robin said, 'just as a matter of course. I can't see them doing much about it.'

'We'll have to tell Duncan in the morning too.' The multiple problems were sending Eve's stress levels into overdrive. She took a sustaining sip of her drink. 'I can't help feeling it must be connected with the box. I need to discover what it means, and who's behind all this. I don't see how I can write *Icon*'s article otherwise and if I let them down, they won't trust me again.'

Robin nodded. 'How do you want to play it with Duncan tomorrow?'

'Let's confront him with the eggs first, and see how he explains it. Then we can feel our way as far as the box is concerned.'

He drained his drink. 'Agreed.'

. . .

At nine o'clock the following morning, Duncan was standing with Eve and Robin outside Hideaway House, running a distracted hand through his thick, dark hair, his eyes wide.

'I'm so sorry.' He turned his palms up. 'What can I say? It's the most terrible bad luck that this should happen while you're here. I've never seen anything like it.'

Eve was pretty sure he was acting; everything about his body language was exaggerated. She guessed this wasn't the first time he'd been targeted. It was disturbing, but it could help Eve tackle Angela. If she and Duncan had experienced something similar, it might relate to her troubles. Eve would push a little and see if she opened up.

Gus was investigating bits of eggshell and Eve called him away, then met Duncan's eye. 'I wondered if it was someone with a grudge. It's a bit of a coincidence that it's happened when you've got a journalist on site.'

'A grudge?' She glimpsed anxiety in Duncan's dark eyes before he masked it, his frown morphing into his trademark smile. 'Surely not. If someone had a grudge against me, they'd throw eggs at White Cottage, not this place.'

'Perhaps it's something to do with Hideaway House itself.'

'But it was a beautiful bit of history going to wrack and ruin. Who could object to me stepping in?'

Now was Eve's chance. 'What about previous tenants? Did anyone have to move out to enable the sale?'

Duncan looked wary now, and hesitated, as though making some sort of calculation. 'Well, there was a squatter, but he was making everything worse. And although Fifi and Edward evicted him, the process went smoothly. Tod was a city boy really. I suspect he was glad to go back to London.'

The same person whose belongings were in the box. Eve didn't look at Robin, but she bet he shared her thoughts. Being forced back to the capital with nowhere to live would be frightening. But maybe Tod hadn't gone that far. He could have

thrown the eggs. Eve was hoping the reference to blood in the
note was just melodrama.

'I hate to ask this,' Duncan said hesitantly, 'but could it have
been someone with a grudge against either of you?'

That threw Eve, and angered her too. It felt as though
Duncan was manipulating her. If he'd read about her involvement in police investigations, he'd know she might have
enemies: connections of people who'd been prosecuted thanks
to evidence she'd found. And as for Robin, he'd kept a lower
profile in the media, but most people in Saxford knew his background: that he'd had to change his name after informing on
corrupt police colleagues. Their network was behind bars now
and Robin was free to be himself, but he could never relax
entirely.

'We haven't had problems before,' Eve said, though it wasn't
entirely true.

'Apologies again. It was just a thought. I'd want you to be on
your guard if it was a possibility.'

Eve rarely made snap judgements, but she didn't believe in
his concern.

'In any case, I'm truly sorry for what's happened,' Duncan
went on. 'Look, why don't you head off for a walk? Enjoy the
sights, and I'll have it all cleared up by the time you get back.'

He hadn't suggested reporting it to the police, Eve noted. 'If
you're sure?'

'Definitely. If you don't mind me fetching water so I can
mop up?' He gestured at Hideaway House.

'Of course.' Eve was glad she'd hidden the box.

'And then Hattie and I will see you at the lodge at eleven as
planned.'

He still wanted to keep the appointment then. He hadn't
given up hope of a good write-up.

Eve and Robin collected what they needed for the walk,
then took the opposite direction to the evening before.

It was still early, but the day was mild and sunny again and they didn't need coats. The warmth brought out the smell of the grass and Scots pines, and where the sun filtered through, dew glistened, picking out delicate cobwebs. Gus meandered here and there, investigating at will.

Eve waited until they were out of earshot before unpicking the situation. 'I'm still smarting at him suggesting we might have been the targets.'

Robin gave her a grim smile. 'I could tell you weren't pleased. It shows a certain amount of low cunning. I reckon he knows you'll find it harder to give him a bad review if you feel there's the faintest chance that you or I attracted the egg thrower.'

Eve nodded. 'It's manipulative and I don't like it.' It was working, that was the trouble. Robin was right, she was already questioning the decision she'd made during the night to focus her article solely on the restoration, pulling back from the review. 'I was convinced he was acting his surprise about the attack, yet I'm still doubting myself.'

'I think you should trust your gut,' Robin said. 'Duncan's a businessman with years of experience, dealing with the media. He's bound to go for damage limitation.'

It mirrored the way he treated Angela, saying whatever it took to keep her onside. Of course, Eve had already decided he must have learned to live by his wits, after the Landerses turfed him out of the hall.

She was still brooding over the situation when a glimpse of a house down a side path distracted her. It looked even older than the hall, thatched and timbered – late medieval, she guessed.

She set off towards it. 'If I broaden my article, that place looks interesting.'

Robin followed her. 'It's beautiful, but isn't it just off estate land?' He took out the map they'd brought with them.

'Oh yes, so it is, but it looks special.' She could see two men outside carrying mugs of tea to a garden table, and there close by was Cesca. Eve was interested. She'd seen the girl with the older man before and had guessed he might be Angela's dad, given Duncan's parents were both dead.

Eve walked towards the house, glad of an excuse to say hello. The grandpa figure might know more about Angela's unhappiness, and she was curious about the building too. It looked like the sort of place to interest Duncan – not that he had the capacity to work on anything extra.

As she got closer, she saw the house was in better repair than Duncan and Angela's rental, but the fabric still needed attention.

Cesca rushed up to Gus, and Eve and Robin bent to supervise and say hello.

The younger of the two men set his tea down, came over, ruffled Cesca's hair and grinned at Eve and Robin. 'You three have met already?' His hair was untidy, with a floppy fringe which he pushed out of his eyes.

Eve explained what they were doing there, and how, in another role, she worked with Angela.

His look was warm. 'I'm Byron Acker.' *Quite a name.* He shook her hand. 'I rent this place from Duncan, as a matter of fact. I'm an artist, you see, and it's a beautiful view. Marshes, a lake, woods and everything.'

Duncan already owned it? How many places did he have?

The older man had come over now. He was receding on top and slightly portly, with a neat iron-grey beard and black-framed glasses. He looked sad but kind, Eve thought, his eyes full of emotion. 'I see you know my great-niece.'

Eve rallied her thoughts. 'You're Angela's uncle?'

He smiled but shook his head. 'My late wife was Duncan's aunt. Duncan and Cesca are all I have left of her now. I'm Jack. Jack Farraway.'

'I'm so sorry for your loss.' Eve explained their presence again and Jack blinked quickly and shook her hand.

'Jess died two years ago now, but it feels like yesterday. Cancer.' He sighed. 'I hear from Angela that you had trouble in the night.' His intense, dark eyes were on Eve's. Perhaps he was worried about what she'd write too. After all, the success or failure of Hideaway House would affect Duncan and Cesca, two blood relatives of the woman he'd clearly adored.

Poor Cesca. She hadn't got it easy, and Eve didn't want to make it worse. 'Duncan suggested it might have been someone with a grudge against us.' She wondered if Jack would leap on that idea too, but instead he choked slightly on his tea.

After a pause, he pointed to the house and changed the subject. 'My wife left this place to Duncan and now Byron rents it.'

That explained it. At least this house must bring in some money. 'It looks like a special place.'

Jack nodded, turning away slightly – to hide his emotion, Eve suspected. 'Jess and I spent many happy days here. We used it as a holiday home when we lived in London and she came back here to die. It was before Duncan and Angela started the Kesham projects, but Angela came to Suffolk for a few weeks to help nurse her.'

He took out a hanky and Eve's heart ached for him. The place must hold so many memories, good and bad.

'I moved down here full time after she died,' Jack went on, taking off his glasses and polishing them. 'I wanted to stay near where we'd felt happiest, so I found another place just outside the estate.' He took a deep breath. 'Of course, when you said the building looked special, you didn't mean on a personal level, and you're right. Cotwin Place has ancient origins.'

'It's an unusual name.'

'And a very old one, locally. Cotwin means a friend who provides shelter.'

That was even more touching.

'It's a precious rarity,' Jack went on.

Byron nodded solemnly. 'The inside's quite something.'

'Would you mind if I showed them?' It must be hard for Jack, caring so much about the place but having to defer to Byron.

'Oh, er, be my guest.'

Eve thought Byron looked slightly uncomfortable, but he stood back to let them in, and she was too curious not to go for it. 'It's very kind of you.'

Inside, there were beautiful, exposed beams forming the structure of the walls. What Eve hadn't anticipated was a high-ceilinged hall with ancient-looking timber trusses to support the roof. 'Heck, this looks even older than the rest.'

Jack nodded. 'Built around 1250. A very rare example.'

His knowledge made Eve wonder if he shared Duncan's passion. 'You're an expert?'

Jack gave a self-deprecatory shrug. 'I worked in building preservation before I retired. Duncan and I crossed paths then, as well as having the family connection. I'm still involved with his current projects in a small way.'

'Jack's being modest.' Byron spoke quickly. 'He's put in a lot of the finance, and he's started to restore this place too, on the side. It's a big job.'

Jack shook his head. 'I did a very small amount while Jess was alive, but I had to prioritise projects that paid a wage. And Jess hated me working during our holidays.' His eyes glistened. 'She said our free time together was too precious for that.' He fell silent.

He must mind about Cotwin Place desperately and Eve felt for him. No wonder he'd wanted to help do it up. It might be tough going though, if he'd already sunk a lot of money into Duncan's projects.

'Duncan must be pleased that you're working on this place,

Jack,' Eve said. Privately, she thought Duncan should have tackled it himself, before embarking on anything fresh.

Byron and Jack exchanged a glance.

'He doesn't actually know,' Byron said after a moment. 'We thought it might cause awkwardness.'

It was left to Eve to guess in what way. Duncan might feel he should pay Jack if he knew, but only if he was more scrupulous than he seemed. Of course, from Byron's point of view, the improvements might lead to a rent hike. Eve could imagine Duncan seizing any opportunity to increase his income. She thought again of his tough upbringing. It must have been sink or swim. She imagined that maxim had carried through to his later life, but it wasn't fair to exploit people because of it.

As her thoughts on Duncan faded, she studied the room in more detail. It looked as though Byron had been having a sort-out. There were book-shaped gaps in the dust on his shelves. It was chilly, despite the warmth outside, and smelled of damp plaster and oil paint. Close to a window, an easel supported a large, partially completed painting of an estuary, reeds and wading birds.

'The scene's just over there.' Byron waved a hand away from the woods. 'That's why I love it so much here.'

'It's a beautiful painting.'

Gus was perilously close to the easel and Eve called him away, but as he whipped round, he upset a pile of paperwork on a low table, and it cascaded to the floor.

'Oh Gus!'

He spun in a circle to see what had happened and more chaos ensued. Sheets of A4 tore, trapped under his paws.

Eve dashed to the rescue, but Byron blocked her way, his floppy hair bouncing. 'Don't.' Now he was in position, he seemed to shake himself. 'I mean, please, you mustn't trouble.'

His abruptness had made Eve start, and she backed off. 'Well, thank you, and I'm so sorry.'

'It honestly doesn't matter.' He was smiling again but he didn't retrieve the papers until Eve was too far away to study them.

It felt best to change the subject to ease the tension and she sought for something to say. 'Your garden's lovely.' She pointed through the window.

'It is, isn't it?' He tucked the rescued papers into a drawer and there was silence once again.

'Perhaps we should get outside before anything gets broken,' Eve said, and Robin did some dachshund herding.

'Who do you think might have thrown the eggs at Hide-away House?' Eve asked Jack as they left the room.

He frowned. 'I can't imagine.' But he didn't meet Eve's eyes.

Outside Cotwin Place, they said their goodbyes. Eve and Robin walked off, but before they'd got far, Eve put a hand on his arm.

'Let's go round the back of Byron's garden. He's clearly hiding something, and I suspect Jack has an idea who threw the eggs too. They might talk about it, now we've gone.' Eavesdropping wasn't ideal, but Eve really needed to get to the bottom of the secrets at Kesham. She'd never work out how to help Angela or write her article otherwise.

They crept around the back of the garden and paused beyond the hedge that marked its boundary. Eve stroked Gus, looked him in the eye and put her finger to her lips. He responded with a disgruntled look.

On the other side of the hedge, Jack sounded tired. 'We both know he's been asking for trouble. It's one long string of broken promises.' His voice cracked with emotion. 'I sometimes think Angela and Cesca would be happier without him.' There was a long pause. 'In fact, I wish he were dead!' The last word came out on something close to a sob. 'Forgive me. That's a terrible thing to say, but I'm at the end of my tether. I don't think I can hide it much longer.'

He went quiet and when he finally spoke again, it was about his restoration work on Cotwin Place.

If they'd said anything more revealing, Eve had missed it, but Jack's words made her shiver. There were so many problems at Kesham. Who had left the note about the former squatter at Hideaway House? And had the same person thrown the eggs? What had Duncan done to make Angela so unhappy, and Jack Farraway so full of hate? And where had Duncan sneaked off to the night before, after lying to Angela about going to the lodge?

It added up to a worrying mesh of grievances and tensions, and Eve had witnessed that sort of turmoil before. She feared for what might come next.

4

'It sounds as though Jack and Byron have become close,' Eve said to Robin as they walked back towards Hideaway House. 'I suppose Jack must spend a lot of time at Cotwin Place, given his restoration work.'

'And if he often minds Cesca, it explains why she's at ease there too,' Robin put in. 'Any thoughts on what Jack said?'

Eve nodded. 'He talked about Duncan's "string of broken promises". One might be failing to look after Cotwin Place before embarking on other projects. I'm sure it would hurt – I don't suppose Duncan's aunt imagined he'd let the place crumble when she left it to him. And it clearly means the world to Jack. But he's obviously got other grievances too.'

'Maybe the money he put up was a loan and there's no sign of Duncan repaying it,' Robin said.

'Very possibly. And then there's the way Cesca is having to live.' The great-niece of his adored late wife. Jack had many possible reasons for his resentment, but wishing Duncan dead was extreme. There had to be more to uncover.

'As far as Cotwin Place is concerned, I guess Byron was prepared to rough it and Duncan decided to take the rent and buy the other properties while he could.' Robin's shoulders were hunched. 'It doesn't say much for his principles.'

'No, but it figures. Byron makes me curious too. He seemed so friendly but he's hiding something. I wish I knew what that paperwork was.'

'It could have been nude sketches. Perhaps he was embarrassed.' Robin dug her playfully in the ribs and she laughed.

'The pages were typed. I saw that much.'

'Maybe he's writing a novel with bad sex scenes.'

'Perhaps, but I somehow doubt it.'

Back at Hideaway House, Duncan had gone and so had the mess. The walls and windows were almost dry, thanks to the sun, but the memory was harder to erase.

The more Eve thought about it, the more tense she felt. For Cesca and Angela's sake, she wanted Duncan to finish his restorations, let the houses out and move on. Without that, they might be stuck in that damp, crumbling cottage for years. If their welfare were the only consideration, she'd praise Hideaway House to the rafters in her review. But unless she knew the troubles were temporary, she couldn't rave about it with a clear conscience. She'd have to stick to her plan to talk to Angela and try to find out more.

She glanced at her watch. That would have to wait. It was time to meet Duncan and Hattie at the lodge.

The Kesham estate seemed extraordinarily peaceful given the antics the night before. It felt as though time had stood still but in reality, the place had seen much upheaval. Owners had come and gone, including the Landerses, who'd provided Duncan with some security, only to whisk it away again. Eve was looking forward to her Saxford gang coming to tea that afternoon. She wanted to grill them on Duncan's local past. After only five and a half years in Suffolk, there were gaps in her knowledge.

At last, they reached Kesham Lodge.

'Heck, Duncan's got his work cut out.' It looked almost as run-down as White Cottage. It had been whitewashed too but the paint was peeling and discoloured. It was an interesting building though, tiny and single storey, with arched windows, just like Hideaway House. Gus was lagging behind, his attention caught by rustling in the trees, so they approached the lodge slowly.

As they got nearer, they heard Duncan's voice. Eve couldn't see him, but his words were clear; he must be outside.

'That wasn't part of the deal! No one takes me for a ride and gets away with it!' His tone was threatening and Eve was glad to listen in. The person he was talking to might have thrown the eggs.

'What the blazes do you mean? Don't you threaten me! You watch yourself or I'll come for you, now I know I can.'

He let out a fierce cry of fury and Eve guessed he'd cut the call and was letting off steam.

A second later, they saw him. He must have been sitting just inside the boundary wall of the lodge.

Robin took Eve's hand as Gus caught them up, and nodded very subtly towards the lodge's window, where a pale, elfin face looked out.

Hattie – Duncan's apprentice and casual bartender at the Cross Keys in Saxford. She looked as watchful as ever, and if she'd been there all along, she'd know they'd listened in. Not the best news, but it was too late to worry now.

Hattie's past flitted through Eve's mind, however hard she tried to blot it out. She'd done her time and there'd been extenuating circumstances, anyway. All the same, the facts were stark. She'd been found guilty of stealing a gun with intent to endanger life and been sentenced to four years. Eve closed her eyes for a second and shook her head. That was the past. She'd only been eighteen when it happened. She'd got out on licence and worked hard ever since. Moving on was admirable.

Eve took a deep breath, and she and Robin walked up to the lodge's door as casually as they could, just as Duncan noticed them. His muscly shoulders were hunched, as though he was set to snap, but as he turned to face them, his expression cleared.

'Ah, excellent.' He shook their hands warmly. 'Glad you came. I'm sorry again about earlier.'

'It can't be helped.' Eve still felt irked that he'd suggested she and Robin were the egger's targets.

'Come inside and talk to Hattie.'

He ushered them through the low front door and they entered a room with a fireplace and one of the beautiful arched windows. The bones of the building were attractive, but there was rubble on the floor and daylight visible through the roof.

Duncan looked up. 'We're replacing the slate, and we've already rebuilt the east wall. There are only three rooms, and a combined wash and bakehouse outside. That'll be rebuilt too.

'And here's Hattie Fifield, my right-hand person on this project. You'll have met her at the Cross Keys?'

They nodded.

'She's learning the ropes so fast I can hardly keep up. Hattie, Eve's the journalist I told you about who'll review Hideaway House.' Eve felt the desperate urge to backtrack. Each time he said it, it felt more inescapable. 'And Robin's her husband, who's doing us the honour of trying out the facilities too. And Eve's dog is Gus, that's right, isn't it?'

It was one point in his favour that he'd remembered, but Eve felt it might be calculated. She nodded as Hattie bent to pet him. The apprentice's cool gaze was on Eve and Robin, not Eve's beloved dachshund. Eve bet she *had* noticed them snooping.

She met Hattie's eye and hoped she looked calm. 'So, what's the plan for the lodge?'

'We'll remodel it – keep the original sitting room and one of the bedrooms, but divide the second to form an en suite and a galley kitchen.'

It sounded set to be another cosy retreat like Hideaway House, and Eve fought to imagine it. At the moment, the place smelled of damp and brick dust.

'Hattie's worked wonders,' Duncan said. 'She's a fantastic all-rounder. She repaired the windows and doors at Hideaway House and she'll do the same here, as well as sorting out the floor and re-rendering the walls. Her research has been a godsend too.' He winked at Hattie. 'Understanding the past can make a vast difference to getting the result you want.'

Eve felt cut out, as though they were sharing a private joke, but she couldn't fathom it. 'It sounds amazing. Is everything going according to plan, or has anything surprised you?' After the disastrous additional costs at the manor house he'd bought, she felt bound to ask.

Duncan rubbed his chin, glanced at Hattie and laughed. 'Well, it turns out we've got to run a new water supply from the nearest building, so that's a bit of a bind.'

'Wow. How far is it?'

'I'm trying not to think about that at the moment.'

It sounded horribly expensive. Surely he should have looked into it before buying the place? It was further evidence of his gung-ho attitude. It had added to his charisma on TV, but he hadn't been in charge of budgets then. Now, it set Eve's teeth on edge. Angela was probably worried sick.

'At least Fifi's given us permission to dig the trench,' Hattie said. 'You know her? She owns the hall jointly with her husband Edward, but the wider estate is hers. She's the richest,' she raised an ironic eyebrow, 'but he's got a title.'

Eve had heard that Lord Edward's family's wealth had

dwindled, and as a younger son, he wouldn't inherit the family pile either.

'Fifi's very happy to be a Lady.' Hattie looked amused.

'She's been good to us though, hasn't she, Hattie?' Eve wondered what Duncan meant by that. 'And our plans fit with her vision,' he went on. 'I'm hoping she might sell me the Warrener's Cottage too, if I can raise the cash.' A big if, Eve imagined. 'Incidentally, Fifi would like to meet you. She suggested coffee this afternoon at two if you can make it? The hall's quite a place, so it'll be worth it.' He looked nostalgic. 'Fifi's hoping you'll mention her project when you write the piece about Hideaway House.'

'Her project?' Alarm bells were ringing. If Eve did go ahead, she wouldn't make her piece a free-for-all.

'A plant nursery with day courses,' Duncan explained. 'We're hoping my tenants might spend money there and that her customers might see my rentals and spread the word.'

'Right.' Despite her misgivings, Eve was keen to talk to Fifi. It was she who'd evicted Tod from Hideaway House, according to Duncan. That, the mysterious box, and the eggs were probably related. 'We'll be there.'

Duncan nodded. 'I'll text her to confirm.'

After they'd talked more about the project, she and Robin left. They hadn't gone far when Gus ground to a halt, turned tail and dashed back towards the lodge again.

Eve swung round to look. A squirrel. *Honestly.* He still hadn't learned that victimising small creatures wasn't on.

She called to him, while giving chase, and managed to catch him just outside the lodge's boundary wall.

'No,' she muttered. 'I've told you a hundred times.'

As she squatted to attach his lead, she heard Hattie's voice. 'I wish you wouldn't big me up so much. People will guess you're favouring me for a reason.'

'Who cares if they do?' Duncan replied.

'I care. You need to explain to Angela first.'

He heaved a sigh. 'It's not as though I was unfaithful. It all happened years before we married.'

'I know, but it'll still come as a shock. And have you let it slip to Fifi? She made a snide comment.'

'I had to tell her. She knew something was up. But you're right. I'll talk to Angela at lunchtime. Promise. But you really are talented, you know.'

'I'm waiting for you to claim it's all down to genetics.'

Hattie sounded entertained and Duncan laughed.

'You're certainly a chip off the old block, that's for sure.'

5

Gus was still looking indignant as Eve rejoined Robin on the path.

'You can come off the lead if you promise to behave.' She looked him in the eye, then removed the offending article, her mind full of what she'd just heard. She relayed the news to Robin.

'So Hattie's Duncan's daughter?' he said in an undertone, as they walked back through the woods.

'It certainly sounds like it. I hope Duncan really does tell Angela soon. It'll be all round the village, if they're not more careful when they chat about it.' Hattie was lodging in Saxford with a woman called Marjorie – a friend of Moira, the village storekeeper. Eve could only imagine the pair's glee at such prime gossip. 'I can't believe Fifi Tuppington-Hynd knows already, yet Angela's still in the dark.' Eve would be terribly hurt if Robin had kept something so momentous from her.

'It all seems like part of Duncan's casual attitude.' Robin walked on, but his eyes were on Eve. 'Maybe Hattie's working for Duncan for mates' rates.'

'Quite possibly. I'm not sure how he'd afford her otherwise.

I imagine that trench for the lodge's water supply will cost a fortune.' Eve's mind ran on. How would Angela feel, accepting Hattie as Cesca's half-sister? Inviting her in for mugs of tea while wondering about Duncan's relationship with her mother. Thinking of how Hattie had pointed a loaded gun at the foster family who'd taken her in after her mum's death. Of course, if Angela had already found out, it was likely contributing to her misery.

Eve wished she could wipe the knowledge from her mind.

Approaching Kesham Hall for coffee with the Tuppington-Hynds was like walking onto the set of a period drama. Eve felt a mix of awe and curiosity as she strode up the long, wide gravel drive. It was all so formal and imposing, with a central porch, two wings and three storeys, topped with grand octagonal turrets, one of which sported a weathervane. At the end of the lawn was a ha-ha ditch for keeping livestock off the gardens without spoiling the view.

Eve wondered what Duncan's childhood home had been like and how he'd felt, making the transition to somewhere like this. She'd have to find out where he'd lived.

A woman in a dark dress and white apron let them in and showed them to a wood-panelled sitting room. There was a huge antique rug on the oak floor and high-backed red sofas. Eve would feel shifty, living in such a big place, though it must be an adventure growing up here. She'd seen the Tuppington-Hynds' two boys as they'd approached, playing on the lawn – identical twins of around eight or nine. Their father, Lord Edward, had been with them, racing around as the twins squealed with delight, his smile as boyish as theirs. It was touching.

But inside, the house felt still – almost stifling. A handsome Bengal cat stalked across the sitting room as they entered, looking regal. It deigned to let Eve stroke it, then walked past Gus with a superior look in its eye.

Fifi Tuppington-Hynd rose to greet them.

'Eve Mallow? I've seen you in the village. And your husband Robin?' They all shook hands. 'Delighted, delighted.' She looked younger than Eve – in her mid-forties perhaps. Attractive and well turned out. 'Let's have some tea.' She glanced at the woman in uniform. 'And call Edward and the boys, would you?'

'Oh, please don't trouble.' Eve didn't want to drag them inside.

'No, no, it's high time they came indoors.' There was an edge to Fifi's voice as she nodded to the maid. 'They barely paused for lunch. Other than that, they've been out there for hours.'

But the weather was glorious. It was just the day for it.

They arrived moments later, the boys looking crestfallen though not actually grumpy, which Eve thought was impressive. Perhaps they were too well trained to kick up a fuss.

'Here's Jasper and Louie. And Edward of course,' Fifi said.

'I'm so sorry.' Edward dashed forward to shake Eve and Robin's hands. 'I hadn't noticed the time.'

'Please don't worry. It's good to meet you properly, Lord Edward.'

'Just Edward, please.' He was older than his wife, and craggy looking in a pleasant way. He seemed a lot more sombre, now he was indoors.

The boys sat on uncomfortable-looking chairs and proceeded to say nothing as the maid brought the tea. Eve took Gus over to be introduced and eventually they unbent enough to tickle his tummy.

The Bengal cat saw what was going on, swished over and inserted itself between Gus and the children, leaving the poor dachshund to right himself in an undignified manner.

Eve turned to Fifi. 'Duncan explained you were hoping I might write about your business venture as well as his.' Might as well tackle it head-on.

Fifi nodded and showed her the plans for the plant nursery and the barn she intended to convert into a tearoom.

'The stables would have been ideal, but the boys have their horses there at the moment, so that's no good.'

It gave first-world problems a whole new meaning. Eve remembered Duncan's dad had worked at the stables and mentioned it. 'I wondered where they lived back then? Has Duncan said?'

'They rented the same cottage he's in now.'

Wow. It might not have been so dilapidated then, but moving to the hall would definitely have felt transformational.

'Ah, you've seen White Cottage.' Fifi must have read her expression. 'It's run-down, but we're not charging them rent. Duncan's doing it up in return for free lodging.'

It could have been a reasonable deal, but working on it with a four-year-old on site would be plain irresponsible. And he wasn't anyway, as far as Eve could tell. No wonder Angela was upset; it couldn't be healthy, living somewhere so damp and rickety.

'Of course, he's done wonders with Hideaway House,' Fifi went on. 'And I'm glad I sold him the lodge too. He's a known quantity.'

She would think that, after his TV appearances and position at the Built Heritage Trust. She probably didn't know about his less-well-publicised disaster at the manor. Eve wondered if Edward also trusted Duncan, but Hattie had said Fifi owned the wider estate. If he didn't like it, there probably wasn't much he could do.

Fifi pulled Eve out of her thoughts by darting to the window. 'What on earth is *she* doing here?'

Eve followed her gaze and saw it was Hattie, walking

purposefully up to the grand front door. A moment later she'd turned, her neat dark bob swishing, and was on her way down the drive again. She must have been delivering something.

'Thank goodness.' Fifi watched her retreating back. 'I don't want her anywhere near the boys.'

'Why's that?' It was Robin who asked.

'Her history is appalling,' Fifi said. Eve felt guilty because they shared the same prejudice; Fifi was simply more honest. 'She used to go out with the squatter at Hideaway House before we sold up, too. It was lucky that Duncan knew the ropes. He helped us get him evicted – handled the whole thing in the end.'

Eve's pulse quickened. So Tod or his allies might blame Duncan for what had happened, then. She stayed silent, hoping Fifi would say more.

Edward had a hand on her arm, as though urging restraint, but she carried on anyway. 'He didn't just break in and live there without permission, he stole from us. The day he left, he sneaked through a side door and walked off with some candlesticks.' Her hand was shaking slightly.

'We don't have proof it was him,' Edward said quietly.

'Who else could it have been?' Fifi turned to her children. 'He certainly came up the drive. You saw him, didn't you, Jasper?'

Eve had never seen a child look so withdrawn – a world away from the boy who'd frolicked on the lawn earlier. But at last, he nodded.

'After that, Tod disappeared to London,' Fifi went on. She shuddered. 'He had it in for us. I was glad to see him go. He ended up living rough, I'm afraid.' Her voice turned flat. 'I hear he's dead now.'

Eve felt a jolt of shock at the news, despite what the note had implied. And had Duncan known about his death too, but not said anything, to avoid looking bad? It was pretty low, if so.

It would have been natural to mention it when she'd probed about former residents.

'It's tragic, but there it is,' Fifi finished, and another shiver ran through her, more violent than the first. She was still very glad Tod had gone, Eve decided. Unless she was totally heartless, he'd really frightened her.

Edward was gazing anxiously at the boys who sat stiffly in their chairs and stared at their mum.

'I'm sorry,' Fifi said, 'but he honestly was a nasty piece of work and it's so hard to trust anyone. Duncan's very fond of Hattie – well of course he is – but I don't think he should take *her* at face value either. Not after her relationship with Tod.'

Eve sensed Fifi was close to tears. Perhaps it was the way her children were looking at her, as though she repulsed them. Eve would be heartbroken if her adult twins looked at her like that.

6

The visit to Kesham Hall didn't do anything to dispel Eve's uneasiness. When she'd read the note in the box she hadn't taken the reference to blood literally, but now it felt close to the bone. The young man who'd owned the Stephen King book, the diary and the beanie was dead, and someone felt Duncan was to blame. He'd advised Fifi over the eviction and it was he who'd wanted to buy Hideaway House.

Eve imagined Tod, young and desperate. Hattie might be Duncan's biological daughter but who knew what she felt underneath? Perhaps she blamed him for the death of her boyfriend. She could have left the note and thrown the eggs. She might be working for Duncan to put him off the scent. And if she was out for revenge, it was possible she'd only just got started...

She shared her worries with Robin. 'Hattie's so hard to read. I could imagine her plotting something without any of us realising.'

He nodded, his eyes serious. 'It's certainly something to bear in mind.'

It felt like the strongest lead they had. If Eve could find out more, she could tackle her about it, but nothing would bring Tod back.

Not long after they'd returned to Hideaway House, the gang from Saxford arrived. As well as Viv there were Eve and Robin's neighbours, Sylvia and Daphne, and Viv's brother Simon. They'd all wanted in when they'd discovered that Eve would be sampling Hideaway House. The afternoon was mellow and they took their tea and scones up to the roof, setting out deckchairs from the fourth tower. Eve sat bathed in sunshine and the gentle country air.

'It's idyllic,' Daphne said, stretching back in her chair, her smartly cut silver hair catching the sun.

'It is if you ignore what's going on around us,' Eve replied.

Viv sat up straight. 'Tell!'

So Eve filled them in.

Daphne looked sober as she swallowed a mouthful of tea. 'I'd heard the rumour about the young man, Tod. It's desperately sad.'

'I'd be angry if someone stole from me too,' Sylvia said, flicking her long grey plait over her shoulder, 'but I wouldn't throw a squatter out with nowhere to go, and if they died, I'd be past complaining about missing candlesticks. But I'm not surprised. Fifi's very brittle. I've often wondered what made her that way but she never chats about her past. Her life before Edward is a closed book. She photographs well, though.' Photography was Sylvia's profession and the reason she'd spent time at the hall. Fifi had commissioned regular formal portraits.

'She's very good-looking, of course,' Simon said.

'Yes, thank you, Simon.' Viv threw a bit of scone at his head. 'Handsome is as handsome does. Moira admires her of course. She's almost as keen on her as she is on Edward. Always going on about her wardrobe and the tastefulness of her jewels. "Very well bred. You can always tell."'

Viv's impression of the storekeeper was so good that Eve almost spat out her tea.

'It's Edward who really sends Moira's heart a-flutter though,' Viv went on. 'She quotes everything he says. "Dear Edward tells me…" "Edward was saying only the other day…"'

'You'd think he'd avoid her store if she pounces on him each time he visits,' Sylvia said.

Viv waved a hand. 'She stocks his favourite cheese and everything. Paul had better look out.'

Paul was Moira's taciturn husband. Eve would be astounded if he'd noticed what Moira thought of Edward or Fifi.

'It's a real charm offensive.' Viv sat back in her chair. 'Offensive being the operative word.'

Eve laughed. 'What do *you* think of Edward?' He'd struck her as gentle and a fond father.

'From what I hear, he spends a lot more time with the twins than Fifi does.' Viv's response confirmed her thoughts. 'Doesn't mind getting his hands dirty.'

Simon leaned forward in his deckchair. 'There are some interesting stories about him. Seems he's an adventurer-turned-family-man. He swam the Channel once, then won the money for his plane ticket home in a bet.'

'Sort of dashing,' Viv said dreamily. Perhaps Moira would have competition.

'There are tales of him rock climbing, skydiving and frequenting casinos,' Simon went on. 'All very glamorous and James Bond. And if you're after heroics, Viv, you're going to love this. Once, when the twins were young and the family still lived in London, he was alone with them one evening while Fifi attended a do. He heard a noise outside, went to investigate and got locked out. The boys were far too young to let him back in, so he sat in the shed, waiting for Fifi to come home.'

'That doesn't sound very heroic,' Viv said.

Simon tutted. 'I haven't finished yet. When he left the shed twenty minutes later to see if his beloved was back, he found the house was on fire.'

Eve couldn't imagine his horror; the mere thought sent a chill through her. 'He saved the boys?' Someone had, obviously.

Simon nodded. 'He called the emergency services as he broke into the house, then ran through the smoke and flames and got them out. He had quite severe burns apparently, but they were unharmed.'

Eve thought of him dashing around on the lawn with the boys. His utter absorption in their world. He must feel so grateful every day that he'd left the shed in time to see what was happening. If Eve were Fifi, she'd watch them and Edward like a hawk too, after such a near miss. But of course, Fifi had been presented with the happy ending, not the gut-ripping fear beforehand.

'Edward never found out what made the noise in their garden?' Robin said.

'Asked like a true detective,' Simon replied. 'He guessed it had probably been a fox or something.'

'All this,' Sylvia said languidly, sipping her tea, 'yet it strikes me that it's his title that Fifi loves most.'

'And what do you all know about Duncan's childhood here, and his relationship with Jojo Landers?'

Daphne shook her head. 'I know everyone felt sorry for him. Such a young man to be left so alone.'

Viv nodded and took another scone. 'There was a lot of bad feeling towards Jojo.'

'Moira still talks about the way she let Duncan down,' Sylvia added. 'Several locals froze her out when she decided to leave with her mum and dad.'

'It sounds harsh to expect her to break away from them when she was still in her teens.'

'There was more to it, from what I heard,' Daphne replied. 'The Landerses had married young, so it didn't strike them as odd when Jojo and Duncan talked about getting engaged. And Duncan was already developing a passion for restoration. He'd done some work on the hall and I imagine Mr Landers thought he had a bright future. Apparently, he promised him a role on the estate once he was trained, as heritage manager.'

Sylvia rolled her eyes. 'From what I hear of Mr Landers, that was probably code for general dogsbody. He was a canny businessman. But if Duncan ended up as their son-in-law, he might have given him special treatment.'

'Losing all that was down to the Landerses moving away, of course,' Daphne went on, 'but I gather Jojo's decision to cut off ties made a big difference too. Mr Landers had intended to fund Duncan through university up until then.'

'So Jojo deciding on a clean break left Duncan alone and penniless.' Eve could only imagine his feeling of desolation.

'I think people were especially upset for him because it came as such a shock,' Daphne said. 'They were very young, but they'd seemed inseparable until then.'

Sylvia nodded. 'And according to everyone, she left without a backward glance. The villagers felt even sorrier for Duncan when someone saw him back at Kesham a few months later, trailing round like a lost soul. I hear he was in tears.'

It hadn't been about the money then. It sounded as though he'd been pining for Jojo.

'It's hard.' Daphne sighed. 'But Jojo must have had a reason, even if we don't know what it was.'

'Her parents ought to take some of the blame,' Viv said. 'Even after the break-up, old man Landers could have stumped up the cash he'd promised. I hear his job in the States was very well paid and the hall went for a fortune. Think it's relevant to what's happening now?'

'It's bound to be; it's part of who Duncan is.' Eve could see how he'd become a fighter, intent on self-preservation.

After that they discussed Eve's theory that it could have been Hattie who'd egged Hideaway House and put the box of Tod's possessions outside.

'I heard a bit of gossip about her this afternoon,' Simon said.

Viv looked thunderstruck. 'What? You haven't said.'

He looked sheepish. 'I wasn't sure I should. I got it at the village store and you know what Moira's like. But she claims Duncan is Hattie's father.'

Eve nodded. She hadn't liked to mention it either, but there was no point in holding back if Moira knew. She only hoped Duncan had told Angela as planned. She might be stoical but there were limits.

Viv turned accusing eyes on Eve. 'You knew too?'

'Not officially.' She sighed. 'I overheard the pair of them talking about it. What else did Moira say, Simon?'

'That Duncan was terribly happy that they'd found each other and that Hattie's mum had cut him out completely. He'd had no idea where she was until Hattie found him.'

Eve wondered if Duncan was telling the truth. He'd clearly known he had a child out there, and he'd probably known her surname. Even if he'd never met her, you'd think he could discover her first name through mutual friends. Perhaps he hadn't bothered.

'Now he's saying it makes so much sense,' Simon went on, 'because Hattie's such a talented restorer. He's in talks with his old production company about a new father–daughter TV series.'

Angela would see even less of him. There he'd be, making a huge fuss of his long-lost daughter while she carried on rising at dawn, cleaning, waiting tables and caring for Cesca. Thank heavens Jack Farraway was there to help, but it was hardly ideal. His words replayed in her head. 'I sometimes think

Angela and Cesca would be happier without him. In fact, I wish he were dead!'

'I was worried about the effect on Angela,' Simon went on. 'But you can imagine what Moira said.'

Eve could. 'That we must make allowances, after Duncan's upbringing and the way Jojo Landers treated him?' Moira never blamed the men.

Simon nodded. 'Got it in one. And then she said, what could you expect, because Jojo wasn't "proper gentry".'

Everyone groaned.

'They were just kids!' Sylvia threw up her hands. 'No one should have expected the relationship to last.'

Eve saw her point, but the thought of Duncan's loneliness at the time was powerful and teenage romances could be incredibly intense. She bet the experience had echoed down the years.

She considered his key contacts nowadays. 'I need to revise Hattie's history.' Inevitably, it was village gossip at the forefront of her mind, not the facts, which dated back several years.

She looked up contemporary news reports on her phone.

Teen found guilty of gun crime.

'What does it say?' Viv was trying to take Eve's phone.

'Hattie was found guilty of stealing a gun with intent to endanger life, as we know, and sentenced to four years in prison.'

Sylvia topped up their teas from the pot as Eve continued to relate the tale.

'She was eighteen at the time. A local family had taken her in after her mum died and they were the people she threatened. She told the court that she'd never intended to shoot them and seemed astonished at the idea.' Eve checked her phone again.

'According to this report, she got off with the minimum sentence because it was a first offence, and it looked as though she'd acted on impulse, dashing in with the gun immediately after stealing it. It also became clear that the family had treated her very badly. She was expected to cook and clean while the others had fun. They had her getting up at dawn, with no time for schoolwork, friends or a part-time job. At eighteen of course, she could have moved out, but she didn't have any money.' There were certain overlaps with her and Duncan. 'It sounds as though it was relentless, and her lawyer said she'd snapped.' Eve could imagine her feeling bitter at the world for what had happened. Someone should have protected her, but they hadn't.

'It sounds as though she was badly failed,' Daphne said, echoing her thoughts.

Eve nodded. 'And if Duncan had been around she'd never have ended up with the abusive family. We've only his word for it that he wanted to find her. But if she secretly hates him, perhaps she'll keep her revenge attacks anonymous until the TV deal's in the bag.'

Sylvia smiled. 'I certainly would, if I were her.'

At last, the gang got up, stacked their crockery and carried everything down the spiral stairs.

Eve and Robin waved them off with promises of more updates the moment they were back in Saxford. The chat had been good, but going through everything had only exaggerated Eve's anxiety. She sat down to make notes for her article, but ended up writing about the dynamics. Hattie might hate Duncan for not being there for her, and for his part in evicting her late boyfriend, Tod. Angela was deeply miserable and clearly wished she, Duncan and Cesca had never come to Kesham. Eve guessed the discovery that Hattie was Duncan's child would only accentuate that. Jack, Duncan's uncle by marriage, his funder, and sometime co-worker, wished he were dead and Jack's friend Byron, Duncan's tenant, was hiding something. On top of all that, someone was attacking Duncan's property.

Her musings were interrupted by a text. Sylvia.

Hate to add to your concerns but if you look from your roof due west, you might see something interesting.

Eve dashed back up the spiral stairs, slowing as she reached the top and crouching low to peer through the balustrade without being seen.

At first, all she could pick out was the empty pathway and the trees to either side. Then gradually she adjusted focus and picked up movement.

Heck. She was all but certain it was Fifi Tuppington-Hynd and Duncan Blake, locked in an embrace.

'That doesn't look very platonic,' Robin whispered in her ear.

7

Robin was right. Fifi Tuppington-Hynd and Duncan Blake were acting like a couple who'd been starved of romantic company for some time. But that wasn't the worst of it. Before Eve could retreat from the roof, she heard voices. Happy shouts and thudding feet. Still crouched, she swivelled awkwardly to look.

Heck. It was Jasper and Louie, just the other side of Hideaway House, with Edward hard on their heels. If they carried on, they'd probably run into Fifi and Duncan.

Eve made a dash for the spiral staircase and in seconds she was on the ground floor, tugging open the door and acting surprised to see Edward and the boys. 'Oh, hello, Edward!'

The moment the words were out she felt embarrassed. She sounded like the hammiest of actors, projecting to the back row, but she really wanted Duncan and Fifi to hear her and move on. It would be awful if Edward saw them, worse still if it was the twins.

Edward waved and walked over.

'Can we come inside?' Louie said.

Eve practically dragged them through the door, despite

Edward's protests that they'd be intruding. 'Of course you can. We've got some scones left if it won't spoil your supper?'

Both twins looked pleadingly at their dad who smiled and nodded at last. 'Go on then.' He turned to Eve and Robin. 'If you're sure?'

They assured him they were.

Robin was already reaching clean plates from Hideaway House's hideaway kitchen.

'It's a bit like a playhouse,' Eve said. 'I'd have loved it when I was a kid too.' She was glad the scone idea had been a hit. She'd made masses of the things, as an over-cautious over-caterer, but now it was paying dividends. Robin put them on the table which would hopefully stop the boys asking to go on the roof.

Eve offered Edward some tea and soon they were all seated. 'What do you think of Duncan's efforts?' She was almost worried to mention his name in case Edward knew about the affair.

'Impressive.' His tone was neutral; she simply couldn't tell.

'You and Fifi didn't want to use the place?'

'*We* did!' Jasper said, and Edward ruffled his hair.

'We've still got the Warrener's Cottage to play in. And you couldn't come here once Tod moved in, anyway.' He turned to Eve. 'His arrival highlighted the problems of keeping empty buildings. It was Fifi's decision to sell – she owns the wider estate – but I agreed. The maintenance was a burden.'

'What about your work? I'm sorry, I don't know what you do?'

'I commute to the City, though I've got some time off because of the school holidays.'

'You can't have much chance to focus on the estate either then, with such long days.'

Edward nodded. 'And the last thing I want is more responsibility. I don't see enough of the boys as it is. I'd like to find a different job, closer to home.'

The move from London to Suffolk must have made his life harder. But perhaps he and Fifi had wanted the boys to grow up somewhere rural.

The twins had finished their scones and were asking to play outside. For a moment, Eve was anxious. If they went into the woods, they might still find their mum and Duncan, but Edward told them to keep to the clearing.

As soon as they'd gone, he leaned forward. 'I'm afraid Fifi sounded harsh when she spoke about Tod. It certainly wasn't ideal, evicting him, but of course we had no idea he'd end up in such dire straits. And truth be told, I really wanted to see the back of him as well.'

Eve raised an eyebrow. 'It can't have been easy, knowing someone had taken over one of your properties.'

'It left us on edge. You have to understand that Tod didn't keep himself to himself. It was as though he was watching us. He'd come and play music at full volume, close to the garden.'

It explained the complaints about the noise. Eve was desperately sorry that he was dead, but she could see that must have been unsettling for the family. Perhaps Tod was angry at the Tuppington-Hynds' ostentatious wealth.

'It was as though he was taunting us,' Edward added. 'He started to feel like a malign presence. When he went, I can't deny I was relieved.'

By the time Edward had finished his tea and left to find the boys, Eve was confident that Duncan and Fifi would have moved on. She sighed with relief, but trouble was still simmering. She'd no doubt it would boil over before long.

She and Robin had a scratch supper of bread and cheese, too full of coffee, tea and scones to eat much else.

'Fancy walking off the food and tension?' Robin asked.

Gus leaped up and Eve nodded as she reached for a cardigan. 'Sounds good. I keep wondering if Edward knows about Fifi's affair. It must be torture, if so, and the same for Angela of course.' It would explain her desperation. 'It's not as though Duncan's likely to leave until he's finished restoring the lodge.' It might take a year. Quite possibly longer. 'He said he'd like to buy the Warrener's Cottage too. He could be here indefinitely.'

They headed for the door.

'I must say, if you moved a lover into our garden shed, I wouldn't like it.' Robin gave her a hug.

'Not sure he would either.'

He laughed. 'Where shall we go? Anywhere you want to revisit for the article?'

Eve took a deep breath. How on earth would she tackle it? Staying at Hideaway House felt like living in a soap opera. 'Let's have another look at the hall. It's got some beautiful architecture and describing it properly will help me put Duncan's restorations in context.' She could make the piece about history, facts and Duncan's work, leaving out any recommendation. No matter how much she wanted to help Angela, she couldn't be dishonest. She'd find another way to support her and Cesca.

Robin gave her a sidelong glance as they left the house. 'I'm sorry things haven't gone according to plan.'

'At least I know a lot more about Angela's circumstances, which can only help. I'll talk to Duncan about tweaking the article, to manage expectations – the eggs are enough of an excuse. But I'm still not sure what to do about the box of Tod's belongings. If I tell him, he might guess who left it here. I wouldn't want to trigger any repercussions.'

As they walked through the woods, Gus dashing ahead in the early evening sun, Eve tried to relax and enjoy their surroundings. The air was still warm, the sky blue with only the odd cloud.

Once again, the illusion of a rural idyll was powerful as

Kesham Hall came into view with its turrets and mullioned windows. As they got closer, Eve grabbed Robin's arm.

'Look. Isn't that Duncan and Edward?' The pair were chatting, close to the hall with almost-empty glasses of whisky. Eve got the impression that Duncan was trying to convince Edward about something. He was laughing, nodding up at the hall, but Edward wore a frown.

As Eve and Robin got nearer, Duncan's carrying voice became audible. 'Surely you must have?' His eyes were wide. 'What, never been tempted?'

In the distance, on the lawn, Eve could see the twins playing football.

Edward was shaking his head.

'Well, if you won't, I will!' Duncan leaped at the wall of the hall and started to climb.

He did it so quickly that he was quite high in a matter of seconds. Eve was dumbstruck, her heart was going like the clappers.

'I heard you used to be an adventurer,' Duncan called down. 'But perhaps those days are behind you.'

'Heck.' Eve found her voice and spoke in an undertone to Robin. 'I wouldn't bank on the stonework holding Edward's weight if he goes up too.' He was taller and more solidly built than Duncan.

Duncan was clambering higher still, using the hall's decorative stone dressings as hand and footholds.

'Oh no.' *Don't be taken in by Duncan's goading, Edward.* Eve wanted to shout it out, but the words seemed stuck in her throat. Surely, he'd be too sensible to follow suit?

But in another moment, Edward was climbing too. He was slower than Duncan, more laboured – used to desk work, not tearing down walls and lifting beams. He looked fiercely determined though.

Eve watched as he joined Duncan at the height of the third

floor. The drop was sickening. It was only when the pair looked stable, standing on the top of one of the bay windows, that she dared to tear her gaze away.

The twins were watching. What if they tried it next? She was sure they looked up to their dad. But it wasn't just Edward's risk-taking that made Eve uneasy, it was the way Duncan had played him.

'Perhaps he does know about the affair after all,' Robin said quietly.

It was just what Eve had been thinking. It made her angry. They were both old enough to know better and it was hugely unprofessional and cruel of Duncan to cheat with Fifi under Edward's nose. Or anywhere, for that matter.

She'd hoped they might climb into the house to descend to ground level, but presumably the windows were shut.

'Let's watch to make sure they get down safely,' she said to Robin, 'and then I'm off. I've seen enough.' It stiffened her resolve to talk to Duncan. She was fuming. What a ridiculous, childish way to behave. For a second, she imagined her article copy. *Come and see local alpha male and old silverback compete for territory.* No. She'd tell him she couldn't recommend Hideaway House and her article would focus solely on Kesham's history and – if he was lucky – his restoration work. She wouldn't mention Fifi's pesky plant nursery either.

Edward and Duncan still hadn't made their way down. Eve's heart was in her mouth as Edward, looking slightly unsteady, climbed up onto the edge of the highest bay window. He teetered there for a moment then made a leap onto an adjoining one, a good three feet away, over a sheer drop.

He made it, but his landing was clumsy. Eve had bitten her cheek in her anxiety. She could taste blood.

Duncan grinned, looking satisfied, not bested, and repeated the leap Edward had made. He landed like a dancer. Even at this distance, Eve could see Edward's anger.

The descent looked even more hazardous than the climb and Robin had to gently prise her fingers from his forearm.

She realised she'd dug her nails in. 'Sorry.'

'Think nothing of it.'

When Duncan and Edward were nearly down, Duncan leaped from the top of the ground-floor bay, landing neatly once again. Eve could see Edward didn't want to copy him. She had a feeling he'd hurt his ankle during the previous leap. He hesitated long enough to see Duncan laugh, then made the jump, pain creasing his face as he stumbled.

As Eve and Robin turned to go, Eve realised they and the twins hadn't been the only ones watching the excruciating spectacle. Slightly closer to the hall, tucked behind a tree, was Hattie. As she turned her head to look at the twins her expression was as cool and inscrutable as ever.

8

'Can I make a suggestion?' Robin asked, as they walked away from Kesham Hall.

'Please do.'

'Let's find Duncan tonight, so you can tackle him. You won't relax until it's done, and we might as well make the most of our last night here.'

He was right – it would be best to get it over with. Eve's stomach was full of cheese, scones and tension. 'If you're sure.'

He nodded.

They could see that Duncan was leaving now too.

'Let's follow him at a distance,' Eve said. 'I don't want to have this talk in the open. If he goes home and Angela and Cesca are there, we can ask him to come back with us to Hideaway House. I'd text to arrange it, only...'

'He might guess you're upset and weasel out of it.' Robin nodded. 'I agree. Let's go.'

At first, it looked as though they'd be in luck. Duncan made for the lodge, not his home, and disappeared inside. She and Robin were about to close the gap and knock on the door, when Cesca's great-uncle, Jack Farraway, stepped from behind the old washhouse. He reached the door before Eve and Robin had shown themselves.

'Want to wait?' Robin asked quietly.

'Yes please, assuming he's not there for ages.' She couldn't bear to go through the build-up all over again. Besides, it would be the first time she'd seen Jack interact with Duncan. She might find out why he'd wished him dead.

As they waited, Eve reviewed what she knew about Jack. His late wife had been Duncan's aunt, and she had left Duncan Cotwin Place, which Byron was now renting. Despite its medieval hall, Duncan had failed to restore it, opting to let Byron move in immediately in return for a fast buck.

Eve was distracted by the sound of Duncan's voice – so loud suddenly that it made her jump. The evening was still warm and he'd opened a window the moment he'd entered the lodge.

'Byron let it slip!'

'I might have hoped you'd be grateful.' Eve had to strain to hear Jack. He was keeping his cool. 'Cotwin Place was my wife's, your aunt's home! I care about it, and it's a lot more historically significant than this place.'

'If you have free time, you could spend more hours helping me!' Duncan was still bellowing.

Seriously? He was telling Jack off for working on Cotwin Place, presumably at his own expense? Eve's blood pressure was rising again.

'Do you have any idea how close to the wind I'm sailing?' Duncan went on.

'As one of your creditors, yes I do.' Jack paused. 'It's time to admit it, Duncan. You're in love with the past. With your life when you had the run of the estate as a teenager. It's not doing you, Angela or Cesca any good. And as for this thing with Fifi—'

'What "thing" with Fifi?!' Duncan's voice was as loud as before. 'Are you serious? It's nothing.'

'I doubt Angela sees it that way.'

Perhaps she knew about the affair too then.

Duncan let out a howl of frustration as Eve's fury with him mounted.

'Look, let's not fight,' Jack said. 'I'm here now and I can help – assuming you've come to crack on, not for an illicit meet-up with your lover.'

'As if someone like Fifi would come here.' Duncan sounded dismissive.

'Well then.'

For a moment, Eve heard nothing but the sound of one of them working with a hammer and chisel. Jack appeared outside and dumped some rubbish into a large sack. He was knotting it again when he paused, a look of confusion on his face.

In a second, he'd reopened the sack and was rummaging inside. A moment later, he stood up straight, as though he'd found what he was looking for. Eve couldn't see it from that angle but it clearly had a profound effect. Jack seemed to forget re-knotting the bag and paced back inside, like a man in a dream.

Eve waited with bated breath.

'I—' It was Duncan who spoke. Just that one word. He must be reacting to whatever Jack had found.

'I can't believe it.' Jack's voice was low and dangerous. 'To know that it was you all along... It takes my breath away. If I could—' But then he stopped himself. 'Nothing matters to you, does it? Only the project you're hellbent on. You can't see further than the end of your nose, but listen here, Duncan. I see you for what you are. There are no excuses. I will never forgive you for this. Never.'

Eve recognised that feeling. It was something she'd experienced only once, when she'd realised that her first husband had coolly betrayed her and that some of their mutual friends knew about it. At that moment she'd been so horrified, so devastated that she really could say no more.

Jack let himself out of the lodge and walked away as though oblivious to the world around him.

Eve felt shaky as she prepared to visit Duncan at last, but again, she was thwarted. Jack paused and turned back towards the lodge. Eve could see he was still fighting his emotions. The thought of him letting go was frightening. But at last, he made for the trees and hid, just like them.

Eve and Robin exchanged a glance and moved back, further into the woods. They couldn't reveal themselves while Jack was watching and the last thing Eve wanted was to be discovered.

She watched as Jack twisted his hands. She had a horrible feeling he was tempted to harm Duncan. Part of her wanted to alert him to her and Robin's presence, to bring him back to normality. But Robin put a hand on her arm when she moved forward.

Perhaps he was right. If Jack did attack Duncan, they could intervene, and holding back would give them the best understanding of the situation.

But a moment later, Hattie appeared from one of the paths through the wood and swept up to the lodge's door. She went inside, and before long, Eve could hear the murmur of voices and the sound of hammers and chisels again.

Jack ran his hands through his hair, pulling at it, then flung his arms out and strode off into the woods.

They'd never know what he might have done if Hattie hadn't appeared.

9

Eve decided there was no point in staying. She wanted to talk to Duncan in private, not in the middle of Kesham's answer to Piccadilly Circus.

She turned to Robin once they'd retreated to a safe distance. 'Sorry. Now I've used up our last evening without talking to Duncan. And it all feels so volatile. I wonder what Jack Farraway found in the rubbish sack. I've rarely seen anyone so angry.'

Back at Hideaway House, Gus went straight to his portable bed. *Very understandable.*

'Why don't you go and test out the bath?' Robin massaged her shoulders, which felt like heaven. 'Be rude not to. Then we'll go onto the roof and watch the stars with a nightcap.'

'Sounds like an excellent antidote to the day. Have I ever told you I love you?'

He grinned and she left the room.

Eve had a good wallow, using some of the complimentary bubble bath which turned the water her favourite shade of green. But try as she might, she couldn't forget the troubles at Kesham. Edward, Angela, Hattie and Jack all had reasons to hate Duncan, but their feelings were bubbling dangerously under the surface. Eve dried herself and dressed, her thoughts still bound up with the situation. It was like a powder keg.

Upstairs, Robin made them liqueur coffees and produced some Florentines. 'Just in case you're hungry again. I bought them at Pepys in Blyworth. Don't tell Viv. Or Moira.'

'You're a marvel.'

'I try.'

She followed him onto the roof and attempted to zone in on the perfect setting. The stars were bright and magical. Eve could even see the Milky Way. She and Robin talked about other things: Viv's commission to cater for a wedding and their plans to make over the garden at Elizabeth's Cottage. The former topic wasn't entirely relaxing, given Viv's chaotic approach and Eve's role as chief administrator, but thinking about their beloved garden was lovely. She'd almost stopped worrying about tomorrow's confrontation with Duncan when she spotted movement, down in the woods.

Hattie perhaps, returning to Saxford after a late stint at the lodge?

Eve turned to Robin to find he'd already moved to the balustrade in complete silence, crouching low.

As Eve crept closer, she understood his quick reaction. The figure amongst the trees was wearing a dark bulky jacket and a balaclava.

Robin moved stealthily towards the spiral staircase. As an ex-cop she knew he'd want to investigate, and she did too of course. He glanced at what she was wearing. Dark jeans and top. He was in navy. They ought to fade into the night, so long as they were quiet.

Gus raised his head sleepily, but Eve stroked him and he settled again. 'Back very soon.'

Outside, they paused for a moment to pick up the figure's route. There they went. She and Robin set off, keeping to the very edge of the path, under the nearest trees. The figure was cutting diagonally through the woods. Eve and Robin gave them a head start, then followed suit.

'I think they're making for the lodge,' Eve murmured.

He nodded. 'Wonder if Duncan or Hattie are still there. We need to make sure they're okay.'

The figure was well ahead of them, but Eve and Robin couldn't risk getting closer. A dry twig, cracking underfoot, would give them away.

In the distance, Eve could see the lodge's dark, closed windows. The place was probably empty.

'Perhaps they're after Duncan's tools,' Robin whispered, but Eve didn't think he believed it.

As they watched, the figure drew a container from under their jacket, prised off the lid and hurled the contents at the lodge. Paint. They had a second pot too. No wonder they'd looked so bulky.

Robin was running forward now, and Eve dashed to keep up. The figure turned swiftly, saw them and started to run too, round the side of the lodge and into the darkness.

Robin hared after them, then fell. What the heck?

Alarm increased Eve's speed. 'Robin?'

'Stop, Eve!'

But she was floored like him before she could react. Someone had tied a thin, tough cord at shin height between a tree bordering the lodge and a gate post.

'Are you all right?' Robin was rubbing his knee.

'Nothing broken.' Her wrist hurt though. Indignation and shock made her momentarily tearful. 'What about you?'

'Same. The person with the paint didn't fall.'

'You think they knew the cord was there?'

'They could have tied it themselves earlier to scupper any pursuer, when planning an escape route. Either that or Duncan anticipated further attacks and he's fighting back. Maybe the intruder did a recce earlier and saw the danger.'

Robin was taking photos. Eve called Duncan's mobile but it was after midnight, and there was no reply. She left a message asking to talk the following morning. This was getting way out of hand. He wasn't responsible for the vandal, but she felt as furious with him as the perpetrator.

Robin was talking quietly into his phone. 'I've reported it,' he said as he rung off. 'No one'll come tonight, of course, but at least that's done.' He took her hand and they started their walk back to Hideaway House.

Once again, Eve felt the vandal might be after bad press for Duncan, and acting because she was there. If so, then altering her article was playing into their hands, but she couldn't give Duncan a free pass.

A sound from the woods made her jump, bringing her back to the present. Her breath caught. Rationally, she knew it could be an animal, but what if it wasn't? The panicky feeling filled her with adrenaline, and she broke into a run. She wanted to get back to Gus and check he was okay. Robin ran too, and Eve's sense of relief when they found all was quiet was overwhelming. Her dachshund stirred and she knelt to give him a cuddle.

'Not the break you were expecting,' Robin said as she got to her feet again.

Eve looked around at the spacious room then up at the grand chandelier. 'It's a special place but I can't tell you how glad I'll be to get back to Elizabeth's Cottage.' She wanted her own space, and a thoroughly normal morning, rescuing Viv from the standard mayhem at Monty's. A forgotten coachload of customers with nowhere to sit would be a breeze compared with all this.

. . .

Once again that night, Eve lay there in the grand bed, looking up at the high, shadowy ceiling, thoughts whirling in her head. She wondered what it had been like when the mysterious Tod had squatted there and how he'd ended up dead. He shouldn't have stolen from the Tuppington-Hynds, but she could imagine his feelings of anger, fear and desperation.

After that, her thoughts turned to Duncan and Edward, scaling the hall. Duncan had found it so easy to goad Edward. The affair was enough to explain it, but unable to relax, Eve used her phone to see if they had a past connection.

She was digging into Edward's background when she found it. A notice in the *Times*, no less.

> *The engagement is announced between Edward, the younger son of Tobias Tuppington-Hynd, 14th Duke of Appleforth, and Lady Mary Tuppington-Hynd of Long Stratford, Suffolk, and Josephine, only daughter of Mr Lionel Landers of Los Angeles, California and Mrs Stephanie Porter of Arundel, Sussex.*

Landers. The very same family who'd owned the hall back when Duncan was a teenager. Josephine. Jojo. Fifi. Eve went cold all over. Jojo Landers, who'd left Duncan to go to America, and Fifi Tuppington-Hynd, Edward's wife, were one and the same.

Duncan's affair was with his lost love from all those years ago.

It seemed impossible, yet it had to be. But why did no one in Saxford know? Fifi would have changed between the ages of eighteen and her early forties, when she and Edward bought the estate. It wasn't that surprising that no one recognised her, but she'd said nothing too. She must be keeping her past a secret. Of course, she'd been frozen out by some of the villagers for running out on Duncan. Idiotic people like Moira had decided she lacked class, too. Perhaps Fifi had wanted to make a new start as lady of the manor. Moira thought of her as gentry now, and had taken her to her heart. Maybe that was why Fifi had wanted to come back: to finally get the respect she felt she deserved.

But Duncan must have returned for a different reason. *For her.* They might each regret their youthful break-up. Not everyone knew what they wanted at that age.

Duncan had already had a property nearby – Cotwin Place, left to him by his aunt. Eve thought of what she'd been told. It must have been around the same time as Fifi and Edward bought the hall that Byron had presented himself as an eager tenant. Eve presumed Duncan had decided buying Hideaway House was a better way of rekindling his old relationship. He'd have needed regular contact with Fifi to convince her the affair was a good idea. Cotwin Place was outside the estate, whereas renting White Cottage and helping her evict Tod would have ensured close contact. Eve wondered why he hadn't cashed in and sold his aunt's place. Perhaps he had enough conscience to avoid it, given the pain it would have caused Jack, but Eve doubted it. She'd have to find out. As it was, he must have scrimped and borrowed to buy the folly, and then, as soon as the work was completed, he'd done it again, buying the lodge to prolong his and Fifi's closeness.

How on earth must Edward feel if he knew the truth? A love affair spanning decades seemed a hundred times worse.

The following morning, Eve told Robin what she'd discovered.

The talk with Duncan felt more pressing still, and they set out to White Cottage immediately after breakfast, but there was no one home.

'I'm getting a bit fed up with this,' Eve said.

'Maybe he's already left for the lodge.'

'Or gone to see Fifi at the hall.'

They were on one of the main paths through the woods and about to turn towards the lodge when Gus dashed off, distracted by a bird on the hall's sweeping lawn. A moment later, he disappeared from view, after which came plaintive barking.

'He's probably stuck at the base of the ha-ha.' It might have been meant to keep out deer, but it would work on Gus too.

Eve was strolling resignedly after him when the bark became a howl. The sound made her skin prickle.

'I'm not sure that's just frustration,' Robin said, striding forward and picking up speed.

When they reached the ditch, Eve was brought up short. Robin had been right.

The sight of Duncan Blake took her breath and left her shivering and nauseous. Robin had dashed into the ditch and was feeling for a pulse, but Eve knew it was only procedure. No one could have survived that battering.

10

Robin dialled the emergency services as Eve agonised over what to do first. They were so close to the hall. The Tuppington-Hynds' twins might easily come out to play and see Duncan's murdered body, but worse still was the thought of Angela and Cesca approaching from the opposite direction. The moment Robin was off the line, she told him she'd go to White Cottage.

He nodded. 'I'll stand guard here. If I see the boys, I'll make sure they don't come near.' He paused. 'Don't tell Angela what's happened, will you?'

Of course, the police would want to do that. They'd break the news with great care, but they'd be watching Angela too. She'd automatically be a suspect and that would intensify once the police started gathering evidence. Duncan had treated her appallingly. A fresh layer of horror descended. 'I won't. I'll just distract her, but you might see her first anyway, given she and Cesca were already out when we knocked.' Poor, poor Angela, and as for her daughter – it didn't bear thinking about.

. . .

In fact, the first people Eve saw as she approached White Cottage were a pair of uniformed police officers who took her name and asked for directions to the ha-ha. And before she got any further, Detective Inspector Nigel Palmer arrived. He looked at Eve as though she was something he'd just sneezed into a tissue.

Eve had dealt with Palmer many times before, when writing the obituaries of murder victims. She interviewed the exact same people as the police, and they tended to be less guarded with her. Unearthing useful information in the past had incensed Palmer. Perhaps he felt she'd shown him up. She'd never claimed any credit, but the local papers had picked up on her role, which hadn't helped. Palmer didn't like Robin either. Eve guessed it was something to do with his past as a detective and the award he'd received for bringing down an organised crime network. Palmer was thin-skinned, lazy and easily threatened.

'I don't believe it,' he said now, with a groan. 'And what might you be doing here, Ms Mallow?'

Gus gave one quick bark as though to tell him off, then stared at him fiercely.

Eve explained about the article Duncan had hoped she'd write, and then about her more immediate mission: to make sure his wife and daughter didn't stumble across his corpse. Quite a good excuse in Eve's book.

'You're not due to stay on the estate any longer, I hope?' Palmer leaned forward, well into her personal space.

'I'm leaving today.'

He nodded. 'A member of the team will be round to talk to you shortly, after which I don't wish to see or hear from you again during this investigation.' Gus let out a low growl. 'Unless of course we have to question you a second time as part of our enquiries.'

Eve was keen to circumvent this, if at all possible. 'I should tell you now that I rang Duncan's mobile last night. You'll find a record of the call. It was sometime after midnight, and he didn't answer.'

'And what were you doing, ringing a murder victim at such an antisocial hour?' Palmer leaned further forward. 'If you and Mr Blake were more than friends, now's the time to admit it.'

For pity's sake... Eve counted to ten and began to tell him exactly why she'd been calling. She was only around twelve seconds in when he waved a hand.

'I don't have time to listen to all this. My constable will get the details. Don't let me see you here again.'

'I'll be pitching to write Duncan Blake's obituary,' Eve said to his retreating back, 'so I will be talking to his friends and relations – after you've dealt with them of course.' She raised her voice slightly. 'I can't guarantee you won't see me around.'

He didn't reply, but she could tell by the set of his shoulders that he'd taken it on board. There was nothing he could do to stop her, unless he could find a judge who'd sign an order to keep her away. Eve hoped that was unlikely.

Palmer was at Angela's door now. It seemed too cruel that the news would be broken by someone like him. Eve wished he at least had another member of the team to share the job. He had some intelligent and sympathetic colleagues, including DS Greg Boles, who was married to Robin's cousin.

As Eve turned towards Hideaway House, heart heavy, she heard White Cottage's door open and close. Life for Angela would never be the same again. She and Viv would rally round, but nothing could protect her from something so devastating.

Robin reappeared half an hour later. 'Greg came to view the body, along with the medic and the scientific support officers. Someone had passed on my message about the paint thrown at the lodge, but I told him we had other information too. DC Dawkins will be along to talk to us soon.'

Eve liked Olivia Dawkins. She had none of the hidden agendas that made Palmer so deficient.

With thoughts of the interview ahead, Eve reviewed the information she had to pass on, and who the police might suspect on the back of it. There were multiple motives, from Angela and Edward, either of whom could have killed Duncan out of desperation and jealousy, to Jack who'd declared he could never forgive him. Then there was Hattie whose life could have been transformed if Duncan had been involved in it from the start. She might easily blame him for the eviction and subsequent death of her boyfriend, too.

Fifi and the artist Byron Acker had no motives that she knew of, but as a lover, Fifi had to be kept in mind. And even Byron had secrets. He'd leaped like a scalded cat to stop her seeing the paperwork Gus had knocked off his side table.

DC Dawkins arrived, and Eve made her tea as the detective stroked Gus, reinforcing Eve's good impression of her.

'Quite a place,' Dawkins said as she sat down.

'But not the idyllic escape Duncan Blake wanted it to be.' Eve felt close to tears.

'DS Boles says you've got information.' Dawkins's pen was poised over her pad. 'Please, tell me all you know.'

After DC Dawkins had finished with them, Eve and Robin packed their things. It felt so strange to think of how delightful Hideaway House had seemed when Eve had first arrived and how numb and sad she felt now. As they carried their luggage back to Eve's car, Eve caught a glimpse of Angela and Cesca in the distance, being comforted by Jack. Byron Acker was hovering in the background, wringing his hands and looking awkward. Beyond them, white-suited scientific support officers darted to and fro.

Reporters with cameras appeared in the small car park, just

as they were leaving. Word had got out fast. The hacks made a beeline for them but Robin told them they'd have to wait for the official statement. He sounded so calm and authoritative that they fell back, and Eve got them away faster than she'd hoped.

Within minutes, they were back in Saxford St Peter. As usual, they pulled up by the village green, ready to carry their luggage home because there was no parking in Haunted Lane. Gus had been uncharacteristically subdued on the journey, but his excitement at being on home turf took over and he bounded out of Eve's Mini Clubman the moment she'd undone his harness.

He wasn't the only one who was energised. A Viv-shaped orange-haired bundle of effervescence bounded across the green from Monty's Teashop as they did their second luggage run.

'Moira says Duncan Blake's been murdered. Is it really true?'

'How the heck did she find out?'

Viv waved a hand. 'Something about a delivery driver not being able to get to the hall. Not sure how he knew the specifics, but he stopped at Moira's to buy a drink. The whole village is buzzing with it. Blimey. I mean, I know I was angry with him for the way he was treating Angela, but I never wished him dead. I can't believe I was having tea with him on Friday.' She paused for breath. 'I keep thinking of Cesca.' There were tears in her eyes.

'I know.' The situation would have a special resonance for Viv, whose husband had died when their three boys were young. Eve gave her a hug, then took a deep breath. 'My worst nightmare is if Angela did it. I suppose Jack would take Cesca in, but it would still be horrific.'

Viv looked scandalised. 'Angela can't have. She's one of the best waitresses we've ever had.'

Not a guarantee of innocence, sadly. 'She's certainly not the only suspect.'

Viv looked sober for once. 'From what you said yesterday, I can imagine. I suppose po-faced Palmer sent you away?'

They hadn't been due back until later that afternoon. 'That's right. But I've told him I'll pitch to write Duncan's obituary, and I'm sure *Icon* will want it – they were keen enough on my original article. As soon as the police have interviewed the key players, I'll go back to Kesham and take my turn.'

'I'm glad.' Viv was nodding vigorously. 'You sound as fired up as I feel. We can't let Angela face this alone.'

Eve agreed, one hundred per cent. 'I can't bear it. She'll need our support. Whatever happens.'

Viv opened her mouth.

'I know. I desperately want her to be innocent, but we have to be clear-sighted. Either way, someone should be rooting for her. She's suffered a lot already – she doesn't need more of the same. And Palmer's bound to shy away from Edward Tuppington-Hynd as an alternative suspect. Pursuing a lord will be his worst nightmare.' He'd be terrified of the career implications.

Eve told Viv how Fifi Tuppington-Hynd and Jojo Landers were one and the same.

She put a hand over her mouth. 'I don't believe it. I mean, we weren't contemporaries. She's a good bit younger than me, but all the same, I'd never have recognised her.'

Eve wondered what had made her break up with Duncan all those years ago, and how he'd convinced her to risk her marriage by rekindling their relationship now.

Viv snorted. 'You realise what this means, don't you? The teenager Moira despised for not being "proper gentry" is the same woman she now idolises because she wears nice clothes and is married to a lord.'

Eve had secretly fantasised about telling her, but at a time like this it wouldn't be fair on Fifi. She'd left as Jojo whom people despised, and reappeared as the lady of the manor. It seemed so sad, if she was still looking for approval. She shared her thoughts with Viv, who seemed very disappointed.

'You mean we can't show Moira the error of her ways?'

'I don't think we should yet, even though it's tempting. It's bound to come out though, when the police and the press dig for information.'

Viv sighed wistfully. 'All right. What will you do first?'

'Send *Icon* the pitch for the obituary and do some background research, both online and in person. I want to know more about Fifi and Edward's relationship.' Ordinarily, Moira would be the natural person to ask, but her crush on Edward would make her too blinkered. 'The key question is, would he have snapped if he'd found out Fifi was cheating on him? Perhaps I'll ask the Falconers.' They ran the Cross Keys and she knew Edward drank there occasionally. 'I'll quiz them about Hattie too. She's quiet and watchful, but I hope she'll have chatted to them during her shifts. Marjorie will probably be a mine of information as well, as her landlady. I want to know more about Hattie's relationship with the squatter, Tod, and what she really felt about Duncan too. I wonder who I could talk to about Jack Farraway...'

'Sylvia and Daphne got to know him and his late wife a bit,' Viv said. 'His wife bought some of Daphne's ceramics for their holiday home.'

The news of the connection was welcome. It was crucial to dig into Jack after the big bust-up between him and Duncan the night before. 'Thanks. And I'll visit Moira too, just as a matter of course.' Eve might as well hear what people were saying. 'As for Angela, I suppose we know her as well as anyone else in the village.'

'And I can't see her murdering anyone,' Viv said firmly.

'But she'd followed Duncan loyally into the middle of nowhere.' Eve sighed. 'And we already agreed he seemed to rely on her for everything from childcare to a stable income. He was supposed to make their rented house habitable, but he never did and he was having an affair with their landlady. We know how stoical Angela is, but if the dam finally burst...'

Viv looked uncomfortable. 'All the same, she's not the type. And she's got a young child to look after.'

'You don't think she could have snapped?' Eve hated even putting the question, but it didn't seem impossible. 'She sounded desperately unhappy when I overheard her on the phone.'

Viv was silent.

11

After Viv had dashed back to the teashop and Eve and Robin had lugged the final lot of luggage to Elizabeth's Cottage, Eve messaged her contact at *Icon* to explain what had happened and suggest she write Duncan's obituary instead of the review. After that, she sent messages to Fifi and Edward, who were both on a local charity WhatsApp group, expressing her sympathy and asking to interview them. She'd approach Angela and Jack in person and send a proper handwritten note to Hattie as Duncan's daughter. Byron wasn't a priority, but she found a contact form for him on his website and asked if she could talk to him too. Robin brought her a sustaining sandwich of tangy cheddar and ripe tomatoes as she worked, then she dashed out to begin her investigations. She dropped off her letter at Hattie's lodgings then went to the village store next door to find that fount of all gossip, Moira.

The store was empty when she entered, which was handy. She took up a jar of Moira's poshest marmalade as a sweetener and went up to the counter.

'Ah, Eve, dear. So tragic about poor Duncan Blake! Tell me, what do you know?'

As ever, Eve was keen to keep the information flow one-way. 'Not too much as yet, I'm afraid, but I wondered what you'd heard, Moira. The store's the hub of the village. I know you'll have valuable information.'

Moira looked suitably gratified. 'Well, Eve, I suppose it's true, people do confide in me.' That was one way of putting it. Giving in to a grilling was another... 'I got the news this morning from a rather handsome delivery driver from that exclusive furniture shop in Blyworth.' Moira leaned forward conspiratorially. 'He let me have a look at the sofa they'd ordered for their children's playroom, since he hadn't been able to deliver it. Dear Fifi Tuppington-Hynd has *such* good taste, and of course, Edward is the kindest of gentlemen.' She flushed slightly.

The urge to tell Moira that Fifi was Jojo Landers was almost overwhelming, but Eve smiled and held her peace. 'That all sounds fascinating. But I wondered, had you heard anything that might hint at what happened to Duncan?'

Moira leaned forward still further, darting a look around the store as though someone might have sneaked in to eavesdrop. 'Well,' she raised her eyebrows meaningfully, 'from what Marjorie says, it's Hattie Fifield you need to keep an eye on.'

'Really? What makes you say that?'

Moira folded her arms. 'Marjorie just happened to be on the landing, near to Hattie's room, putting some towels in the airing cupboard, when she overheard Hattie talking on the phone.'

Hmm.

'Marjorie distinctly heard her say, "I've found my dad. I'd like to kill him for all he put me through. It's no use coming straight out with it, but he won't know what's hit him when I take my revenge."'

On the one hand, Marjorie was a known gossip, just like Moira, prone to exaggerate and embellish. But on the other, that did sound quite specific. 'The police will be interested to hear from her.'

Moira's brow drew down. 'She doesn't want to tell them, because she's frightened of Hattie. She can't just throw her out – it would be against her tenancy agreement – so you can see how awkward it is. She wishes she'd never taken her in.'

Eve bet Marjorie's hair would fall out if she knew Moira was telling all and sundry. It might easily get back to Hattie. 'Maybe you should keep all of this to yourself for the time being and encourage Marjorie to speak to DS Boles. He'll be discreet. What made her accept Hattie as a lodger in the first place?'

'Ah well, that was dear Lord Edward's doing. When Hattie applied for the room, Marjorie went to him for advice. She knew that Hattie was working on the estate, so I suggested he might have an opinion. We went together.' Her cheeks were pink again.

Eve imagined them trotting up the drive to the hall like a pair of giggling schoolgirls. *Honestly.*

'I'm so pleased that he and Fifi put the hall back together again.'

What? 'How do you mean?'

Moira looked delighted to know more than Eve did. 'Well, the previous occupants – the ones who came after the Landers – split it into two dwellings when they divorced. I don't know how they got permission when it's a listed building. I always said it was a travesty, to see such a grand old house altered like that.' She looked very disapproving. 'But they both sold at once, so dear Edward bought the east wing, and Fifi purchased the rest, thanks to an investment that had just matured.' She clasped her hands together, as though the arrangement was akin to achieving world peace. There was definitely no way she'd give an unbiased opinion about either of them.

'And what happened when you spoke to Edward about Hattie?'

Moira's eyes narrowed for a moment – possibly at the thought that Eve was also on first-name terms with his lordship.

'He was kindness itself,' she said, her smile reappearing. 'He gave us each a glass of sherry and told us the history of Hattie's case and how badly she'd been treated by her foster family. He said in his view, everyone deserved a second chance and that from what he'd seen of Hattie, Marjorie didn't have anything to worry about.' Moira was positively glowing.

'Only he might have been wrong, if what Marjorie overheard is anything to go by.'

Her face fell. 'Yes. There is that.'

'Thanks, Moira.' Eve paid for the marmalade and left the store. She wasn't entirely surprised to see Viv again, dashing across the green.

'The customers?' Eve knew Monty's schedules off by heart. It was supposed to be Viv and Angela covering currently, but Eve had texted Angela to express her sympathy and tell her she mustn't think of coming in. Allie, one of their old hands, was coming to the rescue later, but she wouldn't have arrived yet.

'I'm sure they'll be fine,' Viv said. 'Deidre Lennox is in there gorging herself on lemon drizzle cake. She knows to say I'll be right back if anyone asks.'

'You didn't promise her information in return, did you? Because this is for your ears only.'

'I'll be discreet. Scout's honour.'

Eve passed on what Moira had said.

'Wow. So, what do you reckon?'

'I'm not sure. If Hattie was planning to kill Duncan, you'd think she might wait until he'd sorted out the TV show they were due to star in together. Do a season or two maybe and then strike, once she'd made her mark.'

Viv nodded. 'True.'

'I need to find out what stage negotiations were at and what the plan was.' Eve made a mental note to call the production company. It was a legitimate bit of research for Duncan's obituary. 'It's the way Duncan goaded Edward that I can't forget. I could certainly see him snapping.'

Viv nodded. 'That climb of theirs sounds terrifying. What a pair of idiots.'

'That's just what I thought. It's a side issue, but I can't work out why Duncan did it. He already had the upper hand, with his affair with Fifi in full swing. Why make Edward feel even smaller? But whatever the reason, I'll bet Edward feared losing Fifi for good; I'd swear he still loves her.' Eve wondered if Moira's hero was about to come crashing down.

12

Eve went back to Elizabeth's Cottage, googled the production company responsible for Duncan's TV series and dialled their number. Her contact at *Icon*, who seemed to work 24/7, had already texted to accept her obituary pitch, so her request to talk felt official. Eve wasn't surprised when they didn't answer on a Sunday afternoon. She left her number, saying she wanted to cover Duncan's TV plans at the time of his death.

By the time she'd finished, Robin had had a text from Greg Boles, promising updates by that evening, so Eve messaged the gang WhatsApp group to suggest a meet-up over supper at Elizabeth's Cottage. Viv's acceptance arrived in record time.

A visit to the Cross Keys was next on her list. Hattie was on the suspect list, even if she and Duncan had had plans. She had too many potential motives to be ignored. Eve took Gus with her. It would be too cruel to leave him out of the proceedings when Hetty, the pub schnauzer, was the love of his life.

She found both Falconer brothers, Toby and Matt, busy with customers, but Matt's wife Jo, the cook, was free to talk. As soon as Eve had ordered some drinks, they went to sit in a far corner of the garden underneath a cream parasol as Gus

performed his comical greeting ritual with Hetty. The dachshund took a cautious look over his shoulder before relaxing. Jo
was as fierce with overexcited dogs as she was with badly
behaved clientele, but news of the murder had distracted her.
Her eyes were on Eve.

'So, you're looking into this business?' Her brow drew
down as she sipped the Coke Eve had bought her. 'That's
good news. We had a gaggle of journalists in over lunch.
Vultures, the lot of them, present company excepted. You
want to know about Hattie, I take it? She told me in confidence that she was Duncan's long-lost daughter, before the
news got out.'

Eve nodded. 'Is that what brought her to Kesham, do you
know? She was hunting for him here?'

Jo's frown deepened. 'I believe that's right. And then there
was this coincidence that their work passions overlapped.
Though perhaps it wasn't chance. It could be genetic. Anyway,
Hattie did some training in construction as part of her rehabili-
tation after she was released from prison. She did so well that
some charitable specialist took her on and gave her more
training.'

Eve's radar was going off already. She could believe it might
be genetic that both Hattie and Duncan were dextrous and
determined, but you could use dexterity in any number of jobs.
Yet Hattie had pursued a vocation that coincided exactly with
his. Perhaps she'd known that Duncan was her dad all along.
She'd served two years of her four-year sentence. That was a lot
of time for resentment to build up if she blamed him for abandoning his parental responsibilities.

'Did you ever hear Hattie say anything against Duncan?'
Eve asked Jo.

The cook looked thoughtful again. 'No. She said there was
nothing Duncan could have done for her when she was
younger.'

But if Hattie was secretly planning revenge, that's just what she would say.

'He knew about her,' Jo went on. 'She had a photo of him and her when she was a baby, and a letter from him too. Her mum had returned it – she didn't want him in Hattie's life.'

Duncan must have known her full name then. Eve was sure he could have found her if he'd wanted to.

Jo pursed her lips and carried on. 'Reading between the lines, I had the impression Duncan and the mum had had a bad break-up and she didn't want Hattie's feelings pulled this way and that. The result was that Hattie's mum never told her who her dad was and forced Duncan to butt out.

'Hattie was all smiles when she showed me the DNA test she and Duncan had had done, but she's bitter about her child-hood, all right.' Jo's eyes were on the middle distance. 'You can hear the anger still.'

Eve thought about the gun she'd stolen. 'Did you have any qualms about taking her on?'

Jo folded her arms. 'I'd be lying if I said I didn't, but it's like Toby said: everyone deserves a second chance, and she *was* hard done by. Edward Tuppington-Hynd put in a good word for her, so that helped make up my mind.'

Edward again. Was there any chance he'd got fond of Hattie? She was young and pretty and his wife was having an affair. 'What do you think of Edward?'

'Seems like a decent sort. A family man, these days. Loves those boys of his. He often talks about them when he's in here.'

'What about Fifi?'

She frowned. 'She rarely visits, but they came in as a couple once. He was very attentive, but I'd say she was holding back.'

That figured. 'You've never heard him get angry, or seem jealous?'

'Never, but I think he was sad. As though he couldn't reach Fifi, if you know what I mean.'

Perhaps he blamed Duncan, not Fifi, for the affair. Eve stored the information away. 'And what about Hattie's boyfriend, Tod? Did you ever meet him? I wondered what she felt when he was evicted from Hideaway House.'

Jo snorted. 'Good question. Not very happy, you'd think. But no, she's barely talked about him. I heard on the grapevine that he'd stolen from the Tuppington-Hynds, and that he'd died, but Hattie never mentioned it. I decided not to bring it up, in case it upset her, but Toby told her he was sorry. She just shook her head, then asked if she could work an extra shift the following day. Still, people deal with grief in different ways. It was Duncan who advised the Tuppington-Hynds on the right procedure for getting Tod out, from what I hear.'

Eve remembered Fifi saying the same thing. Hattie's apparent lack of emotion was interesting. Eve still thought she was less likely to have killed Duncan when he was about to unlock her TV career, however angry she was. She struck Eve as iron-willed, never giving anything away. But Eve had questions about her, and she could imagine her being ruthless. If Hattie had already done a deal with the production company, it was possible she'd have gone ahead.

Eve thanked Jo, finished her Coke and relied on some heavy cajoling to get Gus to leave Hetty. She mentioned going to visit Sylvia and Daphne, which sparked some excitement in his deep brown eyes, but that cooled when he realised Eve intended to call on them at their place. Gus had a profound dislike for their marmalade cat, Orlando.

A moment later, Eve knocked on the door of lopsided Hope Cottage and Sylvia welcomed her in.

'Viv mentioned you might drop round to ask about Jack Farraway. Come and have some tea. Daphne's got the kettle on.'

Eve followed her through to their tiny kitchen which was painted a deep red.

'You poor thing.' Daphne looked at her anxiously. 'Viv said it was you who found Duncan's body.'

'Robin, Gus and I discovered him together.'

'It sounds dreadful. Please sit down.' She put a beautiful deep-green teapot in front of her. It was one of Daphne's own creations, and Eve loved it. 'I'll pour.'

'Because tea cures all ills,' Sylvia said, with an ironic smile. 'Though of course, Viv says that magical quality belongs to cake, so we bought some vanilla and raspberry confections from Monty's in anticipation of your arrival.'

'You're too good to me.' Poor Gus was less impressed. She felt him tense at her feet as Orlando walked into the room. Eve had tried telling Gus that he had the upper hand in their relationship, but it never worked. The marmalade cat reigned supreme.

'Viv mentioned you got to know Jack Farraway when his late wife commissioned a tea set from you, Daphne?'

She nodded. 'Poor Jess, that's right. She wanted it for their holiday cottage, but when she died, the place went to Duncan. That was hard, I always felt. But I could see the logic. He was brought up at Kesham and although he must have done well out of his career, I had the impression things were tight. And of course, Jack still had his and Jess's London house. When he decided to move to Suffolk permanently, he sold that to get the money he needed.'

'I wonder how Jack's doing now, financially.' Eve sipped her tea. 'I hear he loaned Duncan money.'

'You'd think him having Cotwin Place would be enough,' Sylvia said tartly. 'As for Jack's financial input, it felt like throwing good money after bad. Foolish, in my opinion.'

Daphne sighed. 'But Jack adored Jess, and Cesca is her great-niece. I believe he wants what's best for her above all things. And before Duncan died, I suppose the same applied to him. Jess had no living children. If Jack wanted to support the next generation, then Duncan was it.'

But Eve knew that things had cooled between Jack and Duncan.

Sylvia shook her head. 'I suspect any help he gave Duncan was unlikely to filter through to Cesca, especially after what you've told us, Eve. If Jack finally realised that, it'll have hurt. He was taken for a fool.'

'Did you get any impression of their relationship? Jack and Duncan's, I mean.'

'I barely knew Duncan,' Daphne said, thoughtfully, putting her cup down. 'But I gathered they were old friends – back when I made the tea set at least – and that Jack's marriage to Jess had reinforced that.'

'So Jack knew Duncan first, before he met and married Jess?'

Daphne nodded. 'I believe Duncan introduced them. He knew Jack through work.'

'He and Jess were quite mature by the time they married?'

She nodded again. 'It wasn't the first time for either of them. Jack was divorced, but Jess lost a husband and child in a car accident. I can't imagine anything more painful.

'Jack's love for Jess was strong and touching. When she was in her final days, we went to visit and Jess was very confused and distressed. She was calling out for her late husband and child. It almost seemed as though she'd forgotten who Jack was. I really felt for him. But his reaction will tell you everything you need to know about his character. He was only upset for her, not for himself.'

Sylvia was nodding. 'He scoured the house for her favourite photo of them, but he couldn't lay his hands on it. It was horrible. She got more and more upset and he was frantic. The worst of it was, she somehow remembered that I was a photographer and was convinced I could produce the photo, but it wasn't me who'd taken it. In the end, Jack sketched the pair from memory, and gave Jess the drawing to hold.'

'Angela helped with the nursing.' The pain was still there in Daphne's eyes. 'She told us Jess finally fell asleep once she had the sketch. She died an hour later.'

'Jack sounds like a kind man.'

'The sort who feels things very deeply,' Sylvia said.

Eve had been thinking the same, and of course, that sort could snap spectacularly if pushed to the edge.

'Why are you so interested in him?' Sylvia asked.

Eve explained the stand-off she'd heard at the lodge the night before and told them how Jack had hung around afterwards. 'I wasn't sure what might have happened if Hattie hadn't arrived.'

Daphne went pale, but Sylvia was nodding. 'We need to unpick more of this this evening, when Robin gives us Greg's updates.'

Eve decided to nip back to Moira's before she went home. Some nuts to serve before supper might be nice. She was distracted from thoughts of Jack as she crossed Saxford's green. Hattie Fifield had just emerged from the village store and Eve watched as her expression relaxed from one of pain to a look of calm determination. A second later, a man who must be a reporter swung out of the Cross Keys, camera in hand, looked up and spotted her. The grieving daughter. Hattie must have caught sight of him too, and lo, the look of pain was back again.

13

That evening, Eve and Robin sat in the dining room at Elizabeth's Cottage surrounded by their friends. As usual, Simon's wife Polly had made her excuses. She'd gone on a girls' night out to the cinema in Blyworth.

Sauvignon Blanc had been poured, crab and samphire pasta dished up, and everyone looked at Robin.

'Cheers.' Sylvia raised her glass, which glittered with condensation in the evening sunlight. 'What news from Greg?'

Robin put his glass down. 'Plenty. The estimated time of death was between eleven and one in the morning. The murder weapon hasn't been found, but unless the post-mortem provides any shocks, Duncan Blake was killed with several blows to the head using a blunt instrument.'

'Several.' Eve put down her fork, the sickening image of Duncan's body back with her.

Robin squeezed her hand. 'I'm afraid so. It looks as though the killer was driven by intense fury or fear.'

'So a spur-of-the-moment thing?' said Simon.

Robin frowned. 'Yes, but that covers more than one option.

We might be looking for someone who'd never thought of killing Duncan before last night. Or conversely, someone who'd wished him dead for years, before something pushed them over the edge.'

'What about the weapon?' Eve asked.

'Probably one of his own tools. They got Hattie Fifield to check inside the lodge and there's a hammer missing, which would fit.'

Daphne looked sickened, and Eve wondered belatedly about the wisdom of serving the crab. It was very rich.

'Angela says his tool belt's missing as well. It's possible he was wearing it, with the hammer in its holster. If so, then both items were removed from the scene.'

'So someone could have grabbed the hammer and attacked him before he could react?' Eve pictured it. She assumed it must be easy to slip a hammer from a belt like that. It would be impractical otherwise.

'That's about the size of it,' Robin said. 'If so, it's likely that the killer made the decision to attack him then and there. They may have just seen their opportunity, or Duncan could have said something that made them see red.'

'So awful to think of him carrying the weapon that killed him,' Daphne said.

Robin nodded. 'Let's move onto witness statements, who the police suspect and what we think.'

It was good to have a concrete plan. Eve hoped to goodness for Angela and Cesca's sake that they or the police made headway quickly. She couldn't imagine what they must be going through. She took a deep breath and sipped her wine. 'Shall we go through the key players one by one?'

Robin was glancing at some notes he'd made. 'Sure.'

'We should take Angela first, as Duncan's wife.' Eve wanted to grasp the nettle and get it over with. Viv opened her mouth to say something, then shut it again.

'I think we have to agree she has a motive,' Robin said. 'Duncan was sailing very close to the wind.'

Eve nodded. 'Angela was working all the hours God sends and living in squalor. Duncan was prioritising his affair over doing up their cottage. And he was about to tell her that Hattie was his daughter too. Or maybe he already had. Do you know, Robin?'

'She claims he hadn't, but Greg says she didn't look surprised.'

Viv huffed.

'Either way, she had plenty to upset her,' Eve went on. 'As well as what we've just mentioned, Kesham's beautiful, but it's very cut-off. She wasn't likely to pick up any stonemasonry work there, other than what Duncan needed. And I imagine they were amassing debt, despite Angela's long hours. Duncan seemed unable to see beyond his determination to buy and restore those two estate buildings. He claimed he was doing it for Angela and Cesca, but in reality he'd rekindled his relationship with Fifi, aka Jojo Landers. I sense Angela still loved Duncan, but if she'd discovered his affair, you can only imagine the hurt. The question is, did she know? I presume she didn't mention that to the police?'

Robin shook his head. 'But that doesn't mean much.'

'I agree. She might keep quiet to avoid looking like a suspect.'

Sylvia shot Eve a sidelong glance. 'What are the chances she had no idea?'

Eve had to admit they seemed slim.

'There's something else you should know too,' Robin put in. 'Angela's a wealthy woman thanks to Duncan's death.'

Eve put down her fork. 'Seriously? I thought he'd leave nothing but debts.'

'He certainly left plenty of those. The properties he'd

bought or inherited will probably be sold to cover them. I doubt there'll be much change.'

'So how...' Eve paused for a moment. 'Wait, don't tell me Duncan's life was insured? How did he afford that?'

'Jack Farraway paid for it. He told the police it was for Cesca's sake. She was his beloved wife Jess's great-niece, and he wanted to make sure she was secure.'

'I suppose one can see that,' Daphne said.

Sylvia was goggling. 'I like Jack as much as you do, Daphne, but it does make you wonder.'

Eve's heart sank at the extra motive it gave Angela. It didn't mean she was guilty, but she bet Palmer would jump to that conclusion. 'She'll be comfortably off at last.'

Robin gave her a rueful look. 'It'll be transformational. The police have asked her to stay where she is for the time being, but it won't be long before she sees the back of that damp little cottage.'

Eve's head was in her hands. 'What does Greg think?'

'He's convinced that Angela's devastated by the death, but as he pointed out, if she'd lashed out, that would still fit. And she's Palmer's number one suspect.'

It was as Eve had feared, and of course, Greg was right too.

'We have to do something.' Viv stabbed violently at her pasta.

'We will.' Eve gave her arm a squeeze and hoped that it wouldn't be providing evidence to confirm Angela's guilt.

'Perhaps we should tackle Jack Farraway next, as he stumped up the money for the insurance.' Eve topped up everyone's drinks. She invited Sylvia and Daphne to tell Viv, Robin and Simon what they'd told her.

After they'd finished, Eve said: 'He minds about family – Jess's especially, because he loved her so much. And I've seen him with Cesca. They're close. What if he thought Cesca's successful upbringing rested on the removal of her dad? It's pretty much what he said when Robin and I eavesdropped on his conversation with Byron. If I'm right, and Angela still loved Duncan, Jack might have decided that killing him was the only way to set her and Cesca on a better course.'

Robin nodded. 'Though that doesn't fit so well with a spur-of-the-moment murder in a fit of fury.'

'No, but he and Duncan fought that evening. Perhaps, after innocently arranging the life insurance, he'd started to fantasise about how convenient it would be if Duncan died, then that last row pushed him over the edge. He was so angry he could hardly speak.'

Daphne looked distressed, but Robin nodded. 'That could work. He's certainly got questions to answer. He told Greg he was at home when Duncan was killed, but unfortunately for him, the artist, Byron Acker, called in at half eleven on his way home from an evening at the Pied Piper in Long Stratford and got no reply. Interestingly, Greg said Acker looked quite uncomfortable when he mentioned it.'

'As though he was lying?'

'Possibly, but Greg reckoned he just didn't want to drop Jack in it.'

'That figures. They're clearly friendly. The police went back to Jack, I guess, and asked about the discrepancy?'

'They did, whereupon Jack claimed he'd been out for a walk. He said he'd lied because *he* knew he hadn't killed Duncan, and he thought it would be simpler not to mention it.'

'Blimey,' said Viv. 'What an idiot. I'll bet Palmer's got him high up his list of suspects too.'

'What are you thinking, Eve?' Robin must have spotted her expression.

'That Jack Farraway's no fool. He must have had good reason to lie, and whatever he was really up to, he doesn't want the police to know about it.'

He nodded. 'That's certainly what Greg thinks.'

'I told DC Dawkins about his and Duncan's row. I presume they asked him about it?'

'They did. Farraway said he found a receipt in the rubbish sack which showed Duncan was cutting corners on the renovation of the lodge. He said it made him furious because it was crucial that Duncan was "faithful to the original fabric of the building" or something like that.'

'Sounds like codswallop,' Sylvia said.

Robin gave a quick laugh. 'Greg says he answered readily enough.'

Eve could imagine. 'Maybe they'd had that argument before, so he fell back on it when he needed an excuse. But I agree with Sylvia; I don't buy it. Jack's tone suggested it was something deeply personal. I think he might have gone back into the lodge and fought with Duncan physically if Hattie hadn't turned up.' Eve remembered feeling frightened and suspecting they'd have to intervene.

'He could have found out that Duncan was betraying Angela,' Daphne said.

'He had. He called Duncan out on it when we overheard them, but he didn't issue any ultimatums about it.' Duncan's affair *could* have made him murderously angry, though Eve thought it unlikely given what they'd heard. She suspected it was something even closer to home.

Everyone ate in silence for a moment.

'Who's next?' asked Simon.

Eve rallied her thoughts. 'What about Byron Acker, since we've touched on him? He was obviously wandering around during the time when Duncan was killed too.'

'Turns out his real name is Colin Sanders,' Robin said.

Eve put down her wine. 'Really?' *How did you go from Colin to Byron?* 'Anything dodgy behind the name change?'

Robin shook his head. 'Probably not. He said it was his artist's name and that Colin Sanders sounded boring. Greg said he was blushing when he explained, and he felt a bit sorry for him.'

Eve could see his point.

'They've got no reason to suppose he had anything against Duncan – he paid his rent on time and seems to have been happy with his accommodation. He says he went straight home when Jack Farraway didn't answer his door. He's in the mix, but the police think he's probably an innocent bystander.'

Eve swallowed some more of the crab and samphire, which was delicious. Robin was a seriously good cook. 'I agree. Byron has a secret, but until we know what it is, there's no reason to suppose it has anything to do with Duncan.

'So, we're onto Fifi. She and Duncan were having an affair which automatically makes for a volatile situation, so she has to be on the list. But there's no other reason to suspect her. She and Duncan looked very close when I saw them kissing.'

'But Edward has a big, fat motive,' Sylvia said, spearing her last bit of pasta with her fork.

Eve nodded. 'I'm pretty sure he knew about the affair. Duncan got him involved in that stupid dare and I can't imagine him falling for it unless he felt threatened. I hope Palmer's taking him seriously as a suspect.'

'I'm afraid he hasn't entirely bought your suggestion that Fifi and Duncan were involved.' Robin grimaced.

'But I told Dawkins I saw them kissing.'

'And I did too.' Sylvia's back was ramrod straight, her look indignant.

Robin sighed. 'Even I did, but unfortunately, it's our word against hers, the light was fading, and we were all watching them through the trees. Plus, there's no useful evidence on Duncan's phone. Angela gave them the passcode but Greg reckons she'd only got it by snooping. She went bright red as she admitted she knew it. And lastly, Palmer's not our number one fan, Eve.'

Eve didn't need telling. 'Did they at least ask Fifi about it?'

He nodded. 'Greg and Dawkins made sure of that, but apparently Fifi looked surprised, asked how far away their witnesses were and claimed it wasn't her.'

'I'm sure it was.' Eve thought back. She really was. 'They must know that she and Duncan were an item back when they were teenagers.'

'Fifi says that was a long time ago, and that she loves Edward now.'

It was deeply frustrating. 'What did Edward say about him and Duncan climbing the hall?' That wasn't normal behaviour.

'That it was too much fun to resist – took him back to his youth.'

Honestly...

'I'm sorry.' Robin must have read her look. 'All in all, Palmer's not the sort to push it. Edward's the younger son of a duke and Fifi's loaded. They're both influential in their way and he won't want to cross them.'

'You would hope things had moved on,' said Daphne.

Sylvia gave a hollow laugh. 'That'll be the day.'

Robin turned the page in his notebook. 'Let's move on to Hattie.'

'She's an interesting one.' Eve sipped her wine, then relayed what Moira had told her. 'I'm not sure if Marjorie's reported what she said yet. Moira said she's nervous.'

Robin shook his head. 'Greg didn't mention it. We can let him know informally, but it's not much use when it's idle gossip.'

'I could see Hattie blaming Duncan for her boyfriend's death, and for not fighting harder to keep in touch with her as a child. If he'd kept tabs on her mum, he'd have known she'd been left parentless. Hattie might even blame him for her spell in jail; from the phone call Marjorie overheard, it certainly sounds that way. What's more, she specifically talked about taking her revenge. But he was helping launch her career when he died. Looking at it coldly, killing him now would seem counterproductive.' She explained her plan to talk to Duncan's old production company to see what stage negotiations had reached. 'One other thing to note is that it was Edward who spoke up for her when Marjorie and Jo Falconer wanted a character reference. It made me wonder if he's fallen for her. He could have felt tempted, given what was happening between Duncan and Fifi.' She sipped her wine. 'Did Greg pass on anything interesting about Hattie, Robin?'

He nodded. 'She claims Tod was a one-night stand and she doesn't even know his surname.'

Eve had the dispiriting feeling that everyone was lying. 'How did she know he'd died then?'

'She says someone called her to say, having found her number on his mobile, but they didn't identify themselves. She assumed he'd died in London because that's where he'd been headed. It's on the team's list to check the mobile, but what's the betting it was pay-as-you-go with no contract?

'Palmer's keen on her as a suspect too, of course. He's not one to look past her record.'

That sounded about right. 'She's in the mix from my point of view, but Jack and Edward come top.' Eve decided not to mention Angela again.

14

After she and Robin had cleared away, Eve handed round coffees and amaretti biscuits.

'What about next steps?' said Sylvia.

Viv had taken out a notebook. She'd adopted Eve's habit of writing things down, but not in quite the same way that Eve would have done it. This particular notebook had been donated by Eve and was relatively new, with secure pages, but Eve could tell it wasn't dedicated to this project. The page Viv had open already had a circle of letters in the middle, (an attempt to solve Wordle, Eve guessed), as well as an elaborate doodle and several times and numbers. Eve sincerely hoped they weren't bookings for Monty's that ought to be on the teashop calendar. It wouldn't be the first time.

She took a deep breath and decided to ask later. She needed to focus. 'There's a general question to answer: did the person who vandalised Duncan's properties also kill him? We need to know who it was and what motivated them. I'll have it in mind each time I conduct an interview.' If Eve was lucky, she might spot paint splashed on someone's shoes or something like that. 'Have the police said anything about it?'

Robin nodded. 'It wasn't just the lodge and Hideaway House that were affected. Someone egged White Cottage the night before we arrived at Kesham too. Angela says Duncan was worried about it but he guessed it was a one-off and it was too late to cancel our visit. It was Angela who washed the mess off.'

It would be...

'Interestingly, the scientific support officers say the paint thrown at the lodge wasn't hard to remove. They're getting it analysed.'

'And of course, the eggs would have been quite easy to wash off too.' It was curious. Why not use something harder to shift, like a standard spray paint? For a moment, Eve imagined Duncan doing it himself, but she couldn't think of any reason he would. 'Maybe it was someone who wanted to unnerve Duncan – drive him away even – but who cared about the buildings.'

'It's possible.' Robin's brow furrowed. 'You're thinking Jack or Hattie?'

Eve nodded. 'I wondered, especially about Jack. Restoration seems like his lifeblood.'

Viv scribbled away.

'Moving on to the murder itself, my top suspects are Edward and Jack, as I said, and I'll need to focus especially hard on Edward if Palmer's giving him a free pass. I'd like to find evidence of Fifi and Duncan's affair to force the police to take him seriously as a suspect. Perhaps either he or Fifi will slip up during my interviews.

'The rivalry between him and Duncan was intense, clearly. The affair's enough to explain it but there could be something more.' For a moment, the story of Edward rescuing his children from the fire came back to her. He'd only got locked out because he'd heard a noise in the garden. A wild and horrific thought emerged: what if it had been an intruder, and Edward had secretly discovered it was Duncan? He could have known that

Edward was home alone with the boys and decided to rid Fifi of her commitments by starting the fire. After their painful break-up, she might have become an obsession. If he'd bought Hideaway House to get close to her, it certainly looked that way.

She reminded the gang of the story, then googled it. There were news reports of course, full of atmosphere and dread. It had been the depths of winter, with snow on the ground, melting rapidly as the house was engulfed in flames. A photo showed Edward in a ragged coat, burned by the fire, a paramedic draping him in a blanket as he staggered across the small front garden to a waiting ambulance. Eve guessed someone had stopped the hacks from photographing the twins. That was a mercy.

Once again, she thought of how Edward must have felt, knowing his children were trapped in the house. It filled her with an animal-instinct fear for her own twins, adults though they were.

'Does the article mention the noise that drew Edward outside?' Sylvia asked.

Eve read further and nodded. 'He didn't find anyone in the garden, according to this. And in fact, the last paragraph says the investigators' conclusions were unequivocal. The fire was caused by ancient wiring that had been in the house for decades.' She should have read the whole thing before going down a rabbit hole. 'It's still interesting though. It might explain why Edward didn't give Fifi an ultimatum, despite her affair with Duncan. I believe the boys and their well-being are his top priority.'

'So he might kill Duncan in preference to breaking up the happy home?' Robin said.

Eve nodded. 'I could imagine it. Talking to him and Fifi will be key. As we said before, we don't have any motive for her, but love triangles are always volatile. I'll keep my eyes and ears open.

'Moving on to Jack as the second top suspect, I need to know what he found in Duncan's rubbish bag that was so devastating and why he'd wished him dead, even before that. And if he wasn't out killing Duncan when Byron stopped by, where was he?'

'For Hattie, I want to know if she's lost her chance with Duncan's production company now he's dead, which would be a big point against her killing him. I must also find out more about Tod. If they were closer than she's admitting, she could have killed in revenge.'

'How will you go about it?' Viv asked, underlining Hattie's name several times.

'If she minded about him, she must have wanted to know how he died. I'll try to find out if she went to London after people heard he was dead – it might hint that she was investigating. And I'll get Moira and Marjorie on the case too. Ask them to let me know if they see her do anything unexpected.

'I need to know what she really thought of Duncan. She won't be candid, I'm sure, but I can track down friends of her mum. They might know if Duncan really tried to stay in touch.'

'So that's the top three suspects taken care of,' Viv said.

'But what about Angela?' Daphne said quietly, running her finger along the grain of the wood in the dining table, back and forth. 'It's so terribly delicate.'

Eve took a deep breath. 'With any luck, our investigations into the others will prove one of them guilty. But you're right, it would be wrong to overlook her. I'll ask about her plans. If they're already well formulated that could hint she's been anticipating the insurance payout. It won't prove she killed for it, of course, but if I question her sensitively, I hope I'll find out how she felt about Duncan, and if she knew about his affair. I was meaning to talk to her anyway, the moment Hideaway House got egged. I wanted to see if she'd open up and let us help, but I was overtaken by events.

'Lastly there's Byron. No known motive, and I don't really buy him as a killer, but he *was* wandering the woods when Duncan died and he's hiding something; he looked very shifty when Gus knocked his papers to the floor.' Eve wished she'd got a look. 'I'll make sure I talk to him.'

'Anything we can do?' asked Simon.

'Make excuses to chat to anyone involved – preferably about topics that are unrelated to the murder, once you've expressed your sympathy. Someone might slip up if they're not on their guard.'

When they'd left, Eve texted Marjorie and Moira to enlist their help when it came to Hattie. They'd both be overjoyed to have official roles as spies.

15

Eve felt anxious as she ventured back to Kesham on Monday morning. What if she found irrefutable proof that Angela was guilty? It wouldn't just be her life she was destroying, but Cesca's too.

But at the same time, it was Angela and Cesca who made her mission crucial. She wanted to prove Angela innocent. Being able to grieve without fear of arrest wouldn't be much comfort, but it would be something. On the upside, she could operate without running into Palmer. Greg Boles had told her the coast was clear.

She left Robin to some paperwork he was reviewing for a police case down in London and headed off to Kesham, using the same car park as before. She found it empty, now the reporters and police had gone. Gus squirmed as she got him out of his harness and leaped down the moment he was free. He knew where they were, Eve guessed, and was glad to see the place again. Perhaps the sight of Duncan's body was forgotten.

Despite Edward and Jack being top of her suspect list, Eve made for White Cottage first – she wouldn't start her interviews without offering her condolences to Angela in person. Eve imagined her, sitting with Cesca in the run-down cottage with its damp walls, knowing she'd never hear Duncan striding in through the front door again. Even if she'd snapped and killed him, she'd probably be in pieces now.

She closed her eyes for a moment, but it was no use getting emotional. She needed to stick to her script and find out all she could. It was her only chance to help.

She knocked on the door of the cottage, the rough paint chafing her knuckles.

Angela opened up wearing jeans and a cheerful Breton top, but her bloodshot eyes had dark rings under them and her shoulders drooped. From somewhere behind her Eve could hear Cesca's voice. ('And then they all went home for tea.')

'She's playing with her soft toys.' Angela sounded infinitely weary. 'She hasn't taken in what's happened yet. I'm sorry to let you and Viv down at the teashop.'

'Don't give it another thought. I came to say how sorry we are. You should take as long as you need and if there's anything we can do, we're here for you. You must be completely over-whelmed.'

Angela nodded slowly. 'Thanks. It's such a shock. Would you like to come in?'

But Eve had sprung herself on Angela and it felt unfair. It wasn't ideal, giving her time to prepare before Eve quizzed her, but she was a friend. 'I'd love to stop by a bit later, if that would be okay?' She explained about the obituary. 'In the meantime, I was going to talk to Jack Farraway.' Eve felt so helpless, looking at Angela, knowing there was nothing she could do to ease her pain. She focused on practicalities instead. 'Would you like me to take Cesca to see him, to give you some time to yourself? I could bring her back when I've finished.'

Angela paused for a moment, then nodded. 'Thank you. He'll probably be glad to see her and it would help.' She called over her shoulder. 'Cesca! Come and say hello to Eve and Gus!'

It was just as well that her beloved dachshund was such a hit. He rolled over to have his tummy tickled and Eve reminded Cesca how best to do it.

Five minutes later, Eve was holding Cesca's hand, making her way along a woodland path towards the eastern edge of the estate, beyond which lay Jack's house. Angela had given her directions.

At last, it came into view. It was tiny but pretty, with roses round the door – very isolated of course, compared with being in the village.

She wondered if grief had made him hide himself away, though reaching the gate, she realised you could see Cotwin Place in the distance. Perhaps he'd chosen to move as close as possible to the place where he and his wife Jess had been happiest.

'Does Jack take you to play at Byron's house much?' Eve said to Cesca, thinking of finding the pair there on Saturday morning.

Cesca nodded. 'Byron's nice! He gives me cakes and lets me play with his tea set.'

It was hard to imagine someone like Byron having a tea set but Eve let it go. 'He seems very friendly.'

'He was nice to Uncle Jack when he was crying,' Cesca said, conversationally.

'Poor Jack. What made him sad?'

'He wanted to go into Byron's house because it was his and Auntie Jess's before. He had to stay outside, so he cried, but then Byron said he could come in. Now we go there all the time and Jack and Byron chat and chat.'

Byron's kindness made Eve emotional and her heart ached for Jack. She wondered why Duncan hadn't let Cotwin Place to him instead. But perhaps Jack had wanted somewhere to buy, not rent.

Jack looked almost as devastated as Angela when he

answered the door – drawn, his skin rather grey – but he rose to the occasion when he saw Cesca and gave Gus a pat.

'I'm so sorry for your loss.' They exchanged a few words, then Eve explained about the obituary. 'I know you and Duncan were friends for many years. If you feel able to talk about him, I'd be very grateful, but it must be a hugely difficult time.' Thoughts played in her head: Jack funding the life insurance, wishing Duncan dead and vowing he'd never forgive him. And most damning of all, lying about his whereabouts on Saturday night.

'I'm happy to talk to you,' Jack said. 'You'd better come inside.'

He stood back and Eve took a deep breath and entered.

The interior of Jack's cottage was shady, full of old books and ornaments, with dust motes playing in the air. Everything looked well loved, rather than perfect. It was hard to imagine the owner of such a house being a killer – it was all so normal – but Jack's feelings had clearly built up over time.

He offered to make Eve some tea, which gave her a chance to snoop at the shoes, boots and jackets by the door. None of them were splashed with paint as far as she could see.

Jack returned with the tea and a jug of orange squash for Cesca, then took the lot into the garden. After placing the drinks on a table, he fetched a toy gardening set for his great-niece. It gave Eve the chance to peer at the shoes he was currently wearing, but they looked paint free too. If he was Duncan's vandal, there was no way of proving it. She'd already asked him who he thought was responsible of course, and that hadn't revealed anything.

'I've given Cesca her own bit of garden to tend.' Jack smiled sadly at Eve and indicated a patch covered with sweet Williams alongside some bare earth. 'She likes digging so nothing lasts there. I'm going to put a sandpit in.'

'That's a lovely idea and it's a beautiful garden.' It was

surrounded with a viburnum hedge which made it feel protected and enclosed. 'It must be nice to be so close to where you and Jess lived.'

He nodded. 'It was a bit of luck when it came up for sale.'

'You didn't want to rent Cotwin Place?' Eve wanted to know the background. 'Or buy it even?' If Duncan had sold it to him, he could have used the money to buy Hideaway House, without incurring more debt.

Jack winced, though he covered it quickly and sipped his tea.

'That wasn't an option?' Eve rued the pain she was causing him, but letting it go would be remiss. She needed to know what had happened, for everyone's sake.

'Buying it certainly wasn't. Jess made it a condition that Duncan shouldn't sell the place. She wanted it to stay in the family.'

That explained a lot.

'We talked about me renting it,' Jack went on, 'but the timing didn't work. Duncan was in a hurry to find a tenant and I was still tangled up, selling our London house. Then Byron came along. He was happy to take it as it was, and pay a decent rent, despite the poor state of repair, so Duncan's prayers were answered.' Jack's tone had turned bitter, and his knuckles were white on his mug. He blinked quickly and Eve was sure he was fighting tears.

Not surprising, if Jack's dreams of living at Cotwin Place had been destroyed by Duncan's impatient desperation for cash.

'I guess you'd have started work on the place immediately if you'd moved in,' Eve said.

Jack nodded. 'I'd have put my heart and soul into it. Of course, Byron's welcomed me in and I'm doing bits and pieces for him, so that's something.'

But it was a far cry from living there. 'I suppose Duncan

must have been pleased that you had enough time to help with the other restorations instead.'

Eve knew she'd be touching a nerve; it was horrible, but the only way to tease out the truth. In Jack's shoes, Eve would have told Duncan to take a running jump.

The pain and anger were there in his eyes, but Jack shook himself. 'He was. It made sense for me to help, and I did it willingly. You've seen how hard Angela works and how damp and dilapidated White Cottage is. The quicker they got more income, the better. With Byron installed, the next priority was to finish Hideaway House and let it out.'

But it was clear he'd acted for Angela and Cesca, not out of love for Duncan. 'Did you think Duncan would use the rental income to do up White Cottage?'

There was a long pause. 'It's what I hoped.'

'Only he mentioned he'd like to buy the Warrener's Cottage at Kesham too. I wasn't sure of his priorities.'

'I wasn't either.' He didn't meet her eye, but his words were full of feeling.

Eve imagined he'd given up hope of Duncan doing anything noble or selfless.

As they talked, Cesca filled her watering can from the outdoor tap, then pottered over to the bed with nothing in it and poured out the contents. Gus was close at hand, following her movements with his eyes, doing the odd sideways skip.

Eve decided to change tack. 'When did you first meet Duncan?'

He sighed. 'He worked as an apprentice with me on several projects while I was still married to my first wife. Later, after my divorce, he introduced me to Jess.'

It must have bound him and Duncan together, for good or ill, even if their relationship had soured. 'And what was Duncan like when you first worked with him?'

'Driven. He'd had knocks as he grew up but he came out

fighting. Whatever barriers life threw in his way, he'd find a way around them.'

'That sounds impressive.' Eve paused. 'But I guess it could have made him ruthless.' The way Duncan had let Cotwin Place before Jack made it back to Suffolk bore that out.

At last, Jack nodded. 'He tended to say that the end justified the means.'

Cesca and Gus had been scampering around Jack's lawn happily, but now they were after attention. Eve hadn't quite finished though, so a distraction was needed.

'You could see if any of the flowers need watering,' Eve said to Cesca. The mud she'd been tending was saturated. 'If they're wilting, they're probably thirsty.' She turned back to Jack. 'If that's all right with you?'

He nodded. 'Of course.'

Cesca pottered off again and a moment later she was giving some drooping marigolds a bath. It made Eve think of her own front garden at Elizabeth's Cottage, where there were marigolds by the door. Eve had a feeling the sight of them had influenced Viv's current choice of hair colour. 'Maybe not too much water, Cesca,' she said aloud. 'That's it. Just right.'

Jack reached for the teapot, distracting her from the little girl. 'Another cup?'

'Thank you. Byron mentioned you'd helped Duncan out financially with the restoration of the estate properties.' Eve had been wondering if the financial side of things was relevant. If Jack was out of pocket, he might be repaid from Duncan's estate.

'For the same reason that I agreed to work on them. The sooner they were done, the sooner they'd bring in money and give Cesca some security.' He sighed. 'And I didn't want Duncan letting himself down. I found out he wasn't even paying Hattie; he'd convinced her that volunteering in exchange for experience was the norm. It wasn't right and his name would be mud if it came out. I let him have enough for a small stipend.'

'That was generous of you. Hattie must have been grateful.'

'I told him not to say it was me.' His tone was clipped. There was something he wasn't telling her, Eve was sure of it.

She itched to ask about the angry words she'd heard him and Duncan exchange at the lodge, but showing her hand at this stage would be risky. She'd bide her time.

'I must get Cesca back to Angela and let you get on.'

They stood up and Eve helped carry the tea things indoors as Cesca put her watering can by the back door.

Eve thanked Jack for his time, took his number in case they needed to speak again, and felt his isolation as he closed the door. Cesca skipped ahead next to Gus and that broke Eve's heart too. It was as though she hadn't a care in the world. Angela was clearly right about the news not sinking in yet. Cesca was so young.

Eve was distracted from her thoughts by a sob. She was still close to Jack's cottage and his open window.

She hesitated. It was often telling to monitor a person's reaction just after she'd left them. An interviewee with something to hide might bottle up emotion, which would overflow the moment they were alone.

In this case, it might just be that Jack hadn't wanted to lose face by letting go in front of her. A lot of people still believed a stiff upper lip was essential, especially men. Eve found it achingly sad.

But Jack's feelings towards Duncan had been mixed. On Saturday night, something that felt irreparable had rounded off what was probably months of hurt and frustration. The fact that they'd once been close friends would only accentuate the effect.

She needed to understand, so she hovered close to Jack's window as Cesca skipped ahead. When she peeped in, he had his head down. The sound of him crying was heartbreaking. A moment later, he opened a drawer in a bureau and touched something inside. Eve couldn't see what it was, but his crying intensified. It was probably a photo of his late wife, or perhaps one of him and Duncan, but a sudden flash of anger in his eyes made her want to know for certain. She'd have to call again.

16

Cesca chattered about flowers and the fairies she said she'd seen in the woods as they walked back towards White Cottage. Eve had to make herself focus. Half her mind was still on Jack and the contents of his desk drawer.

Just before they reached White Cottage, Cesca said: 'I wonder if Daddy will be back now.'

Eve stopped in her tracks. 'What did Mummy tell you about it?'

'She said he'd be back if he could, but he can't.'

Eve felt her chest contract and bent to give Cesca a hug. 'I'm afraid that's right.'

A moment later, she was standing at Angela's peeling door again. White Cottage's windows were open on this stifling summer's day, just like Jack's, and Eve could hear one side of a conversation. Angela must be on the phone. Eve bent to show Cesca a pretty pebble in the front garden – anything to buy some time and hear a few words. Once again it was an under-hand approach, but Angela sounded emotional and she could have killed her husband. Eve needed to keep a clear head.

'I still can't believe what I did,' Angela was saying. 'One stupid, rash act and our lives have changed for ever. I was just so angry. And desperate. No. No one knows – well, no one else, anyway.'

Eve held her breath as she passed Cesca a pebble with a hole in it. *Please don't be guilty.* It would be unbearable if Cesca lost this last bit of security.

Angela was finishing her conversation when Eve stood up and knocked on the door. A moment later she heard her slow footsteps as she approached. Everything must feel like such an effort.

Cesca stood up and gave her mum the pebbles and Angela bent to hug her.

'Will you come in now?' Angela said. 'I can answer your questions for the obituary.'

'If you're sure.'

Angela took her through to a small sitting room, covered in books and papers. It felt lived in, but not comfortable. It was too cramped for that. Angela gave Cesca a jigsaw to play with and offered Eve a drink. As usual, Eve accepted as it gave her the chance to assess her surroundings. It really was rotten that Duncan hadn't paid more attention to their home. There was mildew on the wall and the damp would wreck a threadbare silk lampshade before long too. She glanced around for any item of clothing with paint spatters on it, but there was nothing in sight. Of course, White Cottage had been attacked, just like the lodge, but that didn't rule Angela out.

It was a glimpse of white cotton smeared with dirt that got Eve's attention. It was peeping out from behind one of the sofa cushions. Eve glanced over her shoulder, but Cesca was absorbed, jamming a very unlikely pairing of jigsaw pieces together as Gus hovered nearby, looking interested. Angela was still busy in the kitchen, so Eve moved to examine the cotton.

It looked like one of the vest tops Duncan had worn. Or what was left of it. It had been cut roughly. Angrily.

Eve's heartrate ramped up as she wondered when Angela had stuffed it there. If she'd mutilated it before Duncan died, you'd think she'd have disposed of it by now. An alternative was that she'd destroyed it more recently and shoved it behind the cushion when Eve knocked. It didn't mean she'd killed her husband. She could be angry with him for so many reasons – even for leaving her and Cesca alone, however much it wasn't his fault. But under the circumstances, it only added to Eve's worries.

Eve was back by the small table when Angela re-entered the room. 'How did you get on at Jack's? Is he okay?'

Eve made a so-so rocking motion with her hand. 'It must be such a shock for everyone. He explained his history with Duncan, including the money he put towards the estate restorations, and so Duncan could pay Hattie.'

'Ah.' Angela swallowed. From her tone, Eve realised she'd triggered something more than she was expecting. 'Yes, I'm afraid it's true.'

She might be embarrassed that Duncan's uncle had been subbing him, but it felt like more than that. Eve waited, willing her to elaborate.

'I was horrified when I found Duncan hadn't passed the pay on,' Angela said at last. 'No one should work for nothing.'

Heck, so Duncan had pocketed the cash instead. Put it towards buying the lodge perhaps, or paying someone who wouldn't work for free. And Jack had found out, that was clear. Angela had assumed he'd told Eve the whole story. It explained why Jack had been so tight-lipped when Eve had speculated about Hattie's gratitude.

'Perhaps she realised he needed the money for other things. Her earnings from the pub could have been enough to tide her over.' Eve hesitated. 'I hear they had a closer connection than anyone realised.'

Angela's lips twitched as she crushed a tissue she held in her hand. Eve could see how angry she was. 'Yes, I heard that too. But it was the police who passed it on, not Duncan. It seems he was happy for me to hear last.'

She was tearing at the tissue now. She sounded angry and honest, yet Greg Boles had told Robin he was convinced she'd already known. Either he was wrong or Eve was.

'I'm sorry. It must have come as a shock.'

Angela was silent for a moment. 'I ought to be past being shocked by anything Duncan did.'

Perhaps there was even more for Eve to unearth. As for Hattie, Eve privately thought she'd have been unlikely to work for nothing if she'd known there was pay on offer. And if she'd discovered Duncan was keeping it back, it would be another mark against him. Not enough to kill over, but it could have tipped the balance if she'd discovered the truth on Saturday night... Thoughts of a shiny TV career might have faded for a moment. And a moment was all it would have taken.

There was a brief interruption as Cesca started to cry violently, making Gus whine. She'd got a piece of jigsaw caught in her hair. Eve volunteered to help, sat Cesca on her lap, and painstakingly untangled her curly locks as Angela dashed to another room. She returned with a daisy-decorated hair slide. As soon as Eve had managed to separate child and puzzle piece, Angela swept Cesca's hair from her face. 'Duncan bought her this slide as a baby and it's the only one she'll wear.' She burst into tears as she clipped it in place, and Cesca started howling again.

Eve gave them both a hug and eventually, Angela dried her eyes.

After some moments, Eve asked very gently if Angela was okay to carry on, then put some straightforward questions about how she and Duncan had met. She heard how it was Jack and Jess who'd introduced them. 'Jack and Duncan were great friends,' Angela said wistfully.

'Things changed?' Eve would like her take on the breakdown of their relationship.

Angela sighed. 'Nothing's been the same since Duncan realised he could get his hands on Hideaway House.'

His route back to his lost love. This might be Eve's chance to find out if Angela knew about Fifi and Duncan, but she'd have to tread very carefully. The last thing she wanted was to reveal it, if Angela hadn't realised. 'I know he used to live on the estate as a child. And that he knew the Landerses – the family who lived here.'

She watched Angela intently and her face went completely blank. She didn't even blink, and Eve was convinced she was trying to hide her feelings.

'Yes,' Angela said at last, her voice quavering slightly, 'that's right.' She cleared her throat. 'He and his parents lived in this same house, in fact. He said his childhood was happy until they split up.'

Duncan really had slotted back into his old life. Eve wondered what state White Cottage had been in back then. 'I gather the Landerses took him in at the hall for a time.'

'A glimpse of how the other half lived. He and the daughter of the family had a thing going on. They were engaged at one point, and set to stay here for ever, but then the entire family ran out on him.'

She sounded angry at them. If she knew Fifi was Jojo, she must be angry at her too, both for what she did back then, and for her continued hold over Duncan.

If Duncan had come back to see what might have been, and Angela had only realised once they'd arrived, she must have been gutted.

'Do you think Duncan hoped to buy more estate properties?' Eve asked, wondering if he'd told Angela about his hopes for the Warrener's Cottage. It could have made her time at Kesham feel like a life sentence.

Angela closed her eyes for a moment. 'I'm quite sure he did. How he'd have raised the money is anyone's guess.'

'What *was* he like to live with, Angela?' It felt as though they were delving deep enough for her to ask now. 'It can't have been easy.'

She let out a long, unsteady sigh and there were tears in her eyes. 'It wasn't. I knew when I agreed to marry him that he'd be complicated. Life had thrown a lot at him. But I was convinced it would all be worth it.'

'And you carried on feeling that way?'

Angela's jaw tensed, but after a moment she nodded. 'But he gave me more to cope with than I'd ever have imagined.'

Eve sensed she wanted to finally let her feelings out. She waited, hoping she'd elaborate again, but after a moment, when everything seemed to hang in the balance, she folded her arms and shook her head.

'It's history now,' she said at last.

Eve would have to try a fresh tack. 'I gather the vandal who targeted Hideaway House egged this cottage too?'

Angela gave a quick nod.

'Do you have any idea who did it?' Eve wondered why the vandal had changed methods, from eggs to paint. It seemed almost arbitrary.

Angela's shoulders hunched and she looked down at Cesca. 'No. No idea at all.'

Eve didn't believe her. She could be protecting someone or clamming up out of fear.

She'd have to back off again. She asked Angela more about Duncan's work, then finally slipped in her question about her plans for the future.

Angela hesitated. 'I don't want to leave you and Viv in the

lurch, but ultimately, I'd like to move back to London. It would be better for my work – my real work I mean.'

Eve needed to know how far she'd thought it through. 'You certainly mustn't worry about us. But what about Cesca and school?'

'The primary I attended has got a place for her in September.' She stopped suddenly, as though she knew she'd said too much. The hope in her eyes as she'd mentioned the school was gone again, replaced by tears.

All Eve's fears were back. The knowledge of the school place seemed damning. It was a Monday, but schools were on holiday. Checking availability would have taken more than a quick call. Of course, she could have been planning to leave Duncan. It would be understandable. But she must have been anticipating having the money to move back to the most expensive city in the country. The life insurance felt like the obvious source.

Angela blew her nose as Cesca pottered over, put her head on her mum's lap and started to cry. 'I want Daddy to come back,' she said as Angela stroked her hair.

'I'm so sorry.' Eve felt like a bundle of emotions too. She needed to stay calm. 'Viv's been through this, you know. Not in the same circumstances, but her husband died when her three were little. If you want to talk, she'll at least understand something of what you're going through. And either of us are up for chats or childminding. Would you prefer me to leave you to it now?'

Angela nodded and Eve got up to go. 'Can I get you any groceries from Moira's? Anything like that? I could pop them in later.' Eve only wished she could turn back the clock.

Angela looked uncomfortable but at last she nodded. 'If you're sure. I can't face the villagers yet.'

Eve could understand that. 'It's the least I can do.'

Angela asked for some cheese, pasta, milk and vegetables

and insisted on giving Eve the money up front. She did at least have plenty of cash on her. She looked dazed as she viewed it, as though she'd forgotten how money even worked.

As Eve said goodbye, promising to drop the goods off before suppertime, she thought of Angela's phone conversation again. *'I still can't believe what I did. One stupid, rash act and our lives have changed for ever. I was just so angry. And desperate.'*

17

Eve secured Gus in the back seat of the car, then drove home to rejoin Robin who'd paused for a coffee break.

He handed her a cup as she filled him in on what she'd discovered, from Angela's phone call to the lacerated T-shirt she'd found under her cushion. He whistled. 'A productive morning then. Well done.'

'I mustn't distract you, if you're in the middle of things.'

But he shook his head. 'I've got time to talk.'

So they sat at the kitchen table and continued to pore over the situation. 'It's pretty shocking that Duncan never paid Hattie the stipend that Jack provided. I'm still hoping I can find out whether she was resentful. I expect Marjorie will do half the work for me.

'Jo made Hattie sound very cool about Tod's death, which strikes me as odd. Even if he was a one-night stand, you'd think she'd show *some* reaction. But maybe the hard-as-nails veneer is a front; she's had to be tough. If I were her, I'd have wanted to find out more.'

· · ·

In the end, she got her next lead sooner than she'd imagined, via a call on her mobile just after lunch.

Moira.

'*Ah, Eve, I'm so glad I caught you.*' The storekeeper was breathless. '*I've been keeping a lookout, and Hattie Fifield's waiting at the bus stop by the village green this minute. I was just about to call Marjorie for details when she came in. She's with me now.*'

Eve had thought she could hear someone in the background trying to chip in.

'*Now, apparently, Marjorie accidentally overheard Hattie arranging to meet a friend at a pub in London.*'

'*It's called the Wooden Spoon, near Liverpool Street station,*' Marjorie put in, at speed.

'*Just what I was about to say.*' Moira raised her voice, talking over her friend. '*She's due there by five.*'

It might not mean anything, but getting to London was an effort – and expensive too, especially on public transport. It had to be worth finding out more. 'Thanks so much to you both.'

'*Not at all, Eve – I take my civic responsibilities seriously,*' Moira said. '*You know that.*'

Eve managed not to snort, said goodbye and rang off. Moira and Marjorie's nosiness was a boon, but if Eve were Hattie, she'd want to move digs.

Eve passed on the news to Robin, then checked her bag for anything she might need. She was worried about letting Angela down – she'd promised her the shopping – but Robin said he'd sort it out.

'You've really got time? You're my hero.'

He grinned. 'It's true that entering the village store is an act of bravery when Moira's around, but I'm equal to it.' His eyes turned serious. 'You'll be okay?'

She nodded. 'I won't let her see me.' Eve took a sunhat

which would help hide her face, gave Gus a cuddle, Robin a kiss and was on her way.

Eve left her Mini at the station and took the train into London. She kept a sharp eye out for Hattie, knowing they were probably on the same service. At the other end, she looked up the pub, which turned out to be in Whitechapel. She took a circuitous route to avoid being spotted, but that had its downsides. Before long she was heading along a deserted alley where youths slouched against a wall. One of them muttered something unsavoury as she passed. She kept looking over her shoulder, both to see what they were doing and to check for Hattie too.

At last, she found the pub, a lopsided place with sash windows and low ceilings. Eve put on her dark glasses before she went inside and peered through an inner window from the pub's lobby. No sign of Hattie, though it was now a minute past five.

Eve went to the garden next, not daring to pause to order a drink, though the lack of one might attract attention. It was the lesser of the two evils. If Hattie was meeting a friend, they were almost certain to discuss Duncan. What they said could be crucial.

A moment later, Eve caught sight of her, sitting well down the courtyard opposite a young man with a shaved head wearing a black T-shirt that showed his wiry frame. Eve snatched up an abandoned pint glass which still held an inch of lager and walked down the garden. Hattie was facing away from her, thank goodness, and Eve sat at a table just behind, so they were back-to-back. It was taking a risk, but she'd never hear anything otherwise. At least she had her sunhat and dark glasses on. She should look reasonably anonymous if Hattie turned round.

'You're still beating about the bush, Hattie.' That had to be the man with the shaved head. 'I haven't got all day. Why are you really here?'

'You're so suspicious. Could I really not have requested a meet-up for old times' sake?'

The man laughed. 'Ha! No. You're like me, Hattie. Not the sentimental type.'

'You're wrong about that. I wanted to catch up. Hear how life's going back on Beckshaw Street.'

'Yeah, right.' His tone was curt. 'Like I said, what do you want?'

She sighed. 'Money. You owe me. I covered for you.'

She'd lowered her voice and Eve strained to hear, tense.

'Yeah, thanks for that. Speaking of, what happened? Did Duncan start to suspect you were in on the theft too?'

Oh my. Everything came clear in an instant. Now Eve understood why Hattie had said Tod was dead.

'What? No, of course he didn't.'

'If he did, you might have killed him to stop him talking, even if it was rubbish. With your record, it wouldn't look good, would it?'

'You are so full of it. I'm still furious with you for going off with stuff from the hall. But since you did, you must be in the money, and I could use some right now.'

'You'll be making piles of it soon, your face on TV.' He knew about the deal Duncan had been brokering, clearly.

'If it still works out. And it's beside the point anyway. It's your fault I'm having to pay out, after you gave away my secrets. Too much beer, too much chit-chat. It's always the way with you, yet you don't learn your lesson. You should stop talking to Rattler. You know that's how he got his nickname, right? Because he won't shut up. And it's not just my business you've been spilling. Duncan would never have found out you were alive if you hadn't called him. What possessed you? It took me ages to convince him I hadn't known. So I'm in a bad mood, and unless you want me to tell the police exactly where you are...'

There was a long pause. 'All right, all right.' Eve presumed he was counting out some cash, but it was too risky to look.

'Good boy, Tod. Your secret's safe with me.'

And she had a blackmail-worthy secret too, by the sound of it. Something that Tod had let slip to a third party. He hadn't pushed back when she'd blackmailed him, so Eve guessed whatever he knew about her was damning, but not worse than the theft he'd committed. That didn't mean Hattie was innocent of murder, though.

Hattie passed within a couple of feet of Eve as she held her breath, her heart thudding.

After that, Eve heard Tod curse under his breath and waited until he left too before she also exited the pub.

18

On the journey home, Eve thought about what she'd learned. The theory that Hattie could have killed Duncan in revenge for Tod's death, following his eviction, was dead in the water. He was alive and kicking and she didn't sound bothered about him anyway. But she could still have killed Duncan for abandoning her as a child if something had tipped her over the edge – like him not passing on the money from Jack. And it looked as though someone was blackmailing her too. Hattie had blamed Tod for that – his habit of drinking too much, then gossiping. Eve couldn't imagine what he might have let slip, but one of the key players hearing about it and demanding cash felt like an avenue worth exploring.

Angela had had plenty of money in her purse when Eve visited, but she was about to come into a large sum anyway. She didn't seem likely.

Fifi had ample cash of her own and Jack had tried to give Hattie money, via Duncan. Edward might not be as wealthy as his wife, but he worked in the City. He couldn't be hurting.

Eve's mind floated to Byron Acker. She googled his art to see how much it went for, then sat staring out of the window as the outskirts of London gave way to fields. Byron's paintings were wonderful, but they only sold for a hundred or two. He'd have to shift a lot to make a living.

How was he managing to pay his rent? Thoughts of the papers Gus had upset spooled through her head. Byron had been so quick to stop Eve picking them up. If he was involved in something criminal, he could have added blackmail to his repertoire. She pinged Robin a message to ask if the police had looked into his finances, but she guessed they'd had no reason to.

After that, she turned her mind back to Tod. It seemed less likely that it was Hattie who'd left his things for her and Robin to find now. She wouldn't want Eve investigating his fate after what had happened, especially given he had dirt on her. If the person who'd left the box of belongings was also the vandal, then Hattie probably hadn't thrown the eggs or paint either.

Eve followed her out at Blyworth Station and hesitated once she was on the platform. She didn't want to leave her car stranded but she was keen to see where Hattie went next. If Eve drove, she might never find out. She watched as Hattie boarded a bus for Long Stratford, the village just south of Kesham. She could be heading there, or to the estate.

When Hattie climbed to the upper deck, Eve made her choice and got on the bus too, hiding herself near the back downstairs. She messaged Robin to explain. She'd fetch her car later.

Thankfully, several people got out at Long Stratford, where Hattie alighted, so Eve was able to sneak out too, unseen.

Within minutes Hattie had entered the village pub, the Pied Piper. Eve dashed in after her, hoping to hear another conversation, but it was instantly clear she wasn't there for a drink. She wove between the customers, who were eating early dinners, taking a circuitous route until she reached the back door. She caused enough of a stir to distract people – they were probably gossiping about the murder, given she was Duncan's daughter – but Eve didn't see her talk to anyone. She didn't spot any familiar faces in the pub either, but the place was surprisingly busy for a Monday evening; she couldn't check every table. If she didn't hurry, she'd lose track of Hattie. She followed her into the garden, then down a side passageway and back onto the street.

Once again, Eve was torn. She wanted to know what Hattie had been up to in the pub. She'd just acquired money to pay a blackmailer. Perhaps she'd handed it over to someone. If Eve went back to watch the clientele, she might guess who, but now Hattie was dashing off down the high street. If she was going on to Kesham, Eve wanted to see what she did there.

After a moment's indecision, she followed. She'd come back to Long Stratford; maybe the pub staff could tell her if anyone from the estate had been in that evening.

Hattie did indeed cut through the fields to Kesham. There wasn't much cover – no hedges, just the odd tree – so Eve kept well back and was primed to flatten herself against the ground if need be, but Hattie didn't turn. She seemed intent on her mission.

Following became a lot easier once she reached the woods and it wasn't long before Eve realised where Hattie was going. The path she'd chosen led to the lodge.

It might be an innocent visit after all. She probably had things there that she wanted to pick up. Guilty or not, Duncan's death had upended her day-to-day life. As a volunteer, she hadn't lost an income, but the TV deal would likely fall through. Hattie had sounded doubtful about it when she'd talked to Tod. It still seemed like a big barrier to her killing Duncan.

Eve watched from the trees. Hattie didn't make for the main lodge building, but for the washhouse and bakery next door. She tried the handle, but it wouldn't budge. Perhaps the police had locked up since she'd last visited. A moment later, she glanced over her shoulder, then took something from her pocket.

Eve could only see her back, but from her movements and muttered curses, she guessed she was trying to pick the lock. That was interesting. She'd clearly come prepared, which suggested the operation was secret. If her mission was honest, why not ask the police to let her in?

At last, the door came free, and Hattie stepped into the cramped, dark space. She appeared less than a minute later, holding an A4 folder which she tucked inside her jacket. After closing the door behind her, she spent five minutes making sure the lock was fast again, then strode off along a main path in the direction of Saxford.

What on earth had she hidden in the washhouse that was so secret? Eve didn't think she'd find out by following Hattie, but she needed to head that way anyway. Robin had texted to say he'd give her a lift to Blyworth to pick up her car and Eve didn't want to keep him waiting. He'd answered her question about Byron too. It was as she'd thought. Sadly, the police had no excuse to look into his financial affairs.

She kept close enough to Hattie to monitor her, which turned out to be useful. Just before they left the estate, a figure emerged from the woods.

Edward Tuppington-Hynd. Eve paused. She'd already wondered if Edward had fallen for Hattie after he'd given her a character reference.

'Hattie, hello!' He raised a hand and Eve saw her start.

She was reluctant to stop, Eve could tell, but after a moment she turned towards Edward and returned his greeting.

Eve crept closer. They were talking now, but their voices had dropped.

Worry lines creased Edward's brow. 'I'm sorry – I hardly had the chance to talk to you after Duncan was killed. Are you okay?' His intent look told Eve he really wanted to know, but he didn't take her in his arms or show any sign of being more than a concerned friend.

Hattie nodded at last. 'It was a huge shock of course, and I'm sad. Very sad. But it's not as though we knew each other well.'

At last, Edward nodded. 'Your feelings must be all over the place. Who do you think killed him?'

Hattie shook her head, stepping back a little. 'I don't know.' But after a moment, she went on, her words coming out in a rush. 'I'm scared of Jack Farraway. His and Duncan's relationship had broken down and he's got a temper. He took a sledgehammer to a box Duncan had made just over a week ago. It looked like kindling by the time he'd finished.'

Eve wondered what had triggered Jack's fury. Perhaps he'd just discovered Duncan was cheating on Angela, but if so, she didn't think he'd have killed over it. She'd heard him discuss it with Duncan later. He'd been angry, certainly, but it was out in the open – not a grudge Jack had been secretly nursing, until it got out of control.

'Have you told the police?' Edward asked.

She nodded. That was interesting. Greg hadn't mentioned it to Robin. Perhaps Hattie had just made it up, to deflect attention from herself. She'd know it would be believable if she'd seen the tensions between Jack and Duncan.

'Do you think Jack did it?' Hattie went on.

Edward looked unhappy. 'I don't know.' Eve's thoughts turned on their head. Perhaps he'd done it himself and had been checking Hattie hadn't guessed.

19

When Eve got back to Elizabeth's Cottage, Robin drove her straight to Blyworth in his van. She called Greg Boles on the way and told him about the folder she'd seen Hattie pick up at the washhouse. She asked him about the tale Hattie had told Edward too, and it was as she'd thought. Hattie hadn't mentioned Jack smashing up a box belonging to Duncan to the police.

'If she was lying, it smacks of a guilty conscience,' Eve said, after she'd rung off and relayed the details to Robin.

He nodded. 'You didn't tell him about Tod?'

She turned to him. 'I'm sorry. I certainly would have if I thought it would help them solve the case. But as far as I can see, it simply lessens Hattie's motive, without writing her off. That might persuade her to tell the police herself, eventually. I guess she thinks leaving them in the dark is worth the risk at the moment.

'But me telling them feels counterproductive. If they rush in and question Hattie she'll know someone followed her to London. After that, she'll be so careful I won't find out anything. Reporting her break-in at the washhouse is different. Anyone could have seen her by chance.'

He sighed. 'You have a point.'

She felt guilty for giving him divided loyalties. Greg was such an old friend. 'If necessary, I can find out more about Tod myself. She mentioned the street where he's staying in London. I could quiz him while returning his beanie and diary, though it's probably more than he deserves.' It didn't look as though his thieving had been born of desperation after all.

That evening, after a late supper of chorizo and red pepper risotto, Eve sat at her laptop, checking her messages and outstanding jobs.

She hadn't heard back from Duncan's old production company. She'd have to chase them in the morning. Tod had referred to Hattie making lots of money soon, with her face on TV. That might imply that the deal had already been done, though it could still rest on Duncan's involvement.

Hattie had replied to Eve's interview request by email, agreeing to talk to her the following afternoon. It should be an interesting chat. Eve was booked in to see the Tuppington-Hynds at the hall tomorrow evening too – another crucial interview. Beyond that, she'd heard back from an old colleague of Duncan's at the Built Heritage Trust in London who could meet her on Wednesday. And lastly, Byron had replied with his mobile number, inviting her to call to arrange a time to talk.

After getting her admin and to-do lists in order, she researched Hattie's family. She wanted to speak to someone who'd known her mum, to find out how hard Duncan had tried to stay in touch as Hattie grew up. If he'd really made an effort, another of Hattie's potential motives became less likely. On the one hand, Jo at the pub said Hattie had shown her a letter from Duncan, intended for her when she was a child, but on the other, he could have written that any time. If he'd wanted Hattie to work for him for free, currying favour would have been essential. Hattie had been an important asset, and she could imagine Duncan using her without a qualm. He'd kept her stipend for himself, after all.

By looking at the news coverage when Hattie was tried, and cross referencing it with social media, she discovered her mum had been called Posy Fifield. After that, Eve worked painstakingly through old photos which Hattie had put onto Instagram until she'd identified a woman who frequently appeared next to Posy. She was called Susie Parks. Eve found *her* Instagram and discovered she owned the bakery at Long Stratford, the very village she'd followed Hattie to, earlier that evening.

It made sense, of course. Hattie had been brought up locally, just like Fifi and Duncan.

Eve showed Robin what she'd found. 'It makes the trip back there tomorrow all the more urgent.'

Eve was in for two disappointments the following morning. When she chased Duncan's production company, she found the woman she needed to talk to was in meetings all day. She left another message, then headed to Long Stratford, leaving Gus with Robin.

She found Susie Parks' bakery all right, but she wasn't in work that day, something about a domestic emergency, helping her daughter after her garden had been vandalised. It made Eve think of Duncan's buildings at Kesham. Susie's colleague was full of the injustice of it all and muttered about 'youths'.

Eve felt for them, but it was frustrating to have to wait. She did her best to get Susie's assistant onside, then provided her mobile number, with a message to say it was urgent.

After that, Eve went and knocked on the door of the Pied Piper, which wasn't open yet. When there was no answer, she peered through the window of the half-timbered building. She could hear a vacuum going, so someone was inside. At last, the noise stopped and a woman with curly blonde hair and an ample bosom arrived at the door.

'I'm so sorry to trouble you,' Eve said, excuse at the ready. 'I popped in last night with a friend and I think I left my glasses here.'

The woman frowned. 'Haven't found any. Been too busy clearing up after some of the hooligans we get in this place. Someone dropped a slice of beef behind the radiator recently. Stank to high heaven. I ask you! Who does that? And what with that and the blocked loo...'

She really wasn't selling the place. Eve poured out a lot of sympathy, then tried again. 'Could I possibly come in and have a look?'

Finally, the put-upon woman relented. 'All right then, if you must.'

Eve began a search for the fictitious glasses. 'Were you working last night?'

'Nah. My night off. Thank the lord.'

That was bad luck. But then a wiry man with a grey beard and blue eyes appeared. 'I was on last night. What have you lost?'

Eve repeated her excuse for being there and the man started to look too. It pricked her conscience, but his presence was handy.

'It's no good,' Eve said. 'I can't see them. By the way, do you know a woman called Hattie Fifield? Only she's an old family friend and I could have sworn I saw her dash through here last night, though she didn't stop.'

The man didn't answer, so Eve elaborated. 'Petite, huge eyes and a very neat bob.'

His frown deepened. 'Ah, of course. Hattie short for Harriet. But I didn't see her.'

'She was in here a lot a few months back,' the blonde woman said. 'As if we hadn't got enough to do. Her mum was a regular here once, so she wanted people's memories, because she died young.' She huffed but then added, 'Tragic, to be fair,' though it was clearly an afterthought.

'Did she ask about her dad at all?' If she had, it would suggest that she hadn't known it was Duncan all along, nor studied restoration just to get close to him.

'Not in my hearing.' The bearded guy was quickest to answer.

'Nor mine neither,' the blonde woman said.

Hmm. The jury was still out, then. Eve remained doubtful that Hattie had followed the same career as her dad by chance. 'I guess you get a lot of the Kesham crowd drinking in here? You must be their local.' If Hattie had passed money to someone the night before, it might have been to one of them. Eve needed to know who was in the running.

The blonde woman cocked her head. 'That artist comes in a lot.'

The bearded guy nodded. 'He was here last night.'

'And the drop-out who squatted at the old folly used to too.' The blonde woman sighed. 'And Duncan, of course.'

'Poor man.' Eve paused. 'I wonder where the lord and lady of the manor drink.' She knew Edward went to the Cross Keys, but she wanted to see if he or Fifi popped into the Pied Piper too. It would be nearer.

'Ha!' It was the blonde woman who replied again. 'Not here, at any rate. We don't see them, nor poor old Jack Farraway. Not since his wife got ill, which is a shame. He was such a good listener.'

The bearded guy winced. He probably thought it should be the staff letting the customers offload, not the other way about.

'I still see Jack on the estate when I walk the dog though,' the blonde woman went on, oblivious. 'Always a kind word for everyone.'

Eve shook her head. 'Well, I must try and catch up with Hattie. It was odd to see her dash through without talking to anyone.'

But push as she might, she could see she wouldn't get more. They had work to do and the bearded man had become distracted by a smear on the pint glass he was polishing. She thanked them and left.

At least she had confirmation that Byron Acker had been in the pub as Hattie swept through. And Eve knew he was paying to stay at a historic house in a beautiful location, despite his art only selling for modest amounts.

If Hattie *had* been dropping off blackmail money, he seemed the most likely recipient.

20

Back in Saxford, Eve updated Robin over an early lunch, then went to do her shift at the teashop. Viv bounded towards her as she entered, though Eve could hear the timer going off in the kitchen.

She pointed over Viv's shoulder. 'No news until you've rescued the cakes.'

Viv tutted and dashed back through the connecting door. As Eve followed her to stow her bag in the office and put on her apron, the buzzer stopped, bringing relative, merciful peace.

But after that, Viv dogged her every move, snatching bits of news each time Eve went to the kitchen to fetch pots of tea. Eve was finding it very hard to concentrate. It was a great relief when their waitress Emily arrived at two. Eve took some time out in the kitchen to fill Viv in properly as they prepared another batch of bakes.

Viv was suitably impressed by Eve's updates, from Tod's good health to Hattie's blackmail. At one point, she was so distracted that she picked up a wholesale bag of cocoa instead of flour and tipped it up, ready to add to her lemon drizzle mix.

Eve swiped it from her hand just in time.

· · ·

Eve was almost at the end of her shift when Edward Tuppington-Hynd came in. He'd got his twins in tow and Eve remembered he'd taken some time off work because of the school holidays. She was instantly on high alert. She'd anticipated talking to him that evening, alongside Fifi, but here was a way to catch him alone, which could be far more valuable. She was all but certain he'd known about Fifi and Duncan's affair, but would he have killed over it?

She went to serve him, keeping her voice quiet. 'I'm so sorry about everything that's been happening.'

He looked crushed, which would fit if he'd recently killed a man. Eve could certainly see it. Duncan had wound him up, tight as a spring.

He thanked her, his voice equally quiet. Even the twins seemed subdued, despite the menu full of treats in front of them. It took a moment for them to agree their order, then Eve went to fetch the 'chocolate intense' selection. She was still wondering how best to take advantage of this unexpected opportunity. As she made Edward's tea and poured the boys' glasses of apple juice, an idea came to her. She ran through Robin's schedule mentally. He'd be at home right now. A second later, she disappeared into the office to call him, then reappeared, ready to deliver Edward's order.

'I can't believe you sneaked off to make a call before dealing with a customer,' Viv said. 'You never let me get away with anything like that.'

'Exceptional circumstances.'

'What? What's going on? Tell me!'

'All in good time! As you pointed out, I need to get this tray delivered.' Eve smiled sweetly.

Around five minutes later, Robin appeared on the village green with Gus, just as the boys, who were predictably fast eaters, finished their cakes. Edward still had plenty of tea left. Eve had filled the pot as generously as possible with that goal in mind.

Robin was throwing Gus's ball and Eve laughed as she watched to attract the boys' attention. A moment later, they were talking about how cute Gus was and fidgeting in their seats. It was all working out just as she'd intended.

'It's not my place,' Eve said, 'but if your dad says it's okay you can go and play with Gus if you like. You remember him, from when my husband Robin and I came to the hall? If you throw his ball, he'll fetch it for you. Just ask Robin – he'll let you have a go.' She leaned in to talk to Edward. 'I'm sorry. Is that okay?'

He gave a wan smile. 'Of course.'

They watched as the boys tore outside. A moment later, Robin was laughing with them while Gus leaped about excitedly.

Eve topped up Edward's teacup. 'Fifi agreed to let me interview you both for Duncan's obituary this evening,' she said cautiously. 'It's horrible to have to talk to people so soon after a death, but I want to do the article justice. It feels especially important, having been his guest when he died.'

Edward hesitated a moment. 'I understand.'

Eve lowered her voice. 'I realise the story I'll need to tell is complicated and I don't want to say the wrong thing this evening.' It was a low gambit, but she couldn't think of a better way to introduce the topic. 'Did you know he was Fifi's childhood sweetheart when he bought Hideaway House?'

Edward glanced over his shoulder, a tic going in his cheek. 'Perhaps you'd better sit down.'

Eve was breaking all her own rules, but she accepted his offer.

'She didn't explain immediately,' Edward said. 'I pieced the information together.'

Eve decided to take a risk. 'I saw the way Duncan encouraged you to climb the hall.'

Edward glanced out of the window at the boys, who were still dashing up and down the green, and winced. 'I should never have let him tempt me. It's years since I've done anything so stupid. It was just my scene, once upon a time.'

Eve remembered Simon saying he'd had an adventurous spirit.

'Seeing him up there reawakened something in me; that's the only reason I did it.'

It was what he'd told the police too, but Eve didn't buy it. The tension had crackled between them. 'He didn't get on your nerves? Forgive me, but I want to paint an honest picture, and I had the impression he was goading you. If it had been me, I might have played his game too, and regretted it afterwards. Duncan struck me as a difficult man.' It was a fine line, getting him to open up, rather than clam up. 'But Fifi still got on with him, I gather? I guess they went back a long way.'

'Her patience wasn't limitless,' Edward said, his voice tight. A moment later, he looked as though he wished he hadn't spoken.

'She'd got fed up with him too?' This was new. Eve kept deadly quiet after asking her question. She knew the power of a prolonged silence.

At last, Edward spoke again. 'I'm not sure – I was just referring to her character.'

Like heck. He'd been talking about something specific, she was sure. 'What did *you* think of him, as a person?'

'He was goal-orientated and able to compartmentalise,' Edward said, after a long pause.

It wasn't the answer Eve had expected. She guessed Edward had sought for something neutral to say.

'Would you call him ruthless?' Eve scrutinised Edward's face.

'Not necessarily,' he said, as his twins came back indoors. But he was tearing his paper napkin to shreds.

After Edward had left, they had a visitor. Moira, with Marjorie in tow. Paul must be minding the store.

When Eve went to serve them, Moira grabbed her arm.

'Oh, Eve dear, we've just heard the news about Fifi Tuppington-Hynd. That she's Jojo Landers, I mean!' She spoke in a breathless stage whisper.

Eve sensed movement behind her and saw that Viv had appeared to join in the fun.

'Ah yes,' Eve said. 'I'd heard too.'

'Well, of course,' Moira's eyes were wide, 'I always did think there was *something* not quite right about her. She never seemed... top drawer in the way that dear Edward does.'

Viv snorted. 'Moira, you've always commended her on her style and elegance.' She hadn't lowered her voice as much as the storekeeper. To be fair, she was probably too overcome.

'Ah, yes, well, Viv, those are such superficial things, aren't they? But deep down I knew there was a problem, didn't I, Marjorie?'

Her friend nodded loyally. 'I did too.' They were alibiing each other.

'And now it turns out she was Duncan's lover back when she was a teenager. Really quite shocking.' Moira looked delighted, then lowered her voice again. 'She must have killed him, don't you think?'

'What makes you say that?' Moira might be right about Fifi, but Eve bet she hadn't thought it through.

Moira fanned herself with a menu. 'Well, we're not quite sure of her motive yet, but she *was* persona non grata when she left Kesham as a teenager, and she came back in secret. That has to mean something.'

21

———

Between customers, Eve pondered her conversation with Edward. He hadn't admitted that Fifi and Duncan's relationship was back on, but his comment about her waning patience with him felt significant.

Perhaps he knew they'd fought but couldn't be honest without acknowledging the affair, which would highlight his own motive.

If Eve could prove there'd been a fight, Fifi would shoot up the suspect list. And of course, if Edward knew they'd broken up, he'd move down. The trouble was, neither of them was admitting there'd even been an affair.

She was also lightly intrigued by Edward's comment on Duncan's character. Goal-orientated was clear enough. When he found a project he minded about – seemingly one associated with Fifi – he'd go to any lengths to pursue it, from accepting money from Jack to failing to pay his elder daughter a wage. Leaving his wife and younger daughter to rot in a damp house was more evidence, if it were needed. It made his desire to be close to Fifi seem obsessive. But what had Edward meant by

Duncan being able to compartmentalise? It felt like a weird thing to say.

She nipped home after her shift to thank Robin for playing with the twins, then pinged the WhatsApp group to suggest an evening catch-up. Viv was determined to do some Watsoning, as she put it. After that, she walked to Hattie's lodgings, ready for the interview they'd agreed.

It was Marjorie who answered the door. Eve could see Hattie scowling in the background and guessed she rued her lack of independence. Marjorie leaned forward eagerly, peering at Eve through large-framed tortoiseshell glasses. She seemed very reluctant to let Hattie take over.

In the end, Hattie told Marjorie she'd see her later so firmly that she was forced to retreat.

Hattie shuddered as she led the way upstairs. 'Affordable lodgings are few and far between,' she said to Eve as she closed the door.

'You'd move out if there was more choice?'

She gave Eve a wry look. 'You betcha. I caught Marjorie in my room last week. She claimed she'd come to investigate a clanking pipe under my floorboards.'

Eve felt a rush of sympathy. She hated having her space invaded. Marjorie must have been having a snoop, but she'd clearly drawn a blank. The entire village would know if she'd found something juicy.

Of course, Hattie had kept that secret folder safely away from her lodgings until last night. Knowing what her landlady was like, Eve imagined she'd got it well hidden now.

'I'm so sorry for what you're going through,' Eve said as Hattie motioned her to a seat. 'It must be awful to have found your father, only to lose him again so quickly.'

Hattie nodded slowly. 'I was so happy when the DNA test came through.'

Eve remembered Jo mentioning it. 'How did you find each other?'

'I went back to my mum's old village, just up the road, to search for information. A friend of my mum's put me on to Duncan.' It explained why she hadn't needed to quiz the people at the Pied Piper. 'It was such a weird coincidence to find that Duncan was already local,' Hattie went on.

Wasn't it just? And that you'd trained to work in his field. Eve still found it hard to believe it was chance. 'You didn't have any suspicions beforehand?'

She shook her head.

'And you found you got on well? What was he like?'

Hattie gave a secretive smile that convinced Eve she'd hold stuff back. 'Very like me, in fact.'

Eve wasn't sure that was a good thing. When family members were too similar it often led to clashes. 'In what way?'

'He was practical, not easily swayed from his course.'

Practical sounded all wrong. He'd robbed Peter to pay Paul and overspent horribly. But maybe she meant, as in 'unsentimental'. Callous even. On that level, Duncan keeping Hattie's stipend for himself would fit, as would his decision to let Cotwin Place to Byron rather than waiting for Jack. In both cases he'd wanted money and ridden roughshod over others to get it.

'Did Duncan talk to you about his overall strategy?' Eve asked. His approach to maximising funds was high in her mind.

'Oh, yes. Lots.' The knowing smile was back.

'Did he tell you that Jack Farraway would have liked to move into Cotwin Place?'

'He did mention it, but Jack wouldn't have paid so well. He was offering to move in at reduced rent to do the place up. And there were delays.'

Poor Jack. She kept thinking of him and Jess, holidaying

there together. Moving in could have brought him some level of peace.

'I hear you've got a photo of you and Duncan when you were a baby?' Eve was glad Jo had mentioned seeing it. 'Before your mum decided you'd be better off without him in your life. I'd love to see it.'

There was something regretful in Hattie's eyes, but not the anger Eve would have expected if she'd known that Duncan had deliberately abandoned her. At last, she sighed, got up and fished in a drawer by her bed. 'Sure, why not? Here it is.'

It felt like an odd response. Almost as though she was somehow giving in. She handed Eve the photo. She must have been around a year old, cuddly in pink dungarees, with a daisy hair slide.

Eve felt the hairs on her scalp rise. 'Do you know why your mum waited until you were that age to cut Duncan out?'

Hattie sighed again. 'Duncan said they had a row. He wanted to see more of me but she was dead against it. In the end, she threatened to tell the authorities he was harassing us if he didn't leave her alone. He said I cried so much when they argued that he decided to keep his distance until Mum calmed down. Only then she moved, his letters were returned and he lost track of me.'

But neither Posy nor Harriet Fifield were especially common names. Eve was sure Duncan could have found her if he'd tried. Meanwhile, Hattie seemed tired and listless, not angry. That all fitted, of course, now Eve had seen the photo. If only she'd thought of the possibility before.

After she'd thanked Hattie, she crossed the road to the Cross Keys to find Jo Falconer. It wasn't evening-meal time yet, and Eve offered to buy her a drink. She agreed to a small white wine and they perched side-by-side at the bar.

Eve lowered her voice. 'You said Hattie showed you the DNA results she got, proving Duncan was her father?'

Jo nodded. 'Waving it around, she was. She looked gleeful.'

'Yet she was bitter at her dad for abandoning her?'

Jo nodded again. 'She hadn't heard Duncan's side of the story then, I suppose.'

'And did the test have her and Duncan's names on it?'

Jo's eyes widened. 'I'm not sure, now you mention it. I didn't get to look, close up.'

Eve had suspected not. 'She showed you the letter Duncan sent her as a child, didn't she? Did it look old?'

Jo was frowning now. 'It was a bit creased...' Her sharp eyes met Eve's. 'You think it was faked?'

Eve lowered her voice still further. 'All I know is that the baby in the photo Hattie showed me was wearing a hair clip that's an exact match for one Cesca wears. I don't think the picture is of *Hattie* and Duncan at all.'

22

Eve barely had time to ponder the implications of what she'd guessed about Hattie before she was due at Kesham Hall to interview the Tuppington-Hynds.

She told Robin what she'd deduced as briefly as she could, and he promised to update Greg at the station.

Eve thought she understood Hattie's wistful tone when she'd agreed to show Eve the photo now. She knew the truth was bound to come out. Eve might spot it was a fake, but that wasn't the problem. Hattie's DNA was on file, thanks to her conviction. The police would be sure to check it against Duncan's as they looked for motives. The results would probably come through imminently and if Eve was right, they'd show Hattie wasn't his daughter at all.

It would make the way Duncan had treated Angela unspeakably appalling. Jack said he'd believed the ends justified the means, but to allow such a lie to run riot without telling his own wife was breathtaking. He might have told her the next day, of course, if he hadn't died, but that would have been too little, way too late. And would he have told her the real truth, or what Eve now suspected was the fictional version? He might have relied on Angela's patience and stoicism, but everyone had their limits. If she'd found out any part of this by accident, she could have snapped. Duncan had treated her so carelessly.

It took Eve a few moments to calm down, and turn her attention to why the pair had decided to fool everyone. They'd clearly been in partnership and Hattie said Duncan had been 'practical'. If she was telling the truth, her mum's friend had put her onto Duncan when she was trying to find her dad. Presumably they'd got to know each other then and found it wasn't him, but perhaps the possibility had triggered a plan. Father and daughter reuniting was a touching story, likely to capture the public's imagination. Perhaps Duncan had seen its appeal and offered to launch Hattie's TV career in exchange for free labour. Assuming Eve was correct, she wondered what the production company's reaction would be, once the truth came out. The deception would garner some terrible publicity.

But all this sent Hattie down the suspect list. If Duncan wasn't her father, she couldn't have blamed him for abandoning her, and by killing him, she'd ruined a deal that could have made her famous. The moment Duncan died, she was sitting on a timebomb, their lies sure to be revealed. She was still going through the motions, putting off the evil hour when her dreams would be destroyed, but deep down, she must know it was coming.

She thought back to when she'd overheard the pair of them giving away the supposed father–daughter relationship, the day they'd all met at the lodge. It must have been for show. It had felt as though she'd discovered it by accident, after running back near their open window to catch Gus. In reality, they must have heard her calling her beloved dachshund, and seen her too, probably. They'd have spotted their chance to seed the idea. Eve had thought at the time that they'd been unguarded, chatting away with the window open. She should have wondered why. And of course, her 'opening up' to Jo had been odd too.

Eve shook her head. Hattie was the sort to watch and wait, not unburden herself for no reason. Alarm bells should have rung.

Two questions remained. If Duncan wasn't Hattie's dad, then where had she got the positive DNA test? Had her mum's friend suggested other possible fathers? If so, it looked as though she might have struck lucky. Eve really needed to speak with Susie Parks.

And what did her blackmailer have on her? Eve had already decided it wasn't proof that she'd killed Duncan. She was equally sure it wasn't the lie about Duncan being her dad. Hattie wouldn't pay to hide something that was destined to come out anyway.

But for now, she had to focus on her next interview. Edward was still her top suspect, joint with Jack Farraway, but after her talk with him that afternoon, he and his wife might be about to swap places.

When Eve arrived at Kesham Hall, she found Fifi alone. Apparently, Edward had said he and Eve had already chatted at the teashop, so he'd taken the boys into Blyworth to see a film. On the upside, Fifi might be less guarded without him, but Eve wondered if Edward was avoiding her.

Eve was barely inside the hall when something caught her attention: a woman's winter cloak hanging up on a rather grand coat stand, with a pair of binoculars just visible in its pocket. It immediately struck her as strange. Fifi didn't look like your average birdwatcher. Everything she wore was designer and there were no practical women's shoes in the hall. Eve strongly suspected that Fifi had wanted the binoculars for another reason. And why wear the heavy cloak, with its hood, when it was high summer and even the nights were warm? But it was just the sort of thing Robin would approve of for a spot of surveillance. With the hood up, Fifi would disappear into the shadows in the woods. Eve would need to think through the implications once she'd finished the interview.

Fifi took her back to the formal, uncomfortable sitting room she'd visited before, where the Bengal cat was curled up on a cushion. It half opened its eyes, but Eve had left Gus at home so there was no sport to be had. A moment later, it closed them again.

'I'm so sorry for your loss,' Eve said. 'I can only imagine what you're going through.'

Fifi opened her mouth but saw the danger before she spoke. After a second's pause, she shook her head. 'It's very upsetting, especially having it happen on the estate, but Duncan and I weren't close.' The line of her mouth hardened as she made the claim, though her eyes glimmered. There were unshed tears there.

'But you were childhood sweethearts,' Eve said gently.

Fifi flinched, then put her head in her hands. 'I didn't think word had got out, though the police have unearthed the connection. No one from the village seems to remember. I don't remember you.'

'I didn't live here then. I only discovered it because I recognised your birth name when I started to research Duncan's contacts.' If Fifi didn't realise the whole village was talking about her, Eve wouldn't make her feel worse.

'I've heard you work with the police.'

Eve shook her head. It wasn't ideal that word had got around. She didn't want Fifi to clam up. 'That's overstating it. I've very occasionally passed on information. Tell me, why did you hide your past when you came back?' Eve sensed how tense she was. The truth might come pouring out if she let it.

There was a long pause, but then the dam broke.

'Everyone blamed me for abandoning Duncan when he'd been made homeless, but it was all more complicated than it seemed.' She looked up, her eyes hollow. 'I heard later that Dad never came through with the money he'd promised Duncan for his degree. I suppose I should have realised he'd take that line after we broke up, but I didn't. Not at the time. He always said he thought highly of Duncan and I thought he meant it. More fool me.

'And it wasn't just Duncan's world that had been turned upside down. Our move to the States was triggered by our own family drama. It turned out my dad had a mistress and three children tucked away in Blyworth. Mum and I had no idea, but someone saw them and the whole thing blew up in his face. His solution was to run away – leaving his other family standing. I couldn't have abandoned Mum at that point. She was in bits.' She sighed, pushing her hair back from her face.

'I was reeling too, of course. I suppose I felt I needed her as much as she needed me. And I was only eighteen. I'd have found striking out on my own impossible back then. And then, after all that, within five years, Mum and Dad divorced, and Mum moved back here. A good decision, but I wish she'd made it sooner.'

'You didn't want to leave Duncan?'

Without warning, Fifi burst into tears. 'At the time, I thought it was for the best. The enormity of Dad's lies made me look at Duncan in a different way. I felt I couldn't trust anyone. The last thing I wanted was to go through the sort of pain Mum was suffering.'

It sounded like a horrendous situation. Anger rose in Eve's chest at the thought of Fifi's dad, shattering her faith like that. He'd altered the course of her life, her mum's and Duncan's. But Duncan's love had never died. His desire to rekindle things with Fifi had overridden everything else.

'I cried for days about leaving Duncan,' Fifi said, shakily. 'But I was sure he'd get over me. I felt I knew what men were like, after what I'd seen. And I thought he'd be all right financially, thanks to Dad. My father wasn't reliable in a relationship, but he was very good at making money.'

Eve sympathised. Fifi's decisions had been skewed and she'd have been making them against the clock, her parents' departure for the States rushing up to meet her. She doubted many eighteen-year-olds would have done anything different. But she needed to switch focus now and ask about the present.

'Forgive me, but what made you move back to Kesham?' Living a secret life in a place that must evoke mixed emotions sounded like a challenge.

Fifi pressed her lips together and her eyes were full of regret. 'I was happy here once,' she said. 'And I wanted the children away from London. A fresh start in the countryside. I mean—' She stopped. 'It doesn't matter. I didn't see why the villagers should keep me away either. Some of them were a shallow lot. I thought they'd be all over me when I came back as Edward's wife. And so it proved.'

Her words rang true. Eve could hear her bitter satisfaction. But she was leaving something out too.

'Did Duncan talk to you much about your past?' Perhaps she'd give away their current affair if Eve kept her on the topic.

Fifi stared into space before answering. 'A little, as you'd expect. But the restorations were his top priority.'

Eve could see how hard she was finding it to rein in her emotions. Her words were clipped, mouth set, face taut. She wouldn't want anyone knowing they were back together.

It didn't wash, though. If Duncan had only been there for the buildings, he wouldn't have goaded Edward into climbing the hall. And besides, she, Robin and Sylvia had all seen them kiss passionately. Eve decided to switch to a more direct approach and leaned forward, speaking quietly. 'You and Duncan started seeing each other again?'

Fifi started. 'No, not at all. You've got that wrong.'

Eve had a split-second calculation to make. She could

announce that she'd seen the pair of them in a clinch or she could back off. In the end, caution won the day. Go too far, and she might get thrown out; the conversation was too useful to risk sacrificing it.

'I'm sorry. I'd never have put that in the obituary, even if it had been true. I'm afraid I got swept up in the romance of your story. It sounds so sad that fate,' or rather Fifi's dad, 'split you up. But of course, I can see how attached you are to Edward and your lovely boys.' That wasn't really true, but Fifi's response could be interesting.

'Edward's a dear,' Fifi said, as though she was reading from a script. 'He and the boys are thick as thieves. They couldn't have a better dad.'

Her tone had turned wistful, and Eve sensed undercurrents. 'I suppose you must see more of them when Edward's working.'

'They've got to that stage when they shut themselves in their rooms. I never thought it would happen so soon. I'm not sure I...' Her sentence trailed off.

It sounded as though Fifi felt left out. If Edward and the kids were as close as they seemed, she might almost feel unnecessary. At the very least she'd be lonely, rattling around this huge house. Eve felt for her. She'd have found it hard if her own twins had opted to spend all their time with their dad.

She thought of the way Edward had rescued Jasper and Louie from the fire at their London house. Maybe the division had set in as early as that. In Edward's shoes, she wouldn't have wanted to let the twins out of her sight.

Perhaps that related to what Fifi had left unsaid, when talking about her return to Kesham. She'd mentioned a fresh start. It could have been hard to live in their old place, with memories of the fire reinforcing Edward's protectiveness. Perhaps she'd hoped the memory would loosen its grip here in Suffolk, and she'd break back into their tight-knit circle. She might even have liked the idea of Edward's longer commute, giving her more time with the twins. But perhaps Eve was just being fanciful. And even if not, it hadn't worked. Jasper and Louie had remained distant.

As a by-product, Fifi might have been desperate for love and company when Duncan reappeared.

'Did Duncan seem like a family man, do you think?' As his lover, Eve hoped the question might prick Fifi's conscience. It could elicit something interesting.

'Far more than I'd thought,' Fifi said at last. 'You could see how fond he was of his daughter.' If she and Duncan had argued, as Edward had hinted, then maybe she'd wanted him to leave Angela but he'd refused. Even if he'd been obsessed with her, he could have taken that decision – hoping to hurt her perhaps, like she'd hurt him. If so, Fifi could have killed him in a fit of rage. But none of that would explain the heavy cloak in the hall with the binoculars in the pocket. Unless it had hung there since winter, and Fifi really did go birdwatching.

Fifi folded her arms and Eve sensed it would be counterproductive to push further. Instead, she got her talking about Duncan as a teenager. Fifi said how hard it had been for him, even before his parents split up. She painted everything as her dad's fault: their cottage wasn't well maintained, they worked long hours, their pay was poor. It sounded like a strain and little wonder that Duncan's dad ended up having a breakdown or that his mum had needed to go and dry out after they split up. The effect on Duncan must have been dire.

'The Blakes never complained?'

Fifi shook her head. 'I think they were too worn down. And Dad was affable – friendly. He'd invite them in for a drink if they were passing – things like that. I don't think he had any conception of what day-to-day life was like for them.'

'And your dad – and mum – were happy to take Duncan in when neither of his parents could look after him?'

'Yes. Duncan was already keen on restoration and architecture at that stage. He helped sort out the east wing. And Mum and Dad didn't mind us going out together. Dad was lavish with his promises to help Duncan through uni. He even offered him a job on the estate when he graduated, in a vague, handwavy way. Duncan and I adored each other until Dad destroyed my faith in love.'

The events that had made Duncan who he was were becoming clearer, and Eve felt she understood Fifi better now too. It seemed her father had welcomed her relationship with Duncan, then detonated a bomb under it. Its unnatural end might have stopped Duncan letting go.

After Eve had rounded off her conversation with Fifi, thanked her and said goodbye, she left the hall and made her way back up the main drive. She was just about to exit the grounds, into the larger estate, when she heard young voices from beyond a bank of viburnum.

The twins. They must have come back from the cinema.

'What's she doing here?' one said.

'Talking to Mum about Duncan.'

They must be discussing her. Eve paused and listened intently – she could only just hear their quiet voices.

'Why?'

'Dad says she's writing something about him to go in the newspaper.'

'Do you think she knows Mum shouted at Duncan?'

Eve stiffened.

'No. I don't think she could.' The voice was tremulous. 'Do you think it's bad?'

'Maybe.' The reply had come in a whisper. 'She said she wanted him to go away and never come back. And now he won't.' There was a catch in the second twin's voice.

Eve longed to nip round and comfort them, but their words sent a chill through her. It sounded as though Fifi had indeed

fought with Duncan before he died, and judging by the children's words, they feared she might have killed him. This was
horrendous. No one so young should have to cope with that sort
of fear.

As Eve walked swiftly away, thinking of what she needed to
do next, she spotted Edward Tuppington-Hynd in the distance
with Hattie again. Hattie was edging back, as though she
wanted to move on. Was she avoiding talk about the murder in
case she gave herself away? Or did she think he was guilty?

As the pair parted, Eve waved to Edward. He looked down-
cast as he spotted her, but it couldn't be helped.

'I've just finished talking to Fifi,' she said to him. 'I
wondered about extending my walk before I head home. The
woods are so beautiful. Great for birdwatching, I imagine.'

'I suppose they must be.' Edward sounded distracted.

'Not your thing? I could ask Fifi about it when we bump
into each other next.'

But Edward's eyes widened, and he shook his head. 'It's not
hers either, I'm afraid. The local Wildlife Trust might be your
best bet.'

It was as she'd thought, and the presence of the binoculars
needed explaining. She'd discuss it with the gang later.

Eve thanked Edward and said goodbye. She was on her way
home when her mobile rang. It was Duncan's production
company calling back. Eve picked up and explained about the
obituary she was writing.

'I was keen to include anything Duncan had in the pipeline
when he died. I gather he and his daughter were going to make
a new TV series with you.' She needed to pretend she knew
more than she did or they'd probably fob her off.

'*I'm afraid your information's incorrect,*' the executive said.

'That's odd. Hattie Fifield talked about it as though it was a
done deal.'

'*Well, in that case she was either after attention or she's been misled. Duncan made the case for it weeks ago now, but I told him from the start it was a no-go. It's not what people are after these days and we're busy with other projects.'*

Eve paused. 'Could he have got someone else interested?'

'*I hear he tried,*' the woman said. '*But he got the same answer elsewhere. It's a small world; if anyone had bitten, I'd know about it.*'

23

Eve got back to Elizabeth's Cottage just after Sylvia and Daphne had arrived for their catch-up. Robin kissed her and pushed a drink into her hand as Gus mobbed her at the door.

She bent to make a fuss of him as Daphne looked on, her kind concerned eyes on Eve. Sylvia gave her a keen glance too. A moment later, Simon appeared, closely followed by Viv who almost fell through the door in her eagerness.

'What news?'

Robin motioned them to the table. There was the most amazing smell coming from the kitchen. It turned out to be chicken breasts wrapped in Parma ham, with Parmentier potatoes and tenderstem broccoli. 'Let's eat as we talk,' he said as he brought it through.

Eve was all for that. Having washed her hands, she sat down amongst her friends. 'Lots of developments,' she said, as Robin poured wine. 'But what about you, Robin? Any news from the police?'

He nodded. 'Greg called half an hour ago. The check of Hattie's DNA against Duncan's was already in progress, and you were right. They're not father and daughter.'

Everyone gasped, which was secretly satisfying, and Eve explained what had made her wonder.

'It never occurred to me that there was any doubt after Jo mentioned the DNA results,' Daphne said.

'Same. But it turns out she never saw any names,' Eve replied. 'Hattie said she'd gone to a friend of her mum's to ask about her dad. If that's true, perhaps she found him, even if it wasn't Duncan.'

'Any idea who might be in the hot seat?' Sylvia asked, peering at Eve over her wine.

'I wondered about Edward Tuppington-Hynd. I've never seen her look angry with him, but their interactions seem stilted. It left me wondering if he suspects her, or vice versa.'

Sylvia snorted. 'I can see why Hattie pretended she was Duncan's. It looks as though their fake relationship would have launched her TV career.'

'It must have felt like a second chance,' Daphne said, 'after her prison term. Poor Hattie.'

'I'm afraid that's where it gets interesting,' Eve put in. 'I've just spoken to the production company and it looks as though Duncan led Hattie up the garden path.' She explained the details.

Even Sylvia looked shocked. 'So you think he'd promised something he could never deliver in return for free labour?'

Eve nodded. 'That's my theory. Duncan clearly tried to get other production companies interested when his old one turned him down, but he must have known it was no go by the time he died.' She could hardly credit it. Presumably he'd decided to string Hattie along for as long as possible, squeezing every last ounce out of her before the truth came out. And what then? Eve imagined she'd have told all and sundry in revenge when she finally realised she'd been duped. But perhaps Duncan had something on her that he'd have used to keep her quiet. It would fit with her being blackmailed. And even if it didn't get out, the huge lie would have impacted his relationship with Angela and Cesca for ever. It said a lot about his obsessive, short-termist nature that he'd pushed ahead regardless.

Eve sighed. 'I'd relegated her way down the suspect list after discovering Tod was alive and Duncan wasn't her dad, but she's back up there now. I imagine she'd have been incandescent if she found out.' Nothing excused such a horrific crime, but Duncan's behaviour had been despicable. Hattie would have felt so humiliated. And the fact remained, she'd only had to lose it with Duncan for an instant. The killer had hit him multiple times, but after the first blow, they could have carried on in a panic, desperate to finish the job when there was no going back. It was a terrible thought. 'The question is, did she know she'd been fooled?'

Everyone was silent for a moment.

'On the issue of fatherhood,' Sylvia said at last, 'if Edward's the daddy, I wonder how he felt when Hattie told everyone she was Duncan's.'

Eve had been pondering the same thing. 'It can't have been easy, especially with Duncan carrying on with his wife at the same time. He might have felt he'd lost them both to his rival.'

'Then again,' Robin said, 'if he is her father and he's got a test to prove it, he could have told everyone the truth.'

'Perhaps he went along with it out of fondness for her,' Eve said. 'His frustration could have built in the background.'

'Any other evidence he might be her dad?' Simon asked.

'It's circumstantial, but Jo and Moira both said Edward gave her a character reference.'

'He must have had some reason to be so supportive,' Sylvia said.

'He could just be a kind man,' Daphne put in.

'Don't ever change, will you?' Sylvia replied, with a sceptical smile. Daphne shook her head, despairingly.

'Then again,' Eve went on, 'Jack Farraway gave Duncan

money that was supposed to go to Hattie. He could be another candidate. Either way, it would make sense if it was someone local, given Hattie's been around for months now and she got that positive test from somewhere.' She sighed. 'I still can't believe I didn't work out the truth earlier. I kept thinking it was too much of a coincidence that Hattie had studied restoration, just like Duncan. I was blinded by my theory that she'd chosen that career to get close to him and take her revenge. As it turns out, they were just two random individuals, thrown together by luck and self-interest.' She turned to Robin. 'Will the police confront Hattie immediately?'

He shook his head. 'No, so we're to keep quiet about it for now. They want to question her again before telling her that they know.'

'For what it's worth, I'm sure she knows it's coming,' Eve said. 'I guess she was keeping up the pretence for now, but reality was sinking in. On reflection, I think Fifi might have been aware too.'

Simon speared some broccoli. 'What makes you say that?'

'When she talked about Duncan's feelings towards his family this evening she referred to his daughter, singular. I can't be certain, but maybe it was Angela and Cesca that they argued about.'

'So they did argue?' That was Viv, but everyone turned towards her.

Eve felt a quick buzz of pleasure, immediately overlaid with worry for Fifi's kids. She explained what the twins had said.

'Those poor boys.' It was unusual to see Sylvia so moved.

'If they were adults, I'd try to talk to them,' Eve put down her fork, 'but I'm not comfortable in this case. It's too sensitive – it needs to be someone with proper training.'

Robin nodded. 'We can let Greg know; they'll use a specialist interviewer.'

'I think the police should talk to Edward again too. He said

Fifi's patience with Duncan wasn't limitless, though he tried to backtrack when I asked what he meant. Now I wonder if he heard the same row that the twins witnessed. If so, he could have known that Fifi's relationship with Duncan was over. It would make him less likely as the killer. Perhaps the twins can confirm whether Edward listened in.'

'But why wouldn't Edward tell everyone?' Simon said.

'I guess to protect Fifi. She's still denying that she and Duncan had rekindled their relationship. Despite her being unfaithful, it seems Edward wants to maintain the status quo. Jo said he was trying to build bridges with her when she saw them at the Cross Keys.

'The final thing to update you on is the cloak I saw on Fifi's coat stand, with binoculars in the pocket.'

A murmur of conversation rose up.

'What do you think it means?' Viv asked. 'It makes her sound like a peeping Tom.'

'I think she went out in secret to spy on someone. Given the cloak, I'd say she used the hood to hide her face. Whatever she suspected, she thought she'd be able to confirm it using the binoculars.'

'So it would have to be something visual that would be obvious from a distance,' Sylvia said. 'Interesting. What do you think?'

Eve swallowed a mouthful of chicken. 'As I said, I'm starting to suspect that Fifi knew Duncan and Hattie weren't father and daughter. Given that, and the amount of time they spent together, I wonder if she suspected they were lovers. This is all speculation, but if Fifi met him in the woods later, and found she was right, she could have killed him over it.'

'So where are we with suspects?' Viv said, whipping out her notebook and opening it on a page which said 'Call Jonah' in very large letters.

'Jack's still up at the top, but it's possible Fifi will replace Edward to share that spot with him. It all depends on whether Fifi and Duncan had broken up and if Edward knew that. Hattie's still up there too. Byron Acker's at the other end of the scale, though I do wonder if he's blackmailing Hattie.'

She explained the background as Viv scribbled furiously.

'I'm afraid Angela's still very much in the mix though,' Eve added. 'The only reason to doubt her involvement is the fact that we like her.'

Viv didn't add her name to the list, Eve noticed.

Eve went to bed that night with thoughts of Fifi, Hattie and Edward floating through her mind. She'd texted Greg her latest discoveries before she turned in, in the hope that it would settle her, but she was still wound up.

She imagined Fifi, her binoculars trained on Duncan and Hattie, peering through the window of the lodge. But what was the order of events? The lodge had been empty by the time Eve and Robin had seen the vandal throwing paint at the place. Had Fifi spotted Duncan and Hattie there earlier in the evening, then argued with Duncan at the hall later, then later still, gone out, found him on the estate and killed him? The timing didn't make sense. The murder looked spontaneous, which would fit if she'd lashed out just after discovering the truth, but not hours later.

When Eve wasn't thinking about that, she was plotting her trip to London the following day. Her appointment with Duncan's former colleague at the Built Heritage Trust had come round. Planning her questions wasn't enough to distract her from her worries, though.

It wasn't wholly surprising that she woke at two in the morning to the sound of thudding feet down in Haunted Lane. The whole village knew the legend. The ghostly footfalls related to the cottage's history and were said to signify danger.

For years, Eve had told herself that she conjured them up when she was worried, but the fact was, she only ever heard them before a violent attack. A few months back, she'd finally admitted as much to Robin. Her jolting awake must have disturbed him too. He put out a hand and stroked her shoulder. And downstairs, Gus whined.

The following morning, Eve got ready for her trip to London to talk to William Saxton. He had Duncan's old role at the Built Heritage Trust and they'd been colleagues for ten years. His input would be useful for the obituary, and learning more about Duncan could only help when it came to solving his murder.

Eve put on one of her summer suits – a shot-silk dress in emerald green with blue trim and a jacket to match. She wanted Saxton to take her seriously and the right outfit made a difference. After that, she breakfasted with Robin, then went to find her car on the village green, ready to drive to the station. She was just about to unlock it when she saw Moira's neighbour Marjorie stagger towards the village store. You didn't have to be an expert in body language to see something was wrong. All Eve's fears at last night's dream flooded back.

She glanced at her watch. She'd left herself way too much time, as usual. She wouldn't miss her train if she went to find out more.

Nerves made her queasy as she looked through the window and saw Marjorie and Moira were alone. The storekeeper's eyes were wide. The moment Eve joined them, Moira looked up with grim relish. 'Oh, Eve dear. Such a terrible thing. Poor young Hattie never came home last night.'

Marjorie turned a tear-stained face to Eve and took over the story before Moira could stop her. 'I was worried, naturally, and I wake early, so I went to see if I could see her. I tried that building where she'd been working – the lodge place – but she wasn't there. So then I looked up and down the beach but there was no sign.'

She had to take a breath then, and Moira leaped back in. 'So then Marjorie went along the path between Kesham and Long Stratford and that was where she found her. Struck down and killed, just like Duncan Blake.'

24

Eve offered to take Marjorie to the teashop. She felt like sitting down herself – her legs were shaking – but there'd be no time to keep her company. Viv would be eager to take over though, and there were enough servers to allow for it. Eve would have to recover herself on the train and get the details later.

Moira, however, wasn't going to miss out. She hailed her malcontent, people-hating husband Paul and got him to take over so she could go to Monty's too. Eve briefed Viv in the kitchen.

Viv put a hand on Eve's arm. 'Are you sure you should still go to London? You look very pale. You only talked to Hattie yesterday.'

Eve swallowed and took a deep breath. In truth, she felt slightly sick. Hattie had been so young and she hadn't had much luck in life. If what Eve had surmised was correct, Duncan had used her callously, on top of everything else, and now there was this awful, violent ending. It was too cruel.

'Here,' Viv said. 'Take some millionaire's shortbread to keep your strength up.'

Eve swallowed again as the nausea got worse. 'Thanks.'

She sympathised with Marjorie once more, then dashed for her car and drove with the windows down, taking deep breaths.

She was still early for her train. It meant she had time to gather her thoughts and call Robin to update him.

After she'd passed on the news, she added: 'Please could you tell Greg about Tod now, and about Hattie's weird dash through the Pied Piper on Monday evening?'

She felt awful for having held back. She'd been so keen to avoid putting Hattie on her guard but it might have made a difference.

'*I was going to suggest the same thing. And when the scientific support team go to Hattie's room, I'll suggest Greg asks them to look for the folder she took from the lodge. It might contain the DNA results.*'

'Thank you. Poor Hattie. I wonder if the Falconers know yet.'

'*I'll nip over to the pub to tell Jo now,*' Robin replied. '*And I'll get more news from Greg as soon as I can. Good luck in London.*'

Eve tried to focus on the questions she needed to ask William Saxton, but thoughts of Hattie filled her head. All the interactions she'd seen her have with everyone, from Tod in London to Edward at Kesham. And was it really Byron who'd blackmailed her? He was certainly wealthier than you'd expect, and he'd been in the Pied Piper on Monday night. Hattie could have slipped him the money as she'd dashed through.

Of course, blackmailers didn't normally kill their victims, but Eve didn't know enough yet.

She arrived at the Built Heritage Trust's grand, five-storey building overlooking the River Thames with five minutes to spare. The sun bounced off the white frontage as she pushed a buzzer to enter. A moment later, she was directed to the second floor.

She was sitting on a lime-green chair, pretending to look at a magazine and thinking about murder when William Saxton came to find her. He wore a smart suit but still managed to look slightly dishevelled. His hair stuck out at odd angles and his glasses looked as though they'd been dropped recently and possibly sat on.

He took her to a stuffy office made slightly more bearable by a desk fan and rang for someone to bring them iced water. Eve had loved living in London, but she hadn't forgotten how much hotter it always seemed there than everywhere else.

'So, how can I help?' Saxton said, making a valiant effort to tuck his unruly grey hair behind his ears.

Eve explained again about the obituary. She had a sneaking suspicion he'd forgotten why she was there. 'I gather you and Duncan worked together for many years.'

Saxton nodded.

'Could you tell me about him as a person?'

He began to say how passionate Duncan had been, and to recount his achievements, but Eve felt he was pussyfooting around. At one point he said that Duncan had 'taken no prisoners' but shut up like a clam when she gently prompted him to elaborate. It didn't help that the Trust was clearly having a difficult day. In the background, she could hear shouting, then what sounded like a sob.

Saxton managed to ignore it completely, which was quite an achievement. When his PA came in to deliver their iced water, she was blushing and gave Eve an apologetic look.

Eve left the office twenty minutes later feeling her journey had been wasted. She could have got what Saxton told her from old press releases. She was sure he'd been holding back.

She passed the PA again on her way out.

'I'm so sorry about the noise,' the woman said.

'I'm sorry too – it sounded like an awkward situation. What happened?' Most people found it hard to deflect a direct question.

The PA hesitated, then explained in a rush. 'Budget cuts, I'm afraid. HR are letting a secretary go and she's been here for thirty years.'

'They're making her leave immediately?' Once again, Eve waited.

The PA lowered her voice further. 'She's been given an hour to clear her desk. HR put people on gardening leave once they've been made redundant. It's supposed to avoid gossip and bad feeling.'

Hmm. Eve doubted they'd skip either of those things, and it was terrible for the poor secretary. She must be in a state of shock. She was still sobbing in the distance, and there were crashing sounds too, as though things were being flung around. It felt questionable to take advantage, but already, a plan was forming in Eve's mind. A woman who'd worked at the heart of the trust for thirty years could be a valuable resource – especially if her loyalty to the organisation was gone. Eve debated the ethics, but at last, she decided to go for it. What if Duncan's history there helped explain his murder? And now Hattie was dead too. It would be terrible to miss something.

Eve waited just outside the building. When she saw a woman emerge with a tear-stained face and a box containing a desk gonk and a fake cactus, she made her approach.

She explained as simply as she could that she'd heard what had happened and how sorry she was. She was totally honest about what she was after. She told her about the obituary, the murder enquiry and her concern for Duncan's wife and daughter. She said she'd pass anything useful on to the police and that she'd be very grateful to talk, but only if the secretary felt equal to it.

She still looked shellshocked and guilt stirred in Eve's stomach. She wouldn't have asked if she hadn't sensed William Saxton was covering something up.

'I'm Eve, by the way,' Eve said.

'Pam.' The woman wrestled with the box to put out a hand.

'Are you on public transport? Would a bag be easier?' Eve pulled out one of the very thin strong sort she kept in her handbag for emergencies. 'You're welcome to keep it.'

Pam looked teary again. 'Thank you.' She transferred her belongings, and Eve tore up the cardboard box for her and put it in a bin.

'If you're happy to talk, I can buy you tea.'

After a moment's hesitation, Pam replied. 'I could do with a sit-down. And if it might help the police then I owe it to Duncan anyway. He was fun to work with.'

Eve found a café just around the corner – a cheerful place with green ironwork tables and chairs outside. She ordered the works. Pam looked like she could do with it.

'Will you be all right?' Eve said. 'You'll look for another job?'

Pam sighed. 'I'm only four years off retirement and I've saved. I'll be all right financially, but it hurts. I've given most of my working life to the Trust.'

'It can't be easy.'

A waitress arrived with tea, scones, cakes and sandwiches.

After Eve had thanked her, she turned to Pam again. 'So Duncan was fun to work with?'

She nodded. 'There was no side to him. He treated me and the chief exec just the same, even after he got promoted to deputy. And when he got the top job he gave me the day off to celebrate. He was impulsive – he'd bring me in a slice of cake to cheer me up if it was raining. Small stuff, but it made it a happy place to work.'

'I wonder why William Saxton avoided saying anything personal about him.'

Pam pulled a face as she took a tiny cheese sandwich. 'I can think of a few reasons.'

Eve sipped her tea and waited.

'Duncan was unconventional, though it often paid dividends. If a project ran into trouble, it was almost always he who found a way forward – something that no one else had thought of. But sometimes, his determination meant he overstepped the mark.'

Eve opted to stay quiet again and ate a cucumber sandwich.

'There was a scandal just before he left. A woman bequeathed the trust a hundred thousand pounds and her family were furious. They said Duncan had exercised undue influence. The board were terrified of bad publicity, so they negotiated a settlement that calmed things down. After that, it was announced that Duncan had "resigned".'

Eve sipped her tea. 'Did you ever talk to him about it?'

Pam grimaced. 'Reading between the lines, I think the family had a point. He'd clearly been flirting with the woman, wooing her into bequeathing the money. He hinted he'd tried to put her off her family too. Joked about it.'

Heck.

'He wasn't ashamed. He said her kids were a rotten lot who had plenty of cash of their own, whereas the trust needed the money, so you see...'

Eve did indeed. It was yet another case of the end justifying the means – in Duncan's eyes at least.

'It was all hushed up, of course, but Duncan didn't take it to heart when he was pushed out. Not like me.' Pam wafted a hand at her tear-stained face. 'He came back to visit a couple of years ago, and then again a year later.'

Interesting. 'I guess you heard why?' Eve picked up a scone, spread thickly with jam and butter.

Pam smiled this time and nodded. 'The first time, he wanted to apply for a grant to restore a beautiful-sounding house in Suffolk. He said it had a rare medieval hall.'

Goosebumps rose on Eve's arms. 'Cotwin Place?'

Pam frowned. 'I think that was the name.'

So Duncan had *wanted* to restore Jack and Jess's old place at least. 'They turned him down I suppose.'

'Oh, no,' Pam said. 'William said the application had merit and the timing was fortunate. Years had passed since the bequest incident, and although there'd already been the fire at that manor house Duncan bought, it was before the news he was under-insured got out. You heard about that?'

Eve nodded.

Pam sighed. 'So I think William felt sorry for Duncan, and he knew how creative and determined he could be. He trusted him to get the job done and to do it well. The only condition was that he should open the house to the public once a month when the work was complete.'

Eve leaned forward. This didn't make sense. 'But I know that building. The work was never done.'

Pam frowned. 'I know. William was furious. He said Duncan had got unforgivably distracted. When William made enquiries, he found Duncan had actually bought a different restoration project nearby and installed a tenant at Cotwin Place.'

The other purchase had to be Hideaway House. Pam's story seemed to support the theory that he'd sought a project that would bring him into direct contact with Fifi.

'I presume Duncan wasn't allowed to use the grant to reno- vate the other building he'd bought.'

Pam looked shocked. 'Certainly not. It's all strictly regu- lated. The grant that had been agreed was never released.'

Eve could hardly credit it. What a terrible waste.

'And then,' Pam went on, 'Duncan came back again, this time to apply for money to renovate not one, but two buildings he'd bought on the Kesham Estate in Suffolk. He was fired up about it – he'd lived there as a child.'

Had he seriously imagined the Trust would gamble on him again? 'I imagine that went down like a lead balloon.'

Pam nodded. 'Even I was shocked. He seemed so blinkered. There was no way William was going to trust him again. The rejection wasn't a surprise to me, but Duncan seemed incensed.' She shook her head. 'I saw him outside after William turned him down. He'd punched one of our windows and broken it. His hand was bleeding.'

25

Eve spent the journey back to Saxford thinking about what she'd learned. She wondered if Jack Farraway knew Duncan had got a grant to restore Cotwin Place. Heck, Duncan could have let Jack move in and do a lot of the renovation himself. She imagined he'd have adored showing people round once the work was finished. He loved the place so dearly.

Discovering that Duncan had carelessly let the grant lapse could have thrown Jack into a fury. Perhaps he'd found the paperwork in Duncan's rubbish sack, the evening he'd been murdered. But he'd have to have killed Hattie too. A second attack on top of the first was a whole different proposition.

Eve longed to get home to see what Viv had found out from Marjorie, hear the latest from Greg via Robin and share more ideas. But just twenty minutes from Blyworth, her mobile rang. A number she didn't recognise.

She picked up. 'Hello?'

'*Eve Mallow? It's Susie here, Susie Parks. You left a message for me at the bakery. You wanted to talk about Duncan Blake. And about Hattie.*' Her voice cracked. She must have heard the news.

Of course, she was the woman who'd been good friends with Hattie's mum.

Eve told Susie how very sorry she was and rallied her thoughts. She'd wanted to speak to her to see if Duncan really had tried to keep in touch with Hattie as she grew up. That question was redundant, but now poor Hattie was dead, the meeting felt even more urgent. Susie might know who Hattie's real father was.

Eve explained about the obituary and asked if they could meet, and Susie agreed.

'There are things I need to say and it'll be good to talk in any case. I remember Hattie as a little girl. I was so fond of her.'

They arranged to speak as soon as Eve could make it to Long Stratford from the station. Eve wondered what was coming. Susie had sounded very anxious to meet.

Eve sat opposite Susie Parks in a back room at the bakery as a colleague carried on serving. The poor woman was in tears.

'I just can't believe she's dead. I knew her so well as a little girl. I'll never forgive myself for not taking her in when her mum died. Things could have been so different. But I had four of my own, and money was tight.'

Eve got up to get her a glass of water and passed her a tissue from a box on the side. 'I'm so sorry, but you mustn't blame yourself. You could never have known how badly things would turn out. It sounds as though it was the family who took her in that was to blame.'

Susie swallowed and nodded. 'Them and her dad I suppose.'

Eve felt her heart rate increase. If Susie could identify him, it would be a real breakthrough. 'I gather Hattie was looking for him.'

'You heard?'

'She told me herself. Though of course, she made out she'd got the answer, and that it was Duncan Blake.'

Susie shook her head. 'I heard about that. I assumed it must be true, but it wasn't?'

'I'm afraid not, but I know she genuinely tried to dig into her past. The staff at the Pied Piper said she'd been in a few months back, asking about her mum.'

Susie nodded. 'The landlord there's my husband, Steve. You might have met him. Thin with a beard?'

Eve nodded.

'And yes,' Susie went on, 'that's right. She finally decided she wanted to know the truth. I wonder if it was her real dad who killed her.' Her eyes looked hollow, her skin pale. 'It might not have suited them to have her showing up and making waves.'

'Do you know if Hattie's mother had relationships with any of the men at Kesham or nearby?' Eve held her breath.

Susie put her head in her hands. 'Yes, yes, she did.' Her voice had lowered to a whisper. 'She admitted she'd slept with Edward Tuppington-Hynd. He was very young and dashing at the time. On the wild side, really. It was well before he was married of course, and he wasn't yet living at Kesham.'

If Hattie had been Edward's, the news wouldn't play well with Fifi. After being sneered at for her lack of class as a child, Eve suspected she'd have seen Hattie as a series of labels. 'Illegitimate'. 'Ex-con'. It would have been a serious fly in the ointment. Eve wondered how far Edward might have gone to stop Hattie from talking. He seemed like a gentle man, but he loved his boys so much – he wouldn't want anything to threaten his life with them. If he and Fifi split up, he might get equal access, but it wouldn't be the same. But would Fifi divorce him over something like that? It wasn't as though he'd cheated on her, though it was a big secret to have kept, if he was Hattie's father. If Fifi had already known, she could have killed Hattie herself, out of jealousy and to protect her new image, though that felt like a stretch.

'Did Edward know that Posy got pregnant soon after their affair?'

'I'm not sure. He didn't live here then – he'd just come home for a holiday. His parents still lived up the road.'

'Do you think Posy would have tried to involve him if he'd been the father? Or was she happy to go it alone?'

Susie's brow furrowed. 'That's a complicated one. She was fiercely independent, just like Hattie, but happy would be an overstatement. She was often red-eyed around that time. Sad. She wouldn't talk about it, but I guessed the man involved didn't want to know. I tried to warn Hattie when she asked about her dad. I wanted to let her down gently, but I don't think she was listening.'

Or perhaps it was what she'd anticipated, if she was already set on revenge.

'Of course, Posy was mates with Duncan too, so the idea of him as her dad didn't seem impossible. I mentioned him when Hattie asked for information, though I never saw any sign of an affair.'

It tied in with Eve's theory that Hattie had gone to Duncan to probe, leading to them hatching their scheme. Either of them had seemed wily enough to suggest it and they'd both have seen the advantages: Hattie imagining a glittering career ahead of her, and penniless Duncan thinking of all that free labour.

'I think there was an older man too,' Susie added at last. 'I saw a grey hair on the collar of a coat Posy used to wear. I guess he was married, or she would have told me about him.'

Back in Saxford, Eve googled Jack Farraway. He could already have been grey back then and Duncan could have introduced him to Posy. He'd have been married to his first wife – the one before his beloved Jess. Eve wondered why they'd divorced. An affair perhaps?

Robin had texted to say he had news from Greg, which fitted in well with the planned gang meet-up at the Cross Keys. Jo had reserved them a table well down the garden, away from prying eyes.

Eve was keen to get home to change beforehand, but on impulse she dropped in at the Pied Piper before leaving Long Stratford. Her best bet was still that Hattie had dropped blackmail money off there on Monday. She knew Byron had been in then, and that he was a regular. If he was there now, she'd like to see how he seemed after Hattie's murder. She still couldn't imagine why her blackmailer would kill her, but uncovering her secret might be enlightening.

She couldn't see Byron inside, though the blonde, put-upon woman she'd met previously swooped down on her with an: 'Oh, you again.'

She proceeded to tell Eve about her ingrowing toenail and her cat's stomach upset.

It was a relief when Steve appeared. She commiserated over Hattie's death, then asked casually after Byron.

Steve's face opened up into one of welcome as he looked over her shoulder. 'It's funny you should mention him; here he is now!'

'Hello!' Byron looked as friendly and innocent as ever and greeted both Eve and Steve as if they were long-lost friends. 'Thought I'd come over after the awful news this morning. I wanted company. I can't get it out of my head.'

Steve nodded. 'Tragic. We'll have a lot in this evening. People always come together after bad news.'

Eve knew Jo at the Cross Keys found the same. Villagers wanted to speculate but also to find comfort.

'What'll it be?' Steve asked Byron. 'If you're eating, you can have anything off the menu except the fishcakes.'

'Yes,' the put-upon blonde woman added, 'made a few folk sick at the start of the week, so they're off. Literally, I suppose.' She laughed at her own joke.

Why on earth had they recruited her?

'Maybe the lasagne,' Byron said, looking slightly anxious. 'Thanks.'

It made Eve wonder about his income again. Steve seemed to assume he'd stay for supper, so he must eat there regularly. That wouldn't come cheap. There was something odd going on.

'I can't believe it about Hattie either,' Eve said to Byron. 'I spotted her in here on Monday, early in the evening. Did you see her?'

Byron frowned. 'No. No, I didn't.'

Eve couldn't decide if he was lying.

He offered to talk to her then and there for Duncan's obituary, but she told him she wouldn't interrupt his supper. Given her current suspicions, turning up unannounced at his home felt like a better bet. She had a feeling she'd find out more that way.

For the time being, she at least knew that Steve had been right: Byron had been present when Hattie dashed through the pub, unlike her other Kesham contacts.

26

An hour or so later, Eve, Robin and the gang sat at a garden table in the Cross Keys under a cream parasol, with views of the estuary, waders and mudflats beyond. The landscape was beautiful, but wild and lonely too, and the eeriness fitted their reason for meeting.

As Eve tucked into her goat's cheese tart, Viv turned to Robin. 'Don't keep us in suspense. What have the police said?'

He glanced at his notes. 'Assuming nothing unexpected comes up at the post-mortem, the cause of Hattie's death is the same as for Duncan. Different weapon though, and this time it was found in the grass near the site of the attack, wiped clean of prints. It's a second hammer from the collection at the lodge, with a different-shaped head. Someone had broken in; the window was smashed. Everyone on the estate will have to provide their fingerprints in case they match up with any found at the lodge. And they want yours too, Eve, I'm afraid.'

'What?' Viv looked outraged. 'Why on earth?'

'Because we were both on site when the first murder took place. And probably because Palmer's itching to cause us trouble. Mine are already on file of course.'

'So the break-in means it was definitely premeditated this time,' Eve said. 'I wonder why the killer didn't use the same weapon. And why they took the first one away but left the second.'

Viv was nodding, scribbling down the details in her notebook, next to a recipe. The word 'murder' sat just below a reference to glacé cherries.

'It's a good question,' Robin said. 'It must mean something.'

'What about time of death?' Eve asked.

'Between eleven p.m. and one in the morning. Hattie wasn't working at the Cross Keys yesterday evening. They're trying to piece together her movements.

'And speaking of movements, none of the key players has an alibi. Edward and Fifi don't share a room any more and the place is so big, either of them could have sneaked out without the other noticing. And Cesca would have been asleep by then. I know it's hard to hear, but Angela could easily have left her.

'The other news from Greg is that the forensics team didn't find that folder you saw Hattie take from the washhouse at the lodge, Eve. Nor any sign of the DNA results she showed Jo.'

'That's a shame but I'm not surprised.' Eve lowered her voice. 'We know how nosy Marjorie is. In Hattie's shoes, I wouldn't have left anything so sensitive in my room.' She took stock for a moment, before speaking again: 'Shall we go through each of the original suspects and see where we're at?'

There were nods of agreement.

'Jack was joint top of our list for Duncan,' Eve said, 'and his motive for that first murder looks even stronger after my interviews today.' She told them about her conversation with Pam from the Built Heritage Trust.

'I can't believe he let the grant to restore Cotwin Place lapse.' There were tears in Daphne's eyes. 'Jess would be so upset if she knew.'

'What about Jack for Hattie?' Robin asked.

'His motive there seems less certain. There's an outside chance that Hattie was his daughter. Susie Parks thinks Hattie's mum could have been seeing an older man. There's no real reason it should be Jack, except that he's got a long-standing connection with this area, Duncan could have introduced them, and Jack put up that cash for Hattie's salary. Either way, I'm not sure it counts as a motive; he didn't have much to lose if the news came out.

'But of course, he could have killed Hattie if she knew he'd killed Duncan, and that's more believable. Duncan must have pushed Jack so close to the edge.'

Daphne looked upset. 'I hate to think of him doing it, though I see he was tried to the limit. But to kill Hattie too, after he'd been so kind to her...'

'If she tried to blackmail him over the murder, his sympathy might have evaporated. And I'm afraid she could have. Someone was squeezing money out of her in their turn, and I'm sure she guessed her planned TV career was dead in the water. She might have seen her chance to make money and grabbed it. She said she and Duncan were very alike. Practical.' It was a miserable thought.

'Shall we tackle Edward next?' Robin asked. 'He was joint-top suspect after the first murder, but I've got news from Greg now. A specialist interviewer spoke to his twins and they each admitted they'd witnessed a row between Fifi and Duncan. What's more, you were right, Eve. Edward heard it too. Louie spotted him in the shadows.'

That was significant. 'And during the row, Fifi told Duncan he must leave, so Edward knew the affair was over. He's far less likely to have killed from jealousy.'

'News indeed,' Sylvia said. 'Does Fifi admit she and Duncan had an affair now?'

Robin gave a wry smile. 'Believe it or not, no. She says she was angry with him for failing to renovate White Cottage as promised. She lost patience and gave him notice to quit.'

'What did the twins tell the police about the argument?' Eve asked.

'Just what you heard one of them say – that she wanted him gone for ever – and that Fifi told Duncan she knew exactly what he'd been up to.'

'That fits more neatly with a second affair than it does with a row over the renovation.'

Robin nodded. 'But it's not conclusive and we can't be sure.'

'And what did Edward say? Any idea of the timing?'

'He says it was around nine forty-five. He noticed because the twins were supposed to be in bed. They backed that up, inasmuch as they admitted that they were in bed reading, heard the rumpus and went to look.'

'So Fifi and Duncan fought a good hour and a quarter before Duncan was killed and Edward knew all about it.' Eve pictured the scene.

'So Edward moves down the list?' Viv said.

'I'd say so, though I have an update on him and Hattie.'

Everyone looked at Eve.

'Susie Parks has confirmed that Edward had an affair with Hattie's mum, around the time Hattie was conceived. He could certainly be her dad. I suppose it's not impossible that he killed Duncan out of jealousy, because he'd claimed Hattie as his daughter. Or he might have killed Hattie to stop her telling Fifi the truth. But I don't think he'd have done both. Either he wanted to claim her or he didn't. And of course, we've no proof he's her father.'

'And even if he is, killing Duncan for claiming Hattie as his daughter sounds shaky,' Robin said. 'As I said before, if he really minded, he could have proved it. With his influence he could probably have helped her establish a career, almost as well as Duncan could have.'

'Better, in fact, given Duncan's promises were all lies.' Eve sighed. 'So perhaps Edward's motive for Duncan doesn't hold water. In which case, Hattie can't have discovered his guilt and become his target. I think he comes right down the list, but I still want to know if he was Hattie's dad.'

'The police asked Edward about his chat with Hattie on Tuesday evening, incidentally,' Robin said. 'He claims he was just checking in with her, in passing. He says he felt sorry for her, losing her dad.' He shrugged. 'He might really believe she was Duncan's, even if it turns out she was his. Though there is that positive DNA test to consider.

'Perhaps we should look at Fifi next, now we've confirmed she fought with Duncan the night he was killed.'

'Yes.' Eve marshalled her thoughts. 'If Duncan was sleeping with Hattie as well as her, then Fifi could have killed him from jealousy. Perhaps she went to find him after they'd fought, hoping to win the day, then saw him with Hattie again. That might explain the delay and the loss of control. And if Hattie was nearby, she might have guessed Fifi was guilty, making her a target too, especially if she stooped to blackmail.'

'So Jack and Fifi are high up the list?' Sylvia said.

'I think so.' Eve sipped her drink. 'Then, I hate to say it, but we come to Angela.'

Viv put her pen down, just like the last time.

Eve suppressed a sigh. 'Sadly, Angela had plenty of motives to kill Duncan.' She looked at Viv, daring her to disagree. 'Then if Hattie found her out, with or without the added complication of blackmail, Angela could have killed her to protect Cesca's future. I can't see her killing Hattie out of jealousy though, even if she and Duncan were involved. The gap's too long. She'd have calmed down.'

'I'm sure you're right,' Sylvia said, meditatively. 'You'd have to be truly desperate. I can't imagine smashing someone's head in.'

'That's a relief,' Simon muttered.

Sylvia smiled placidly at him. 'Still worried about that time you killed our pot plants?'

'Enough of this banter.' Viv had taken up her pen again. 'Who's next?'

'Byron, and I still don't have a motive for him. He looks as innocent as they come, on the surface,' Eve said, between mouthfuls of tart. 'Kind, friendly and affable. But he's up to something and I won't be happy until I find out what. He was in the Pied Piper on Monday night, which was the first place Hattie went after squeezing money out of Tod. If Byron was blackmailing her, she could have slipped him the cash on her way through the bar. It would be a lot more anonymous than visiting his house.

'And he might fit as her blackmailer for other reasons too. His paintings don't sell for much, yet he lives quite extravagantly. It's a shame the police don't have any reason to check his bank account. What if he collects people's secrets and his work as an artist is a front?'

'What leverage could he have had over Hattie?' Viv asked.

'It's a good question. The fact that Duncan wasn't her dad won't wash. I suspect she'd have paid to keep that quiet before he died, but not afterwards, when she knew the truth would come out anyway. And Hattie having murdered Duncan is also a no-go. Whatever her blackmail-worthy secret is, Tod's aware of it, and if he knew she was guilty of murder, I doubt he'd have let her blackmail *him*. I think it's something we still don't know. Maybe talking to Tod is the answer.' Eve was already mulling another visit to London.

'But Hattie could still have been Duncan's killer?' Robin asked.

Eve reviewed the facts. 'Possibly. If she found out he'd got her working for nothing on the back of a fake TV opportunity, that *could* have made her lash out. But if she did, then it's hard to think of a reason for someone to kill her, unless it was to avenge Duncan's death, and I'm not sure any of our suspects loved him enough to do that. I'd guess Hattie was innocent – of Duncan's murder, at least.'

'I suppose Tod could have killed Hattie if he thought the blackmail might continue,' Viv said, doubtfully.

Robin looked up. 'It wasn't him. The police checked; they found his number on Hattie's phone. He and his mates were at some club all evening with multiple witnesses who check out. They spoke to him about the theft from the hall too. Turns out he's got form for shoplifting, but he denies all knowledge. I doubt they'll manage to mount a case against him at this stage.'

'So, next steps,' Viv said, pen poised.

Eve sipped her wine. 'Addressing the top suspects first, I want to know why Jack and Duncan fell out so badly the night Duncan was killed. And if Jack wasn't out killing him, then where was he, and why the heck did he lie about it? I need to talk to him again. Something in a chest of drawers near his front window upset him very badly just after I left last time. If I can get a look at it, then so much the better.

'For Fifi and Angela' – Viv's look turned dark – 'I need to confirm that Hattie and Duncan were having an affair and find proof that they knew about it, or else rule it out. It could have been the final straw that made one of them kill Duncan, putting Hattie in a prime position to guess their guilt.

'It worries me that Angela seems to have planned how to use Duncan's life insurance before he died. Finding an innocent explanation would make me feel a lot better.'

There was silence for a moment.

'So that covers the top three suspects,' Sylvia said, to another filthy look from Viv. 'What about other loose ends?'

'I'd like to find Hattie's folder. I'll bet it contains the DNA results and although it might not relate to the murder, I'd feel happier knowing. Perhaps she moved it from one hiding place

to another. She had a base here of course, as well as at Kesham.'
Toby, Jo's brother-in-law, was passing with a tray of empties so
she hailed him, apologising for the interruption.

'Did Hattie have anywhere secure at the pub to leave
valuables?'

Toby raised an eyebrow. 'The police wanted to know that
too. We've got a safe, but she never asked to use it, and other
than that, no. She didn't have a locker or anything.'

Eve thanked him. 'I hope she didn't destroy it. I'll need to
search every place that she frequented.'

'And then there's Byron,' Viv said.

Eve nodded. 'I want to know if he was blackmailing Hattie,
and why. For that, Tod's a promising lead. Hattie blamed him
for letting her secret out, so he must know what it is.' His friend
Rattler, right there in Suffolk, probably knew the basics too, if
she could find him. But he sounded unreliable. Eve would
rather get the full details, and from the horse's mouth. 'The
information might be more important than it seems. Whatever
her secret was, she and Duncan were thick as thieves, and now
they're both dead.'

Eve wrote up her latest thoughts that evening to get it all off her
chest, but once again, when she went to bed, she couldn't sleep.
She got to that half-dozy state which she hated most, where
ideas jumble without making sense. She was too drowsy to
order them, but still too worried to actually drop off.

And when she did finally sleep, she dreamed of the footfalls
in Haunted Lane again and Gus whining downstairs. She was
so tired that she didn't wake properly and the following morning, she wasn't sure if it had been real or imagined.

27

On Thursday, Eve tried to forget her dream from the night before. All the same, she was relieved when she went to the village store and Moira didn't face her with news of another death. If she hadn't heard, it probably hadn't happened. After that, she presented herself at Blyworth Police Station for finger-printing. She felt strangely uncomfortable, considering she had nothing to hide.

After the frustrating trip, she was finally able to get down to business. She forced herself to tackle one of the jobs she was dreading most: trying to find out if Angela had known about an affair between Duncan and Hattie. Eve could imagine it being the final straw. Deep down, she felt Angela was as likely to have killed Duncan as Jack or Fifi were. The words she'd overheard made her shiver: *'One stupid, rash act and our lives have changed for ever. I was just so angry. And desperate.'*

Before leaving for White Cottage, she texted to see if there was any shopping Angela wanted, then went to Kesham armed with groceries and some cake from Monty's too.

Angela looked as pale and drawn as she had previously, though her eyes were no longer red. If she'd killed Hattie she must have managed to deal with the fact emotionally. That might fit, if she'd decided it was essential to protect her daughter.

Cesca was clinging to her mum's legs, her thumb in her mouth. Even Gus's presence didn't tempt her away. Eve could tell that the new reality had set in. She might not quite understand what death was, but she probably knew her father wasn't coming back. Eve's heart bled for her, especially because deep down, she thought that Duncan had loved his daughter. Eve had seen their closeness when they'd met at Hideaway House. He'd behaved like a selfish idiot of the first order, but none of this was black and white.

'I'm sorry to intrude,' Eve said.

'That's okay.' Angela stepped back to let her in. 'Thank you for the groceries. How much do I owe you?'

Eve followed her through, with Gus at her heels, and tried to protest, but she knew it was no good. Angela would never accept them as a gift.

When Eve told her the amount, she opened her purse and Eve couldn't help noticing she had plenty of cash once again. Angela did a double-take at the sight of it too.

'I could have sworn I'd spent more of it,' Eve heard her mutter.

Was it possible she was acting, and it had been she who'd blackmailed Hattie? She might have spotted Eve's look of surprise at the number of notes.

'Would you like some tea?' Angela asked, after handing over the money.

Eve got up. 'What about if I make it?'

She looked too exhausted to protest. 'Thank you.'

Eve went through to the kitchen and stuck the kettle on, then looked around her. It was always useful to see as much of someone's home turf as possible, whether it belonged to an obituary subject or a murder suspect. Off the small room was a pantry, but Eve could see it had been adapted to be a play area for Cesca. She remembered coming up with similar ploys herself – something to distract her twins as she cooked their suppers.

At the back of the shelves, behind the toys, were cardboard boxes, the logo of a gin brand printed on the side. What if Duncan had had a drink problem too? That would have swallowed up yet more money and made him even harder to deal with.

Eve tiptoed over and peeped inside, but in fact the boxes were full of old books with beautiful bindings. Some of them were for children, such as *The Hobbit*. Eve could see why they weren't on display. White Cottage had almost no space for such things. And wherever they were kept, the damp would get to them eventually. Eve tucked the box closed again.

In front of the boxes, Cesca had a chalkboard, and there were jigsaw puzzles too, as well as a large tin of chalk paint and boxes of felt-tip pens. Something about that triggered a thought, but she couldn't quite grasp it.

Sighing, she took the tea through to the other room.

Cesca was sitting in a small side room off the main living area playing with four tiny espresso cups in pretty colours with delicate handles and gilt rims. They made a perfect dolls' tea set.

The moment they'd got settled, Cesca put down her soft toys and trotted up to her mum.

'Please can I do painting?'

Angela looked as though she might cry.

'I could set it up for her if you like,' Eve mouthed over Cesca's head, but Angela shook hers.

She stroked Cesca's hair. 'Not right now, my love. Come and sit on my lap if you want.'

Cesca started to climb up but then changed her mind and went over to join Gus, who was investigating a corner.

Her request to do artwork had taken Eve's mind back to the chalk paint she'd seen in the pantry. She hadn't heard of it before, only blackboard paint. It must be handy for kids though. Presumably you could wash it off, just like standard chalk. She bet Cesca would love daubing it about the place. Perhaps Angela and unconventional Duncan had let her paint their walls...

It was then that Eve had her idea. She'd been intending to express her sympathy again before digging into her enquiries, but now a different line of questioning sprang to mind.

'I saw the chalk paint in your pantry. It must be handy if you want to be sure you can get it off again.'

She watched Angela closely. She was a professional, like Duncan. A stonemason, committed to restoring old buildings. She must have some feeling for places like Hideaway House and the lodge, because of their historic value. Would she want to ensure they weren't permanently damaged, even if she threw paint at one of them, as a protest?

Colour rose in Angela's cheeks. 'Yes, absolutely. And things do get messy with a little one around. You know that.'

Eve nodded. 'And sometimes when adults are involved too.'

Angela's flush increased and she bit her lip.

'I'm so sorry to ask, but was it you who vandalised this place, Hideaway House and the lodge?' Eve spoke very quietly and gently. 'I remember hearing how easy it was to wash the paint off the lodge and of course, the egg mess was easily reversible too. I can imagine you wouldn't want to damage precious old buildings, but you might want to shake Duncan's confidence in his latest projects. In your shoes, I'd have been desperate to get him away from Kesham.' She paused. 'Away from Fifi. And Hattie too.'

Angela put her hands over her face, as though she couldn't bear to look reality in the eye. Thank goodness Cesca was too involved with Gus to notice what was going on.

Eve put an arm around Angela's shoulders and gave her a squeeze. 'I'm so sorry. You've been in such an awful position.' If only Eve had been able to get her to open up at the teashop. She might have been able to help defuse the situation. Her thoughts ran on. It fitted that she'd leave the box of Tod's belongings too. She was married to Duncan. She could easily have nipped into Hideaway House as he worked and found them. Tod had probably left them in his haste to get away after the theft and Angela would have heard the rumours that he'd died.

'Did you want to scupper Duncan's projects here, so he was forced to go back to London and start over?'

Angela gulped and nodded at last. 'I know it seems awful, but I was at my wits' end. And when you came along, promising Duncan some excellent publicity, I thought we'd be stuck here for ever. I was convinced you'd catch me when you saw me at the lodge. I'm afraid I rigged up the tripwire before I started work. I knew I'd be able to leap over it and get away if anyone came along.' She leaned forward suddenly, her eyes anxious. 'I didn't leave Cesca on her own. Jack came and sat with her.' She shook her head. 'That's why he wasn't in when Byron called, the night Duncan died.'

It explained a lot. 'He knew what you were up to?'

Angela nodded and hung her head. 'He sympathised. He refused to tell the police in case they thought I was guilty of the murder too.'

'What made you swap from using eggs to Cesca's paint?' Eve might not have guessed if she hadn't.

She sighed. 'I'd run out, and I couldn't get into town to buy more. I thought if I stocked up at the village store in Saxford, people might talk, so I looked for an alternative.'

Simple as that. 'Can you remember what time you got home?'

'About midnight. Duncan was still out, of course. With Fifi, I suppose, or working.'

So Jack could still have killed Duncan later, as could Angela in theory, either on her way home or if she'd gone out again.

Eve lowered her voice further still. 'You knew Duncan was having an affair with Fifi then?'

Tears were falling fast now, and Angela nodded. 'I couldn't tell the police about that, either. They'd be bound to think I killed Duncan out of jealousy.'

It was time to bring Hattie into the mix, but Eve could hardly bear to cause her more pain. She needed to take it slowly. 'I'm so sorry about the latest death.'

To Eve's alarm, Angela's upset shifted up a gear. Her sobbing held a fresh sense of desolation, though she was almost silent. Eve guessed she was intent on not alerting Cesca, who was still turned away, preening Gus, who appeared to be loving the attention.

'What is it, Angela?' Eve really was wondering if she'd killed Hattie, her reaction was so extreme. It was hard to keep her voice calm.

'Hattie and Duncan. I feel so guilty.' Her voice was barely audible, and Eve tensed. *Please don't let her have done it.*

'You knew they weren't father and daughter?'

She nodded. 'I discovered that they were meant to be by accident. I heard him mention it to Fifi, of all people.'

That explained why she hadn't looked surprised when the police faced her with the information, even though Duncan had never told her.

'I was knocked for six, as you can imagine. I wanted to understand the background before confronting Duncan, so I went to listen in on him and Hattie. That's when I heard them discussing their scam.'

'They ended up having an affair?' Eve could see she'd got it wrong, the moment she said it.

'No. No...' Angela closed her eyes. 'I followed them often

enough to be sure that they weren't. But I told Fifi that they were, the night Duncan was killed!'

Suddenly, Eve understood. 'To put a wedge between her and Duncan?'

Angela nodded, her red hair falling forward. 'It was a disaster, us being here. He kept telling me he was doing everything for mine and Cesca's sake and the look in his eye – I think he really thought it was true, but it made no sense. The next minute he'd be off and into her arms. So I went to see her and told her they were lying about Hattie being his daughter. And then I said they were sleeping together.'

Eve handed Angela a tissue and could see exactly why she'd done as she had. She must have been desperate to force a change, but the possible consequences didn't bear thinking about. 'What time did you say all this to Fifi?'

Angela blinked, as though that sort of detail was the last thing she wanted to bother with. 'I don't know. Around nine maybe, or a little before? Well before I went out to throw paint at the lodge. Jack came early, so I took my chance. But the next thing I knew, Duncan was dead.' She looked utterly bereft. 'I've been wondering ever since if he was killed because of me. Sometimes I'm convinced of it, but then I talk myself round.'

Angela blaming herself during that phone call Eve had overheard made sense now.

She took an uneven breath, and a tear trickled down her cheek. 'At the time, I couldn't bring myself to confess it all to the police. I was convinced they'd suspect me as much as Fifi if they knew she and Duncan were really having an affair. And my tactics would make me sound desperate. But what if Fifi really is guilty and Hattie knew, so Fifi killed her too? Perhaps I triggered the whole thing. I feel terrible.'

'Only the killer's to blame, and it might not have played out as you think, anyway. Do you have any firm evidence that Fifi's guilty?'

Angela shook her head, but her look was bleak.

Eve rallied her thoughts. 'Listen, I saw a pair of binoculars in the pocket of a cloak at Fifi's house. I believe she'd been out to spy on someone, and something must have triggered that. After what you've just told me, my guess is that it was your story. She wouldn't have wanted to believe it. I imagine she went to see for herself, the moment you left her at nine.'

Angela looked listless, too exhausted to see the implications. 'You're probably right. I saw her leave the hall when I was near the bottom of the drive.'

Bingo! 'The point is, she won't have got proof, from what you say. You're absolutely sure Hattie and Duncan weren't having an affair?'

Angela blinked, as though Eve's words were starting to sink in. 'Certain. They simply didn't act that way, and I never saw them so much as touch, let alone kiss. Their relationship seemed practical. Almost clinical.'

'In which case, if Fifi killed either of them, I doubt it was because of what you said to her.' Eve imagined how things must have played out. Fifi had left her place at around nine, binoculars in her pocket, to spy on the pair, then summoned Duncan. He had arrived at the hall by nine forty-five, when she'd told him he must leave Kesham. Not because of an affair with Hattie, it seemed, but she must have discovered something important. Something she'd seen, or overheard... Eve was starting to suspect the latter. There was only so much you could see that would have that sort of effect, and if Hattie and Duncan hadn't been kissing...

Angela took a deep breath. 'Thank you for letting me know. I've been turning it over and over in my mind. I couldn't sleep for worrying about it.'

Eve felt a lot better than she had, too. Angela had had a plan to end Fifi and Duncan's affair and it hadn't involved murder. She couldn't see her killing her husband while she was busy trying less violent methods. There was just one thing still worrying her.

'Angela, when I spoke to you the day after Duncan's body was found, you were talking about taking Cesca back to London – to get her into your old school. Was that what you were hoping you'd do as a family, before the murder?'

Angela nodded, her eyes filling with tears again.

'I suppose it would have been tricky, financially.' The unrealistic aspiration needed explaining.

She nodded. 'It was just a fantasy really.'

But the plans had sounded concrete, right down to Cesca's school place. Eve found it hard to believe that Angela was guilty, but that one tiny detail left an element of doubt.

28

After Eve left Angela, it felt important to drop in at the hall. She wanted to see both Fifi and Edward's reactions to Hattie's death, though after the talk with Angela, Eve's thoughts were shifting again. She'd imagined Fifi might have lost control later on, after her and Duncan's argument, if she'd gone into the woods and seen him and Hattie together, but Angela was a hundred per cent certain that there was no affair between her husband and his apprentice, so that couldn't have happened. It seemed Fifi had fought with Duncan over something she'd seen or heard between nine and nine forty-five that evening. Whatever it was, she'd told him to leave – not privately, but in the hearing of her husband and twins. Eve couldn't imagine why she'd go out again later to kill him. And even if she'd had a conceivable reason, she'd surely have taken her own weapon.

The visit to the Tuppington-Hynds wouldn't be wasted, though. Eve still wondered if Edward had been Hattie's father. She didn't think he'd kill her to hide the truth, but nothing was certain. Fifi had clearly disliked Hattie, even before the rumoured affair with Duncan. If Edward feared that Fifi might have divorced him over it, he could have panicked. If not for love of Fifi then for the fear of losing full access to his adored twins. Eve still wanted to know why Fifi and Duncan had fought too. It might not be relevant, but she couldn't rest until she understood.

She knocked at the door of the hall, with Gus at her side, sniffing furiously around the frame. Perhaps he could smell the Bengal cat.

When the maid answered, Eve asked if she might see the Tuppington-Hynds.

She was shown to the formal sitting room, where Edward stood by a window, and Fifi perched on one of the uncomfortable, high-backed sofas. Edward wandered over as Eve and Gus entered, greeted her, then sat down next to his wife.

Eve expressed her shock. 'I can't think how Duncan would have felt if he'd been alive. Father and daughter both dead.'

She flicked a look from one Tuppington-Hynd to the other. After what Angela said, she guessed Fifi no longer believed the lie, and Edward wouldn't either, if he'd been Hattie's father.

Edward looked ashen, just as he might if Hattie *had* been his. His eyes were bloodshot, Eve noticed.

Fifi was looking down at her lap, her lips tight. Eve sensed she'd love to put Eve straight and was fighting the urge.

'It's horrific.' Edward had caught her looking at him. 'I almost... we almost... Well, we almost lost our boys once, long ago. It doesn't bear thinking about.'

Of course, it would catch him on the raw, under the circumstances. Eve had never had a close call with her twins, but a jolt of fear flew through her just at the thought. She nodded. 'I'm so sorry. It must bring back painful memories.'

'Edward hates to let them out of his sight now,' Fifi said, and once again, Eve was convinced she envied their closeness.

Eve didn't learn anything more from the Tuppington-Hynds, but after the maid had shown her out, she decided on the same approach she'd taken on leaving Jack Farraway's house, and hung around, close to the window of the formal sitting room. She put her finger to her lips, and Gus settled himself resignedly by her feet as she strained to hear anything the couple might say.

Eve was looking into the room at a shallow angle, but she could see both Fifi and Edward had risen from the sofa. Edward took Fifi's hand in his.

She shook her head. 'It's too late, Edward.'

But he drew her close. 'I don't care about the affair. It's not too late as far as I'm concerned. And as for the boys, let's take off as soon as this business is over. Whisk them away somewhere. Spend all day, every day, all together. I hadn't realised how you were feeling. I... I should have seen.' His voice cracked with emotion and in another moment, she finally relaxed, her head against his shoulder. Eve still didn't know if Edward had been Hattie's dad, or why Fifi and Duncan had fought, but the reconciliation put a lump in her throat.

Eve's next plan was a return trip to London. Hattie had told Tod he was responsible for her being blackmailed, so he must know the background. Finding out more might not help. Her blackmailer would presumably have wanted her alive, but perhaps her secret had been worth killing over in someone's eyes. Eve knew Tod lived on Beckshaw Street, thanks to Hattie mentioning it, which was a good start.

She walked Gus back through the estate, pondering how to identify Tod's house or flat number. The police would have it, of course, having interviewed him, but Eve knew giving it out would cross a line. She was distracted by the sight of Byron Acker, outside Cotwin Place. His phone rang and he instantly looked tense and furtive.

Eve ducked behind a tree as he glanced over his shoulder before taking the call.

'What, immediately?' she heard him say. After a moment he let out a low whistle. 'That's a lot of money. And if you don't pay up, you'll be in big trouble. They're not known for their patience.' He sighed. 'Look, I've got my reputation to think of. Just because I was involved before...' But then his tone changed. 'All right, all right. I'll help.'

He glanced over his shoulder once more, picked up a bag from inside his house, locked up and made for the car park.

Eve might be on the brink of finding out how Byron could afford his rent, and if he *was* involved in something criminal, it suggested a general lack of conscience. It made him black-mailing Hattie believable.

But Eve was on foot; she couldn't follow Byron as he drove off. She called Robin, who dashed straight to his van, hoping to spot Byron as he left the estate. But when they met back at Elizabeth's Cottage ten minutes later, he'd had no luck.

She got ready for her trip to London, thinking of what might have been.

'Tod's an unknown quantity,' Robin said, as she grabbed her bag. 'And there's no knowing how he'll react if you find him. My afternoon appointment's just cancelled. Let me come too?'

Eve didn't have to think twice. Joint sleuthing was one of her favourite things.

She called the teashop to ask one of their waitresses, Allie, if she could look in on Gus later. She'd been hiring her for such purposes ever since her previous ad hoc dog minder – another of Monty's waitresses – had switched jobs. She was much adored by the dachshund. Eve could hear Viv in the background, demanding news, and told Allie that she'd text her en route.

After that, she gave Gus a cuddle and promised a lovely walk on their return. She needn't have worried though. At the mention of Allie, he rolled over twice then ran around the coffee table. He'd found his previous dog minder much more exciting than Eve too.

'Do you think he'd miss me if I never came back?' Eve asked Robin as they drove to the station.

'Almost certainly. But not as much as I would.'

'More or less than he'd miss a sausage, do you think?'

She caught Robin's grin in her peripheral vision. 'Don't ask awkward questions.'

Beckshaw Street was full of dilapidated Victorian terraced houses, each with multiple doorbells. The labels were unhelp-fully anonymous as you'd expect, with just the flat number.

They decided Robin should lurk nearby with an open call to Eve. She'd look less intimidating on her own, but he'd still hear everything, ready for a conflab afterwards. And if there was trouble, of course, he'd be on standby too, but Eve doubted it would come to that. It wasn't as though Tod was directly involved in this business.

She rang bells at regular intervals along the road, and asked for Tod whenever someone answered.

'I'm sorry,' she said to each person who looked mystified, 'I must have got the wrong flat. I know he's on this road somewhere.'

At last, someone told her Tod lived two doors down in flat three. 'Or at least, that's where he used to be. With a gang of mates, yeah?'

Eve nodded. Best to look knowledgeable.

'Yeah, I thought so. He's been back there a while.'

'He moved out, then returned?' That was odd.

'Yeah.' The young woman was looking suspicious now. 'But then you'd know that, right? If you know him. You're not a mate of his mum's, are you?'

From her tone, that would be a bad thing. 'No, nothing like that. I'm a friend of an ex-girlfriend of his.'

The woman whistled. 'That sounds like trouble. Don't tell him I told you his flat number.'

'I won't.'

Eve walked to the house two doors down. Why had Tod left a flat in London he shared with his friends to squat in Hideaway House in rural Suffolk? To be with Hattie? Eve found it hard to believe. They hadn't seemed emotionally attached.

The police had already talked to Tod about Hattie's death, of course, and he had an alibi, but it would be interesting to see if he seemed upset.

She rang the buzzer for flat three of the gloomy-looking house, with its brown paintwork and peeling front door.

She had to lean on the bell two more times before someone answered, and when they did, it wasn't Tod. The guy facing her was solid-looking in trousers and an orange T-shirt that were too small for him.

'What's your problem?' He slouched against the door frame.

'I don't have one. Is Tod in?'

The guy pulled himself up. 'Who wants to know?'

'My name's Eve. I knew Hattie Fifield.'

He stuck out his lower jaw. 'Her death's got nothing to do with Tod.'

'I know. I heard.'

The man she recognised as Tod had appeared behind the large angry guy now. 'So what do you want then?' he asked, stepping forward.

'I know Hattie was in trouble before she died. I think she was being blackmailed and that you know why.'

Tod scoffed. 'Hattie was a law unto herself. Why would I know anything about it?'

'I heard you talk to her at the Wooden Spoon. She said it

was your fault her secret had got out. Then you gave her money.'

Tod folded his arms, his head on one side.

'Why did you go to Suffolk when you were already settled here?'

'I don't want to talk about it.'

Eve took a twenty-pound note from her bag. 'I know I'm taking up your time. If you want something in return, that's understandable.' She hated offering – it felt grubby.

Tod started to close the door, but before he could manage it, Eve locked eyes with his bolshy friend. She'd seen his spark of interest when she'd pulled out the twenty. If Tod was as loose tongued as Hattie suggested, the friend might know something too. 'I'm going to sit in the café round the corner, in case you change your mind.'

'Be my guest,' Tod said sarcastically and slammed the door shut.

Eve had noted the café as she and Robin walked from the tube. The place looked dirty and greasy, but it would be worth ordering a cup of tea if Tod, or more likely his housemate, came to find her.

'Sorry, Robin,' she said, as he rejoined her. 'More waiting around. I guess you could sit at a different table.'

But the café was deserted and Robin opted to wait around the corner. 'Two strangers at once would stick out like a sore thumb.'

After ten minutes, Eve gave in and drank the tea she'd ordered, despite the state of the mug and the horrible-looking filmy bits floating on it. She hoped there wouldn't be any ill effects. She'd just ordered a second cup and was starting to feel shifty when Tod's flatmate swung through the door and made for Eve's table.

The man behind the counter looked relieved, as though Eve now fitted into a context he understood.

The guy from the flat sank into the chair opposite and she fetched him a mug of tea.

'Give me double what you were offering Tod,' he said, as she sat back down, 'and I'll tell you everything I know.'

Eve paused a moment. 'Will it be worth it?'

'How the hell should I know?'

Hmm. 'All right. I'll take the chance.' Eve put forty pounds on the table between them. First things first. 'You know Tod stayed in the country around a year back?'

The guy nodded.

'And that he stole valuables from a rich family while he was there?'

He raised an eyebrow. 'Just some rumour. Though Hattie came round to our place after Tod got back, shouting the odds at him for nicking stuff.'

Eve wasn't surprised he wouldn't admit to Tod's involvement, but Hattie's outrage tied in with the conversation she'd overheard at the Wooden Spoon. It was time to dig more generally.

'So how long have you and Tod been sharing a flat?'

'There's five of us. People come and go but apart from his stay in Suffolk, Tod's been around longest. Three years.'

A stable arrangement. 'So why did he go to Suffolk?'

The man shrugged. 'Don't think it was *for* Hattie, but it was to do with her. She knew Tod from way back and she rocked up at our place a few times. Something about researching her dad. Then later, she came again. Said she'd got a proposal for him and that money was involved. She wanted him to go somewhere with her – back of beyond by the sound of things. And she said she'd got a business contact who would pay him. All he had to do was squat in this old building for a few weeks. He could be as noisy as he liked and treat the place like a dump – if he damaged stuff, all the better. Money for jam, so he went. Eventually they chucked him out and sold the place so back he came. Not bad work, he said. And this hasn't been either. I don't know anything else.'

He took her two twenties and left the café.

29

Eve was full of what Tod's mate had told her as she and Robin travelled home. It felt like a good result and not bad value for money, when it came down to it. She still felt grubby though.

'You think it was Duncan who paid Tod to squat?' Robin said.

Eve nodded. A memory had come back to her. 'We over-heard him on the phone, getting angry with someone, the day after we arrived, remember?'

Robin nodded, frowning. 'He said something like: "That wasn't part of the deal! No one takes me for a ride and gets away with it!"'

'That's the one. And I remember him adding, "Don't you threaten me! You watch yourself or I'll come for you, *now I know I can.*" I think he was letting rip at Tod for thieving. It was long after the event, so I assume he'd only just discovered he was still alive. Hattie said word had got back when Tod contacted an old friend at Kesham.' Rattler – so called because he kept rattling on. 'I'll bet Duncan was less than pleased to hear Tod was still around to tell his tale. He'd be sunk if the police investigated and discovered what he was really doing at Kesham.'

'Making Hideaway House seem like a liability, so Fifi would sell it to Duncan cut-price?'

Eve nodded. That had to be it. 'I can imagine it felt like a burden in the end. She'd have been eager to get rid of it and Tod. Edward said he was hanging around all the time, watching them, making his presence felt. I believe Duncan encouraged Tod to make himself as unpleasant as possible, and to trash Hideaway House too – even more than it was already. I think the notebook we found wasn't so much a diary, as a record of things he'd done to keep his side of the bargain.' Eve remembered the strange list:

The roof leaks now.

Visited the lake. Trespassed.

Tap's broken.

'And we know it was Duncan who advised the Tuppington-Hynds on the eviction process. Fifi probably had no idea what to do and he presented himself as her saviour, sorting the problem. She'd have been relieved and grateful. She probably let him handle everything, which might have helped him win her back. As it turns out, it was within his power to tell Tod to go home – simple as that.'

'All so Duncan could curry favour with Fifi.'

'And make his attempts to get near her more affordable. Paying Tod a few quid to make Hideaway House feel like a millstone could have saved him tens of thousands.'

'So he effectively robbed Fifi to get close to her.'

It had been a terrible way to behave, yet entirely predictable, given his end-justifies-the-means philosophy. He'd probably decided that Fifi didn't need the money, so why worry? She doubted he'd have thought twice.

'What if Fifi overheard Duncan and Hattie talking about hiring Tod?' Eve said. 'She'd have felt cheated and humiliated. *That* could be what caused the fight with Duncan.'

Robin nodded. 'It's certainly possible. If Duncan had only just discovered he was alive, it would be natural to bring him up. He might have accused Hattie of lying to protect him. And if Fifi did discover the truth about Tod, she probably wouldn't tell anyone. As you said, it would be deeply humiliating to admit her lover had tricked her so casually.'

'I need to know for sure. I feel another visit to Fifi coming on. If I hint at what I know, she might really open up this time. Admit her affair with Duncan even.'

They went back to musing over the new information.

'Hattie was up to her neck in it,' Robin said, after a moment. 'D'you think her blackmailer had found out about her scam with Tod?'

Eve nodded. 'Very possibly. Tod could have let his mission and her involvement slip after a few drinks. And I'll bet Hattie would have paid to cover it up. If word got out, it would have been ruinous for her. She and Duncan were con artists.'

'I still don't see Hattie's blackmailer killing her, but I'd like to identify them. I won't feel comfortable until all the jigsaw pieces fit together. More crucially, we need to know if Hattie was blackmailing someone else in turn, to get more money to pay. If so, they could have killed her. Edward's still in the running, I suppose.'

'If he wanted to keep it quiet that he was her dad?'

Eve nodded, but she could see Robin wasn't convinced. Even she felt like it was a stretch.

He cocked his head. 'There's another option. I know you think Byron might have blackmailed Hattie, but alternatively, I'd say he's a possible victim.'

Eve shook herself. 'Of course, if he's involved in something illegal.' It needed investigating.

Eve couldn't quite write Edward off, though. She wished Hattie's folder had been found. If it contained the DNA results it might at least show if Edward had been her dad.

The moment they got back to Saxford she went to pick up Gus, who still seemed high on his visit from Allie, walked him around the village green, then took him to the Cross Keys, while Robin did some paperwork at home.

Gus dashed across the pub to Hetty the pub schnauzer, almost tripping up Jo's husband Matt who was carrying a tray of empties. A moment later, the two dogs were performing their comical greeting ritual.

Eve gave Matt an apologetic look. 'Sorry.'

He laughed. 'Keeps me alert.'

When he was back behind the bar, Eve ordered a Coke and bought him a drink too. 'Mind if I have a scout round? I'm still hoping I might find Hattie's missing folder.'

'Scout away. Toby was looking for it too, when he heard what you were after.'

That wasn't good news. Matt's brother was the careful sort. If he hadn't found it, it probably wasn't there.

All the same, she went around the building, even negotiating her way into the forbidden territory of Jo's kitchen. She found nothing. While she was backstage, Jo asked for updates and Eve explained her quest to find Hattie's father.

'You said it was Edward who put in a good word for her before you took her on?'

Jo looked thoughtful as she nodded.

'Did he say why he'd got confidence in her?'

She pursed her lips. 'Not really. Just that he'd seen her on the estate. He said she had a good work ethic.'

'Would it surprise you if he turned out to be her dad?' He'd recommended Hattie to Marjorie too.

Jo sighed. 'All I can say is, he was ever so pleased when I offered Hattie the job and he bought her a drink to celebrate. I remember thinking what a nice man he was to look out for someone down on their luck. I should have known it would be more complicated than that.'

'We don't know for sure of course. If only I could find those DNA results.' It was tantalising, but as Eve made her way home, coaxing a reluctant Gus away from Hetty, she forced herself to keep a balanced view. It was Jack who'd given Duncan enough money to pay Hattie a wage. He was in the running too. She needed to visit him again and find out how he was reacting to Hattie's death. He was still a top suspect.

But he wasn't her only mission that evening. Before she did anything else, she wanted to talk to Fifi again, and bring up Tod. Her reaction might help Eve guess if she'd discovered the scam. That could certainly have caused her row with Duncan.

And it was finally time to call on Byron Acker. His phone conversation from earlier played on her mind. *'If you don't pay up, you'll be in big trouble. They're not known for their patience.'* She liked both him and Jack and there was something innocent, almost boyish, about Byron. But Robin was right. With his secrets, he was vulnerable to blackmail, and Hattie could have targeted him to raise funds, putting herself in danger. He was definitely a suspect.

30

It was late afternoon when Eve was invited into Kesham Hall's library by Fifi Tuppington-Hynd. Eve had said quietly that she'd like to talk to her in private.

'What a beautiful aspect this room has,' Eve said. 'I love your arbour, and all the honeysuckle.'

'Thank you, but you didn't come to talk to me about the gardens.' Fifi's tone was stiff. She hadn't invited Eve to sit and was standing too, though she'd closed the door for privacy.

'No. I wanted to take you into my confidence.' She was putting a spin on the situation, but it seemed like the safest approach. 'You probably heard from the police that Tod, the squatter from Hideaway House, is alive after all.'

Fifi's rigid face and body loosened. It looked as though the topic of conversation had come as a surprise, which was just as Eve had hoped. She wanted to jolt Fifi out of her formality and get her to open up.

'Yes, yes they said.' Fifi sat down, taking a padded leather chair near the window. 'They told me they'd interviewed him about the theft but they didn't have enough evidence to charge him.' She gripped the chair's arms, her voice still tight. The stealing would have angered her, naturally, but Eve felt it was more than that. Discovering Duncan's scam would explain it perfectly.

Eve took a seat opposite her. 'The truth is, I saw Tod and Hattie together before Hattie died. I heard what they talked about. And earlier today the final bit of the jigsaw fell into place. I know exactly why Tod came here.'

She'd been watching Fifi the entire time she spoke and saw her crumple – her shoulders droop, pain crease her face and renewed disbelief turn her eyes hollow.

'I can see you found out too.' Eve mustn't give her the chance to deny it. She needed Fifi to specify what she'd heard.

Her head was in her hands now. 'I went to speak to Duncan the evening he died, and overheard him and Hattie talking.' She didn't mention the binoculars, or Angela's lie about Duncan and Fifi having an affair. 'That was when I discovered the arrangement he'd made with Tod – all brokered by Hattie of course.' She closed her eyes for a moment. 'God help me, but I wanted to kill the pair of them in that moment. I felt like such a fool. No wonder Tod made our lives a misery.'

'It must have hurt extra if you were still in love with Duncan,' Eve said quietly.

Fifi looked tired rather than angry. 'When he came back here, I remembered *why* I'd loved him but when I overheard him that night, it struck a faint chord. I realised I'd been right as a teenager to suspect he'd hurt me one day. It wasn't just because my dad had made me cynical. It was that I'd already picked up on the ruthless side of his personality. He started to make himself useful to Dad the moment he guessed his parents might leave the estate. He charmed him, just as he charmed me. I suspect he always loved Kesham itself, best of all.'

'I'm sorry.'

But Fifi shook her head. 'It's history now.'

Eve guessed she'd never admit to the present-day affair. It

would be too humiliating. 'Forgive me, but I heard a rumour that you and Duncan fought, the night he died.'

Fifi sighed. 'The joys of living in a small community. But yes, that's right – and now you know why.' She leaned forward. 'I texted him to say I needed to see him urgently. I didn't even want to wait until morning to tell him he had to get out. I said I'd changed my mind about cooperating with him over the water supply for the lodge too. It was childish, but it felt good.'

Eve was sure it was the truth, and it fitted with what the twins had overheard too: her telling Duncan she knew exactly what he'd been up to.

'I suppose I'll have to give the police the full story, now you've worked it out,' Fifi went on, 'but will you please not tell people in the village? They made my life a misery before I left for California, and they know I came back in secret. If they realise Duncan and Hattie duped me, they'll laugh at me for ever.'

Eve nodded. 'I wouldn't dream of spreading it around. The police are the only ones who need to know.'

She'd make sure Fifi kept her word and told them.

Robin had been walking in the woods so he and Eve could catch up between interviews. They met on the path towards Byron Acker's house and she explained what Fifi had said.

'Nice work.'

'Thank you.'

'Any thoughts beyond what you discussed?'

'I suspect she saw Duncan for what he was, the moment she heard him talk about Tod. She's clearly decided he came back for Kesham's sake, not hers. I can see why she concluded that, but Duncan challenging Edward to climb the hall still makes it look as though he wanted Fifi too. Either way, she admitted how angry she was. But she didn't confront him or Hattie on the spot, I'd guess because they were together and she'd have been outnumbered. They might even have laughed at her.

'Instead, she summoned Duncan and made it clear she was withdrawing all support for his projects, from his cottage to the water supply for the lodge which would be essential if he wanted to let it out. And if he had to give up the restoration, Hattie would also be wounded and off the estate. It's the same as with Angela. Yes, she was livid with Duncan, but she'd worked out how to tackle it, and that didn't involve murder.'

31

Robin made himself scarce again as Eve neared Byron's house, though they'd set up an open call, in case Eve ran into trouble. Byron lived alone, unlike Fifi, so it felt justified, given Eve's intention to go snooping. He handed over Gus to go in with her too. It was good to have some moral support.

She took a deep breath as she walked up to the front door. Cotwin Place sat just outside the estate, isolated, looking like something from a fairy tale.

She could see Byron was home. His car had been in the car park and his windows were open. She'd yet to interview him about Duncan, so her excuse for visiting was lined up. Turning up unannounced was important. Uncovering his secret was a major part of her goal, to see if Hattie might have blackmailed him over it. She didn't want him tidying away any clues, but it was a daunting task. She wasn't sure how she'd snoop without him spotting her.

He looked distracted when he opened up, but bent to pet Gus. Eve hoped the dachshund didn't feel used, but he was a godsend in these situations. He made people relax.

'I'm so sorry I didn't call ahead. Everyone on the estate's dealing with such a lot. I was hoping to ask you a few questions about Duncan for the obituary.'

Byron blinked. Eve could see the level of emotion in his eyes and that concerned her. Any loss of life was a tragedy, but he hadn't known Duncan or Hattie well, officially.

'Of course.' Byron opened the door further and let her in. 'That's all right. I— It's just all so horrifying.' He shook his head. 'Would you like a cup of tea? Or something stronger?'

'Tea would be wonderful, thanks.' She needed to keep her wits about her, and setting him a task in the kitchen might give her the chance she needed to have a proper look round.

He left her in the striking medieval hall and Eve thought again of how devastated Jack would have been if he'd found out Duncan had failed to use the grant he'd been awarded to restore the place.

She scanned the room for paperwork that might help her in her quest. There was no convenient pile lying around like last time, but she spotted a closed laptop sitting on a table. Next to it was a cabinet with doors that wouldn't shut properly, thanks to the quantity of papers and folders stuffed inside.

Eve glanced towards the kitchen door. Sneaking a look at the cabinet felt horribly risky but it was that or examining his laptop. Unless he had a revealing screen open, that would probably tell her nothing.

She crouched next to the cabinet, her eye on the kitchen doorway, and eased out a file.

It was full of old water bills. The next she tried held stuff about a savings account. It was no good. From the files' labels, they all contained personal, household stuff. She switched to the laptop, holding her breath. The screen wasn't locked. She opened a file explorer window to see a sea of folders. The most recently accessed were labelled 'PW Vernon' and 'Boxwood Ltd'. She double clicked to examine the first, saw the contents and rocked back on her heels. After taking a moment to digest what she was seeing, she went into the second folder. Byron's kettle had come to the boil, but she had her confirmation. She closed the windows and pushed the laptop lid shut, seconds before Byron appeared with her drink. He'd poured himself a whisky, Eve noticed.

He gave Eve a sheepish look as he sipped it. 'Sorry. Trying day.'

Yes, it must have been. Everything was clear now. What she'd thought she'd known had fallen to bits in front of her.

She remembered the conversation she'd overheard that morning. *'If you don't pay up, you'll be in big trouble. They're not known for their patience.'* She felt faintly hysterical now she'd viewed his files. 'Work related?' she said at last. 'I hear you've got a sideline.'

He flushed. 'Who told you that?'

'I can't remember.' She couldn't wait to tell Viv. She bet Robin was on tenterhooks too, listening in. 'But why do you keep it a secret?'

He grimaced. 'I'm supposed to be Byron Acker, artist. Fake it until you make it, isn't that what they say? I've had a bit of interest in the local press recently. I don't want them seeing me as Colin Sanders, accountant.'

He must have been referring to the tax office that morning. She felt like such an idiot. Robin was doing well not to burst out laughing on the other end of the line.

'You could be proud of both.' From the quantity of correspondence on his computer, he clearly got a lot of business.

'I certainly earned my money today. Between ourselves, my client's been an absolute pain in the backside. I wasn't overly keen on working for him again, because of reputational risk, but I gave in in the end.'

It all fitted so much better with the impression Eve had of Byron's character. He was still blushing, and she couldn't help feeling sorry for him. The upshot was, his secret wasn't black-mail worthy. It was very unlikely that Hattie had blackmailed him for any other reason, so he almost certainly hadn't killed her to put an end to it. He could still have coerced money out of her, though he seemed too nice, and he was clearly solvent.

'So you wanted to talk about Duncan.' Byron sipped his drink. 'I didn't know him well.'

'He was an easy landlord?'

'Not at all interfering.'

Privately, Bella imagined he hadn't given two hoots about Byron or his lodgings, so long as he kept paying the rent. He was too busy obsessing over Fifi, or the estate, if she was correct. 'What did you think of him as a person?'

Byron frowned. He looked as though he was wrestling with himself. In Eve's profession, she knew how ingrained 'never speak ill of the dead' was.

'He had some odd priorities,' he said at last.

'In what way?'

He shook his head and Eve sensed he wished he could back-track. 'Just my sense as an accountant,' he said at last. 'I like balanced books. I think Duncan did a lot of borrowing and not much paying back.'

The last words came out in a rush, with what sounded like relief. He was glad to have found a plausible answer to Eve's question, she guessed. She wondered what odd priorities he'd really been thinking of.

'He borrowed from you?'

'Oh no.' Byron answered readily now.

But it still wasn't surprising that he'd formed that opinion. He was friends with Jack Farraway, and Jack had handed over money.

Eve asked a few more innocuous questions: how Byron had heard about Cotwin Place and what he thought of Duncan's restoration work. She wanted him to relax; she'd never get anything useful otherwise. As the inconsequential chat flowed, Eve took the chance to study the room around her. Byron had tidied up since she'd last visited. He'd polished the shelf where she'd seen the dusty book outlines previously. It was filled with china and glassware now. Eve's attention was caught by two pretty espresso cups with tiny handles and gilt rims. They were just like the ones that Cesca had played with at White Cottage. Eve loved the iridescent glaze the potter had used. Two here and four at White Cottage.

A set of six?

Of course, Jack often looked after Cesca, and he also frequently visited Byron, while working on the restoration that Duncan should have organised. If he took Cesca with him, she'd need entertaining. Perhaps Byron had let her play with the tiny cups and she'd taken a fancy to them. He could have given her some to take home. That was kind.

When their chat drew to a close without further insight, Eve asked him about them.

'Ah no, that's right.' He was blushing again. 'Cesca seemed so delighted with them, and I don't need six for myself.'

A creeping suspicion was stealing into Eve's mind. 'Angela must have been grateful. You and Jack between you must have made all the difference. I don't think Duncan helped with the childcare much.'

'No,' Byron said. 'No, I don't believe he did.'

Eve's mind was back on Byron's comment about Duncan's odd priorities. And then she thought of Angela's campaign to drive Duncan away from Kesham by vandalising his properties. Jack knew. He'd babysat Cesca while she went out. What were the odds that Jack had told Byron? He could have explained how unhappy Angela was. Whether Byron knew or not, he would have seen how badly Duncan treated Angela. And he was giving his belongings to her child to play with. Eve didn't doubt he was a kind man, but his blush hinted it might be more than that.

Eve was starting to think Byron could have fallen for Angela. In their short interview, he'd gone from being a suspect for the second murder, to being innocent in her eyes, then back to a suspect again, this time for Duncan *and* Hattie.

32

Eve sneaked into the woods for a quick word with Robin before going on to Jack Farraway's house.

'It was more striking when you could see the way Byron blushed,' Eve said. 'Heck, Robin. If he's really fallen for Angela, I could see him losing it with Duncan, and it's plausible that Hattie guessed his guilt. Most people would have gone to the police, but we know someone was squeezing money out of her. She could have decided to pay it forward and blackmail Byron in turn.'

Gus looked from her to Robin, as though he sensed something serious was going on, but couldn't work out what.

Robin nodded slowly. 'You think he's got the right temperament?'

'To strike Duncan in a fury for the way he treated Angela? That might be one of the few circumstances in which he'd lash out. It would be different if it looked premeditated. As for Hattie, he might have needed to kill her for his own security. The trouble is, it's nothing but guesswork.' Eve imagined telling Palmer her theories, all based on some espresso cups. There was no way he'd take her seriously and for once, Eve couldn't really blame him. She needed proof. 'I've got one idea for finding circumstantial evidence.'

Robin raised an eyebrow.

'Twice now, I've seen Angela with lots of cash in her purse, when she was paying me back for shopping. The first time she was so upset she just looked dazed as she counted out my money, but the next she double-took at the amount that was there.'

'You think Byron might have slipped money into her bag to help her out?'

'I wondered. Even if Hattie was blackmailing him he could probably have afforded it. His day job must be fairly lucrative. And Angela handed over some of the notes to me for the groceries. What if we ask Greg to check them for fingerprints? They'll have us all on file, after the break-in at the lodge. If there's a nice clear set of Byron's, it would make him look protective of her at the very least. Jack might secretly sub her too, of course, but I'd imagine he's short of cash, after funding Duncan and shelling out on materials to restore Cotwin Place.'

Robin frowned. 'It's a bit unorthodox, but I suspect Greg will agree. He texted me a while ago to say he's on the estate, as a matter of fact, talking to the Tuppington-Hynds again. Let me see if he's still here.'

Robin made the call and five minutes later they were standing in the Kesham car park handing over the notes to Greg, like three dodgy dealers. Even if they got the results Eve hoped for, it wouldn't be proof, but it might lead the police in the right direction. Her heart sank at the thought of Byron being guilty, but she couldn't ignore her hunch about his feelings for Angela. It was too important.

After Greg had driven off, they separated again, ready for Eve's visit to Jack's cottage, but they'd opened another call. Once again, Eve would look for an opportunity to snoop, which made her visit especially risky.

She knocked on his door and after a moment, he opened up. 'Hello again.' He sounded tired and sad. 'Come in.'

She followed him inside. 'I'm very sorry to bother you when things are so awful. I couldn't believe the news about Hattie.'

He nodded, but turned away, as though he didn't want her to see his expression. Eve felt disappointment bite her. Instinctively, she liked Jack, but something wasn't right. If it turned out he was Hattie's dad, Eve still couldn't see why he'd kill her over it, but he might be guilty if Hattie knew he'd killed Duncan and had been blackmailing him. He and Byron were now the strongest suspects in Eve's eyes.

'I had a couple of extra questions about Duncan, but perhaps it's not a good time.'

'It can't be helped,' Jack muttered. 'Drink?'

He still wasn't meeting her eye. 'A cup of tea would be lovely.' She'd pop if she had much more, but as with Byron, it would be helpful to get Jack out of the room. She wanted to search his chest of drawers to find out what had made him so emotional after she'd left last time.

The moment he'd disappeared to the kitchen, she went to investigate, thinking back to what she'd witnessed. They'd just finished talking about Duncan's murder when she left, then she'd spotted him through the window, rootling in the drawer. Whatever he'd found had made him cry. She was sure it must relate to Duncan – why make a beeline for it at that moment otherwise?

Gingerly, her heart beating fast, her eye on the kitchen door, Eve eased the top drawer open. Inside was a complicated muddle of things: string, pens, keys and much else besides. But on top of everything else was a photograph, cut into an oval shape as though it had once sat in a frame. The photo smeared with something brown. Eve smelled it. Varnish? There was brick dust on it too. It was clear it had been on a building site.

Her mind was on Jack, standing over the rubbish bag just outside the lodge, finding something that sent him running to Duncan and swearing never to forgive him. She bet he'd found this photograph, but what did it mean?

It showed a youngish woman arm-in-arm with a man of around the same age, a young boy standing just in front of them. Glancing at the kitchen door again, Eve turned the photo over. Someone had written on the back, before it was cut into its oval shape.

... phen, Jess and Anthony (aged five)

Eve felt goosebumps rise on her arms and tears prick her eyes. Jess, Jack's wife, together with her first husband and son who'd been killed in the car crash. She remembered the missing photograph Sylvia had talked about, which Jess had wanted so desperately when she was dying. Selfless Jack had searched high and low for the picture, listening to her agonised cries, until in despair, he'd done his best to sketch Jess's first husband and her beautiful boy.

If Eve was right, then for some reason this precious photograph had ended up carelessly flung aside, knotted in a bag with rubble and dirty rags. But why would Duncan have taken it? There was only one reason Eve could think of, and the picture's oval shape seemed to confirm her thoughts.

She was almost too overcome to focus, but the sound of clinking china brought her back to the present. In one movement, she replaced the photo and slid the drawer closed. She needed to speak to someone who knew what sort of frame the photograph had been in. She was betting it had been valuable and was no longer in Duncan's possession. It wasn't only money for materials and mortgages he'd have needed, but smaller amounts to pay people like Tod too.

His end-justifies-the-means mantra came back to Eve. No

wonder Jack had been devastated by what Duncan had done, if she was right. He'd made the last few hours of Jess's life even more terrible, because of his selfish priorities. And it looked as though he'd done it casually too. He hadn't thought to dispose of the photo just after he'd stolen it, but later, presumably when he'd happened across it again. It must have sat in a pocket or work bag for ages.

Jack reappeared and Eve fought to pull herself together. It was the same for him as it was for Byron: if either of them had killed Duncan, Hattie could have worked it out.

Eve and Jack sat down and Eve asked the extra questions she'd invented about Duncan – mainly about his relationship with Jess. Jack told her how fond Jess had been of him, but his voice was tight. He was holding back. She guessed that even now Duncan was dead, he couldn't dispel his anger. It was time to steer him on to the latest murder.

'Were you surprised when Hattie said she was Duncan's daughter?' The truth still wasn't public.

Jack paused for a long time. 'I was,' he said at last. 'I'd known Duncan for many years. To have had no hint of it made it hard to credit, and Jess clearly had no idea either. She'd have told me if she had. I still believed it though. At first, at least.'

Eve raised an eyebrow.

'In the end, I wondered if they'd made it up.' When Eve didn't chip in, he added: 'It helped Hattie a great deal, didn't it, to have everyone think her dad was a TV star? She was set to be one too.'

Eve was uneasy. There was a bitterness in his voice. He might have given Duncan money to pay Hattie at one point, but she sensed that by the end, he'd hated the pair of them. And now they were both dead.

She moved the conversation onto safer topics: her visit to Angela and Cesca and how sweet Cesca had been, playing with the espresso cups. 'Byron must be fond of her.'

'I believe he is.'

Neither of them specified which 'her' they were talking about.

As Eve sipped her tea, her gaze drifted over Jack's garden where they'd sat last time she'd visited. She could see the patch of earth where Cesca liked to dig, as well as the marigolds which she'd watered. They'd been wilting – in the heat, Eve had assumed. They looked worse now. Pretty much dead, in fact. Maybe the dry weather had finally put paid to them.

At last, Eve wound up her conversation with Jack and thanked him. She left feeling dissatisfied. Every question she'd asked had increased her worry over his possible guilt, but she'd uncovered nothing concrete.

She began her walk home with Gus, knowing Robin would catch her up.

'Tell me everything,' he said, as soon as he'd joined her. There'd been a lot he couldn't gather, since he'd only listened in.

Eve explained about the photo and her theories, then relayed the rest of their conversation. 'That's it,' she said at last.

At home, they continued to pick the new information apart over supper, but no fresh enlightenment came. It was only later, when Greg rang, that the tempo of the evening changed.

'News on the cash you handed over,' Robin said.

'Already?'

'The pressure's increasing for Palmer to get a result. Everyone's working long hours. The information's interesting. It's not Byron's prints on the notes.'

33

Robin sat back in his chair. 'The clearest sets of prints on the notes from Angela's purse are yours, Hattie's and Jack's. There also appears to be a partial of Tod's. Yours overlay Jack's. And both yours and his overlay Hattie's and the partial.'

Gus had scampered over from his water bowl, and held his head up high, alert, as though he knew this was a turning point.

Eve closed her eyes for a moment and thought. 'If Jack had cash to spare, it wouldn't surprise me if he slipped Angela some. But if this money had been through Hattie's hands too, and Tod's, then there's only one conclusion to draw.'

'Uh-huh. It certainly looks as though Jack got the cash he gave to Angela from Hattie.'

Eve shook her head. 'I was thinking this evening, when I spoke to him, that although Jack gave Duncan money for Hattie's salary, he spoke as though he'd despised her by the end. Do you think Palmer will do anything?'

Robin grimaced. 'I wouldn't get your hopes up. It's like you said, Jack secretly slipping Angela money isn't surprising, and although the prints seem to tell a story, it's circumstantial. Hattie could have paid Jack back for something, which would explain her and Tod's prints. But at least Greg will have the facts in the back of his mind.'

But that wasn't enough. 'I think I should talk to Jack again. I don't have to admit I got inside information from the police. I can just face him with what we've guessed, embellish a bit and see if he cracks.' She had a feeling he might.

'He could still be the killer, Eve – don't forget that.'

'I know. I won't. But we need to understand his emotions. Under ordinary circumstances, I'd say Jack is a kind man. It's possible he was blackmailing Hattie as a sort of punishment for aiding and abetting Duncan. If so, he might have had less compunction about killing her if she became a threat, but her death was very different to Duncan's. Whoever did it went in cold, even if they were driven by terror at what Hattie might do.'

'I can't argue with that.'

Eve gave Gus a cuddle and promised to be back soon as he settled down in his bed, then she and Robin returned to Kesham.

Robin hung back with the same arrangement as before, but it turned out to be pointless. When Eve reached Jack's cottage, he wasn't there.

She couldn't bring herself to give up. As she walked home again, she called him on his mobile. Perhaps she could arrange an appointment for the following morning.

He picked up, and she visualised the woods around him. She could hear twigs cracking and a nightjar singing.

Eve apologised for bothering him and began to explain why she wanted to talk again. As she told him about the meeting she'd witnessed between Hattie and Tod, and what they'd said about her needing money, he sighed.

'*Ah. I see.*'

He sounded so resigned, she sensed she wouldn't have to wait for tomorrow. Next, she told him about Angela being surprised to find extra money in her purse. 'I know how much you want to protect her and Cesca, so it makes sense that it came from you. She'll be short until the life insurance is paid out. But it left me wondering how you'd managed it, when you'd spent so much helping Duncan and restoring Cotwin Place.' She took a deep breath. 'It struck me that you might have got the money from Hattie. I could tell this evening that although you'd once sympathised with her, you'd lost faith with her in the end, so blackmail didn't seem out of the question.'

'*What?*'

Eve could tell she'd got it wrong from the shock in his voice. Yet she must have been on the right track until then. It was the first time he'd interrupted. Her thoughts rearranged themselves. 'No. Sorry. So it wasn't blackmail.' Jack was a kind man, she should have hung on to that. Perhaps Hattie had *owed* him money. 'You felt sorry for her, and you knew Duncan hadn't paid her the stipend you funded. So you scraped together some money to loan her direct?' Perhaps he was her dad after all; it would explain his generosity.

'*That's right.*'

Relief washed over Eve. At last, she was getting somewhere. 'Then something changed your opinion of her, and you demanded it back?' The revised theory sat far more easily with her impression of Jack.

'*I'm afraid so.*'

'I'm assuming your change of heart came when you found out about Hattie helping Duncan arrange the scam with Tod?'

'*Yes.*' His voice shook slightly. She could tell it still made him livid.

So Hattie had known Jack could ruin her reputation if he chose. Eve imagined she'd have felt the same urgency to comply as if it *had* been blackmail.

'I guess you didn't hear it from Tod himself, but from someone else, more recently?' It would explain why he'd only lost faith in Hattie lately. 'An old drinking partner of his, perhaps, nicknamed Rattler?' Hattie had said he liked to talk, and of course, the blonde woman at the Pied Piper had mentioned that Jack was a good listener too.

'*Right again. When I realised the part Hattie and Duncan played, I was appalled. I'm still wondering what to do with the information. It seems to have died with them and that doesn't feel right.*'

'I can understand why you were angry, and why you recalled your loan. I'd have done the same. If you don't mind me asking, where did Hattie bring the cash? It's just that I saw her acting oddly before she died, and I haven't found a way to explain it.' She could no longer imagine Hattie taking her payment to the Pied Piper. The blonde bartender had said Jack never went there these days, and besides, if Hattie had been repaying a loan, there'd be no need for the cloak-and-dagger stuff, but Eve wanted to rule it out.

Jack hesitated. '*Look, perhaps it's better for us to discuss this tomorrow. I can give you the full story then. Ten-ish? It might help me work out what action to take.*'

'Thanks. I'll be there.'

Eve told Robin what Jack had said as they walked back to Saxford again. As he fished in his pocket for his door key, Eve stared down at the marigolds growing in their small front garden. They were doing a lot better than the ones she'd seen at Jack's place.

Absently, she mentioned it to Robin. 'I love the way everything at our place always looks wonderful, thanks to you. When we're embroiled in something upsetting like these murders, coming outside to appreciate nature makes all the difference.'

He smiled as he opened the door carefully in an effort not to wake Gus. 'I'm glad,' he whispered, then he frowned. 'Wait a minute. What did you say about Jack's marigolds?'

Eve repeated it. 'Too much heat and lack of water, I suppose.'

Robin's brow remained creased. 'That doesn't make sense.'

'How so?'

'Marigolds are drought tolerant.'

'Maybe Cesca overwatered them then.' But did that really figure? She'd stopped when Eve told her to.

'When did you first notice them wilting?' Robin asked.

'The day after Duncan was killed.'

He was shaking his head. 'It reminds me of a past case. I'm sorry, but I think I need to go back. I'd like to take a look if I can. You should get some rest, like Gus.'

But Robin's urgency rubbed off on her. 'You have to be kidding! I'm coming too.' Her breath was short as they exited the house again. This time, they took Robin's van.

When they arrived at Kesham, Jack's house still looked empty. A minute later, they were peering through his hedge.

Robin turned to her, not looking any happier. 'I need to talk to Greg, but I know what he'll say.'

They moved away from Jack's place before Robin made the call. 'No, no,' Eve heard him say after he'd explained his worries, 'I understand.' He turned back to Eve after hanging up. 'Getting the police to investigate the marigolds is a lost cause, as I thought.'

Eve swallowed. He'd explained his fears as they'd driven over. 'You really think the missing murder weapon might be buried there?'

He nodded. 'I could be wrong, but I've seen it before. There was a guy down in London who buried a knife under a flowerbed. He thought he'd been cunning, but dying flowers in an otherwise well-kept garden gave him away. In this case, the police don't have the evidence to get a warrant, so I'd like to look myself.'

They knocked on the cottage door before trespassing, just to be certain no one was home, but everything was quiet.

After that, Eve recorded Robin's journey through Jack's hedge on her phone, in case there were queries later. Then she followed him and kept the video going. Robin had snatched up a trowel from his van and he wore gardening gloves too.

He didn't have to dig that deep before he found Duncan's tool belt and his hammer. It still had blood on it.

Eve spent a long time with the police that night. She and Robin spoke to uniformed officers at first. It took a while for Palmer to arrive and when he did, he wasn't happy.

'Do you make a habit of breaking and entering at will?' He was glaring at them both.

'We trespassed, that's all,' Robin said calmly. 'And we tried to involve you first.'

'Then decided you knew best.'

Eve was having to bite her tongue, because in the event, Robin – with his gardening expertise – *had* known best. And what they'd done was something only a private citizen could have got away with.

'We were worried something was off, and after we'd called you, we knocked at the door but there was no reply,' Eve said. 'In the end, we thought it was better to risk getting into trouble than to miss something so crucial.' She put her head on one side. 'I expect the media will take your side, though, and say we should have let sleeping dogs lie.' She smiled at him sweetly. She'd got to know the local reporters over the years. She knew exactly whose side they'd be on, and that Palmer would understand the risk of making this into a big deal.

He looked livid. 'You probably sent Farraway running. He could be anywhere by now.'

'If he left because of what we found then he must have had a premonition. He was already out when we turned up.'

She wondered if her phone call could have spooked him, but she didn't think so. Nothing he'd said made him seem more likely as the killer, the opposite if anything. Of course, Palmer made her go through all that too, and everything she'd discovered so far. It was lucky that she was primed to explain it all away without admitting they'd had inside information from Greg. All the same, she had to take a deep, steadying breath.

She felt sad and anxious. Jack seemed like a nice man who worried for Angela and Cesca. She had plenty of evidence to suggest he was the killer, but she was still loath to accept it. Finding the murder weapon buried like that didn't prove he was guilty.

'It's interesting that the murderer left the weapon that killed Hattie close to her body,' she said to Palmer. 'If Jack killed both her and Duncan, why vary his behaviour like that?'

'There could be any number of reasons,' Palmer said irritably. 'As a civilian, you wouldn't understand.'

But Robin had nodded as she spoke. She was sure he was thinking the same as her, that Jack could have hidden the weapon to protect someone. Perhaps he'd taken a stroll after babysitting Cesca and found Duncan's body, the belt and the hammer. He knew Angela had been out to vandalise the lodge. He could have worried that she'd bumped into Duncan and lashed out. Seen him kissing Fifi, perhaps. Eve had written Angela off as a suspect because she'd had other plans to split Duncan and Fifi up. But she could still have lost control, and Jack might believe that she had.

If Eve shared her thoughts, Palmer might decide that Angela was guilty. Set him on a particular course and he'd never let it go. Eve needed to find out more first. And in the meantime, where was Jack Farraway?

. . .

At last, the questioning was over, and Eve and Robin drove back to Elizabeth's Cottage. The moment they parked by the village green, Viv and Simon appeared next to Robin's van.

'Simon came round for supper and we saw you drive off towards Kesham,' Viv said. 'We've been waiting to find out what's up ever since. Honestly, you've been ages. I've been yawning my head off and Polly's texted twice to ask where Simon is.'

'Long story,' Eve said.

They went back to the cottage, where Gus stirred sleepily and gave them a tired look through half-closed eyes. Eve soothed him while Robin made them all hot chocolate. It was just what Eve felt like. It had got late and adrenaline had made her shivery. A moment later, she found shortbread to serve with the drinks.

Once they were settled, they filled Viv and Simon in.

'So you're not sure Jack did it?' Viv said.

'It's just odd that he'd hide one murder weapon but leave the next one be,' Eve replied. 'And when we spoke on the phone, he was clearly horrified at the far lesser crime Hattie, Tod and Duncan had pulled off, devaluing Hideaway House.' Her thoughts had coalesced. She felt more certain now.

Robin nodded. 'I agree. If he'd committed murder, it would be odd to obsess over something less serious like that.'

They were debating possibilities when a text came in on Robin's mobile. His look turned grim as he scanned the screen.

'Message from Greg. I'm afraid Jack Farraway's been attacked. They've found him unconscious near the lodge at Kesham. Hit over the head as before, but this time with a rock, which was found at the scene. The good news is, his attacker only gave him a glancing blow. They hope he'll survive.'

34

Eve and Robin were late to bed that night, and Robin kept an arm around her, but she couldn't stop crying. The last call she'd had with Jack echoed round her head. He'd been talking about Hattie and Duncan, then said he'd tell her everything the following day. If the killer heard him, they might have thought he was about to unmask them. He'd been chatting quite openly, then cut the conversation short.

What had she been thinking? She'd been too impatient to get answers. She'd never conduct an interview like that in such an uncontrolled way again. But it was useless to vow that now. What if Jack died? She kept a vigil, hoping against hope he'd be okay. He was a kind man, and Angela and Cesca's mainstay. He didn't deserve any of this.

In the rare moments she wasn't consumed by guilt, she thought about other aspects of the case, because this had to stop. Angela had already lost a husband and now, thanks to Eve, she'd almost lost a father figure too. It was desperately urgent to find the truth.

There were still so many unanswered questions, Hattie's father's identity being one. Jack had loaned her money, another kindness, and if he was her dad, then her duplicitous behaviour would hurt all the more. But why keep quiet, if he knew the truth? He could have told everyone she was lying as a punishment, if he disapproved of her and Duncan plotting. Edward seemed a more likely candidate.

Eve got up at half-past six, feeling limp as seaweed, after around an hour's sleep. She found Robin in the kitchen. He walked over and took her hands in answer to her look.

'Greg texted half an hour ago. Jack came round during the night. He's out of danger and there'll be no lasting damage.'

'Thank goodness.' Eve felt waves of tension ease out of her body, though she'd still never forgive herself.

Robin nodded. 'They'll interview him shortly but it's already clear he doesn't know who attacked him. They came at him from behind and there are no prints on the rock.'

Eve drank copious amounts of coffee and tried to rally her thoughts. It was still possible that Jack had noticed something that would make a difference. She wondered what he'd say about the buried hammer and toolbelt. Once she'd heard the latest from Greg, she wanted to hash things over with the gang.

In the meantime, she had places she needed to be. Once again, she wanted to visit Angela, this time to say how sorry she was that Jack had been attacked. She'd be devastated. Surely, she had to be off the suspect list now?

But when Eve voiced the thought, Robin frowned and she knew he was about to say something she wouldn't like.

'I agree, she'd have to be absolutely desperate to try to kill Jack. I'm not sure she'd do it on her own account, even if she was under immediate threat of arrest. But she does have Cesca to consider. I don't think you should discount her. And a failed attack could fit. Even if she felt compelled to kill Jack, she'd find it incredibly hard. I know she'll probably have Cesca with her when you visit, and you're not planning any risky snooping this time. I can't see her trying anything, but promise me you'll be cautious.'

She gave him a look. 'I'm always cautious.' She knew he'd come and listen in if she asked, but she felt she owed Angela some privacy. He'd made her pause for thought, though. She'd watch her carefully as she expressed her sympathy. She could use the visit to test her theory about the missing photo frame too. Angela might know what it had looked like. It wouldn't tell her who'd killed Duncan, but it could certainly reveal more about his character. Her other goal – and much more crucial to the murders – was to find out how Angela felt about Byron. If she might have left Duncan for him, he became less likely as the killer. But if, despite the way Duncan had behaved, Angela was determined to stick by him, then Byron could have lashed out from passion, fury, and frustration.

Eve texted Greg to make sure the police weren't with Angela, then headed to Kesham with Gus in tow.

In the end, she found her on her own.

'Byron offered to take Cesca for a walk.' Her eyes were swollen with crying. 'It's such a relief to let it all out while she's not here. I was so frightened when I heard what had happened to Jack. I know he's going to be okay now, but I can't stop thinking of him, lying there, utterly helpless. We came so close to losing him...'

Eve gave her a hug and felt terrible. 'I know. I'm so very sorry. You've had way too much to cope with.'

Eve bustled around as before, putting a casserole she'd brought into the fridge and making tea. She was finding it hard not to get emotional too. Thoughts of the unwitting part she'd played plagued her. But she needed to focus, and try to make up for it.

She wanted every second to count, so she automatically considered the kitchen's contents again, in case she'd missed a clue last time. But in fact, her thoughts felt inconsequential. She noted afresh the boxes of books in the repurposed pantry. As she waited for the kettle to boil, she thought again of the damp getting to them. If she were Angela, she'd keep them on a higher shelf. She could see mildew on the walls near the skirting board. She, Duncan and Cesca had been at Kesham for over a year now. It didn't take long for things to spoil in those conditions.

It was that thought that made her pause, because she hadn't noticed any damage to the books, last time she'd looked. She peered at them again but it was true: they hadn't suffered. In fact, they were all in good condition. She retrieved the copy of *The Hobbit* she'd spotted last time and opened it.

Wow. A first edition from 1937.

Eve eased it back into the box again, thinking. She finished making the tea and took it through to Angela.

They talked about Jack: how very fond Angela was of him and what a relief it was not to have to explain another death to Cesca.

'Poor man, he hasn't had an easy life,' Angela said. 'It was so hard when he lost Jess.'

'I gather you spent some time nursing her,' Eve replied.

Angela nodded. 'I wanted to help, so I brought Cesca over with me for a couple of weeks.'

'And I heard about the photo she was so desperate to hold as she was dying.'

'Of her first husband and child? That's right. My heart ached for Jack; she hardly knew him by that stage. And yes, there was a massive hunt for the photo. We never did find it.'

'Had you seen it before?'

Angela nodded. 'Jess had it on a high bookshelf in the spare room at one point. When we couldn't find it, we assumed she'd put it away to stop Jack feeling like he was living in their shadow.'

'Do you think Duncan was aware of the photo?'

Angela looked confused. 'I expect so.'

'Can you remember the frame it was in?'

She nodded. 'It was very pretty, but heavy. Floral, bronze with gold. Turn of the century, I remember Jess saying. It had been a wedding present. Why do you ask?'

Eve sighed. 'I discovered by accident that Jack found the photo shortly before Duncan died. It was without its frame, though.'

Angela frowned. 'How odd.'

But not when you considered how badly Duncan had wanted money and how single-minded he'd been about getting it. It made Eve think of the books in Angela's pantry again. Duncan would surely have sold a first-edition copy of *The Hobbit* if he'd known they'd got it.

Eve could only assume he hadn't known. She felt the hairs on her forearms lift. That and the lack of mildew on the books suggested they were recent acquisitions. They might date back to before Duncan's death though – they'd been stored behind Cesca's toys, in anonymous-looking boxes. Had that been an effort to hide them? Eve could imagine Angela doing that to keep them from Duncan's grasp.

And then suddenly, she could guess exactly where they'd come from. She should have seen it before. Memories of dust marks on a shelf came back to her.

'Angela, I'm so sorry to ask, but why did Byron give you his books?'

Her lips parted but instead of speaking, she hung her head and her hair fell over her eyes.

'How did you know?' she asked at last.

'I saw the gap where they'd been in his house. What with that and a couple of other things, I put two and two together. I'd already realised he was fond of you. And of Cesca. He passed the books on before Duncan died, didn't he?'

At last, she nodded. 'He said his father had collected them

but he always reads on Kindle and he didn't want them any more. He told me they might fetch something. He'd guessed how desperate I was to move away, and he said I could use the money to help me get back to London.' She closed her tear-filled eyes for a moment. 'I think he hoped I might use the proceeds to break free of Duncan. Although I let him give me the books, I'd decided before Duncan died that I'd have to return them.'

'Because you wanted to stay with him, and move back to London together?' Eve looked into Angela's anxious eyes.

'I wasn't sure what I wanted,' she said at last. 'It's hard to explain. Even after Duncan died, I was so angry with him, I cut up one of his tops just to let it out. It was hard to get past the hurt over Fifi, and his and Hattie's lies, and I couldn't have it out with him.' There were silent tears running down her cheeks.

That explained the lacerated vest Eve had found. But angry though Angela had been, Eve had no doubt she'd still loved Duncan. It was plain to see, from the look in her eyes to the tone of her voice.

Eve guessed she hadn't lost hope until he'd died. Wanting to drive a wedge between Duncan and Fifi showed she was committed to her marriage. Byron might have decided Angela would never move on unless Duncan was out of the picture.

35

After saying goodbye to Angela, Eve led Gus through the woods, back towards Saxford. She'd texted Robin to say she'd finished, and he walked out to meet her, so they completed the journey together. It was useful, allowing several minutes of calm as they talked and everything settled in her mind. After that, they returned to Elizabeth's Cottage for lunch, before Eve headed to Monty's. Various queries were forming in her head.

Viv demanded a debrief the moment she arrived, of course, which worked all right as they were both on baking detail while Allie and Emily served.

As Eve explained the guilt she felt over the attack on Jack, Viv pulled her into a hug.

'You can't know for sure, and besides, it's like you always say, only the murderer's responsible for what happened.'

Eve didn't truly believe it in this case, but it was still comforting.

'So what are the take-home points?' Viv weighed out icing sugar, clouds of it filling the air so that Eve could taste the sweetness. How had Viv worked in the business so long without learning to be tidier?

'Angela fantasising about moving back to London is explained. She decided against selling Byron's books, but I'll bet she googled their value all the same.' Curiosity would be natural. 'I found a similar first edition of *The Hobbit* which had sold for nearly forty thousand pounds.'

Viv whistled. 'I might search my bookshelves when I get home.'

Eve had had the same thought. 'If the other books are worth anything like that much, she could probably have afforded to buy a house outright. So that revelation reassures me about Angela. I don't believe she was focused on Duncan's life insurance when she talked about returning to the capital. I think she was so tempted by Byron's gift that she investigated a school place for Cesca. But in the end, her conscience won out. She knew he was fond of her, and she couldn't take his money to rescue Duncan from his debts.

'But my discovery makes me more worried about Byron. The books are one heck of a gift. I'd already decided he'd fallen for Angela, but perhaps it counts as an obsession. And, horrific though it is, Jack as the latest victim might fit. The pair of them spent a lot of time together. Jack could have guessed Byron was guilty, as could Hattie, who might have decided to blackmail Byron rather than go to the police. And of course, Byron was fond of Jack. Perhaps he botched the attack on him because that made it hard.'

'So Byron's right up there.' Viv pushed up her sleeve with a sugary hand and Eve tried not to twitch. Attempt unsuccessful. 'Anything else?'

Eve nodded. 'We now know it was Jack who was demanding money from Hattie – not blackmail, it turns out, but the repayment of a loan. But it doesn't seem likely she dropped the money at the Pied Piper. Jack, Edward and Fifi never go there, according to the staff. So why was Hattie there? She was only inside for a minute or two. Whatever she was up to, she barely paused as she dashed through.'

Viv frowned and attempted to dust the icing sugar off her sleeve, adding more in the process. It was all Eve could do not to snatch a drying-up cloth and flick it off. 'It does seem weird. What do you think?'

'I'm not sure, but I need to find out. I'm going to go over there after work.'

'You will tell me what happens, won't you?' Viv had grabbed Eve's arm to emphasise her point, covering her in sugar too.

Eve gave Viv a look and dusted it off. 'When have I ever let you down? We're due to meet in the Cross Keys later, don't forget.' Robin had messaged the WhatsApp group to suggest it. He ought to have the low-down on Greg's interview with Jack by then.

When Eve reached Long Stratford, with Gus in tow, she went to find Susie Parks. She'd been friendly before and it felt right to check in to see how she was doing a second time. Hattie's death had been such a bombshell. What's more, she knew the village and the pub too, with her husband being the landlord there. And she'd also known Hattie. That combination made her more likely than most to come up with useful ideas.

Susie had just finished at the bakery and seemed glad when Eve offered to buy her a drink at the Pied Piper. She waved at her husband as they walked through the door.

'It's good to come in and see Steve. We had our first date here, you know. Sneaked in when we were underage and thought ourselves so daring.' She smiled, shaking her head. 'Never thought he'd end up running the place. What with that and the bakery, we're like ships in the night. Busy, busy, all the time.' Her look had turned wry.

The blonde barmaid served them, and they went to sit in the garden.

Eve had already expressed her sympathy all over again, and they'd shared their shock over the attack on Jack too.

It was time to move on to the matter in hand, and Eve leaned forward, lowering her voice. 'I saw something odd recently, and I wanted to ask you about it. Hattie dashed in through the front door here, but in less than a couple of minutes she'd come out the back way and was round on the street again. I didn't see her speak to anyone.'

Susie frowned. 'That's odd.'

'I wondered if you could think of any reason for her to pay such a short visit.'

Susie's sad, tired eyes met Eve's and she spread out her upturned hands. 'I'm sorry. I can't imagine. When was this?'

'Monday evening. You can't think of anything out of the ordinary that night? Something you saw, or that Steve mentioned?'

She frowned, then leaned forward. 'Monday does stick in my mind, but it's nothing to do with Hattie.' She was already whispering but she lowered her voice further. 'We had some customers complain of upset stomachs after eating here that evening.'

Now she mentioned it, Eve remembered the blonde waitress telling Byron the fishcakes were off the menu.

'Sorry to hear that.' Eve was always glad that she and Viv mainly produced cakes. They felt a lot less hazardous than meat and fish.

'It's never happened before,' Susie said. 'Steve's ever so careful with his hires – the cook's been with us for a couple of years, with no trouble at all. She says the fish must have been off when we got it. Threatened to walk out if we didn't stand up for her. Steve took it up with the suppliers of course, but they weren't having any of it either. It's all been very tense.'

'Poor you.' What with that and the rotten beef the barmaid had found behind the radiator, the pub would be losing customers. Eve tried to imagine something like that happening in the Cross Keys but failed. No one would dare treat the pub with disrespect for fear of Jo's reaction. It had taken Eve at least three years to get used to her fierceness.

Eve mentioned the beef incident to Susie.

'Oh, I know. It's been so warm, so the smell was awful. It took a while to work out where it was coming from.'

'Do customers normally behave like that?'

Susie shook her head. 'No, thankfully. It's a rarity.'

Another attack. A tiny, sneaking suspicion crossed Eve's mind. 'Did you ever solve the mystery of the fishcakes?'

Susie shook her head. 'And the weird thing was, not everyone who had them was affected.'

Hmm. It was a rat Eve was smelling now, not rotten beef. 'You didn't get it checked at a lab or anything like that?'

Susie's frown deepened. 'No, they were all gone by the time we knew people had got sick.'

Taken in isolation, those two incidents might have felt like bad luck, but Eve was struck by the memory of something Susie's assistant at the bakery had told her.

'Did you ever find out who vandalised your daughter's garden?' Eve needed to ask, though she didn't like the direction her thoughts were taking.

Susie looked nervous now. 'No, but my son's car was keyed the day after.' She put her hand over her mouth. 'You think someone's targeting us? That the beef and the fishcakes and the vandalism are all related?'

The blonde barmaid had mentioned a blocked loo, too. 'I'm not sure.' In reality, it was just what Eve had begun to suspect. And worse still, she had an idea why. Eve had been thinking that Edward might be Hattie's father, or that Jack could have been, but there was another prime candidate for that role.

Someone who'd been around at the time and must have spent lots of time with Hattie's mum. Her best friend's husband, the landlord Steve.

It wasn't a good thought, but it was the sort of thing that happened. From their earlier conversation, Eve was sure that the possibility had never crossed Susie's mind, but sharp Hattie who'd seen the world might have wondered. And she'd been in possession of that positive DNA test. Eve couldn't imagine Steve agreeing to take one, but there were bound to be services who'd ignore the rules for the right price. Hattie could have pinched a cigarette butt of Steve's or a glass he'd drunk from to get the sample she needed.

Eve couldn't prove it – not unless she found the missing paperwork – but it fitted. Hattie could have slipped something into a few fishcake dinners as she'd dashed through the pub on Monday evening. And targeting the Pied Piper and Steve's legitimate children made sense. Eve remembered Hattie's phone conversation which Marjorie had overheard. *'I've found my dad. I'd like to kill him for all he put me through. It's no use coming straight out with it, but he won't know what's hit him when I take my revenge.'*

If Steve was her father, Eve imagined there was no way he'd have confessed at the time. Susie had said she'd always felt guilty about not taking Hattie in when her mum died, but they'd already got four children of their own. If she'd ever said that to Hattie – which seemed quite likely – it would have made the hurt even sharper. Always assuming Eve was right. As for the grey hair Susie had once spotted on Posy's collar, that could fit too. Eve's dad had had blue eyes like Steve, and near-black hair, and he'd gone grey very young.

Susie's look of anxiety was increasing. 'Please, tell me what you're thinking.'

Eve didn't want to throw her life into turmoil, especially with no proof. 'I'm not even sure. Take no notice.'

But as she left the pub, she suspected Susie might be putting two and two together.

36

By seven thirty that evening, Greg had updated Robin on the attack on Jack, and Eve was sitting in the Cross Keys with the gang, ready to hear about it. Her head was in a whirl. She wanted to see where the latest discoveries left them, then pool ideas.

The weather had finally broken, so they were indoors. Outside, the sky was an angry indigo and lightning forked the heavens. Eve had Adnams beer-battered fish and chips in front of her. It felt suitably heartening given the storm, and nothing beat Jo's tartare sauce. The cool Sauvignon Blanc alongside was going down well too.

The others were also tucking in. Eve had already filled them in on what had happened at Angela's that morning, as well as at the Pied Piper later on. Now they were all glancing at Robin, waiting for his news.

'As I said this morning, Eve, Jack has no idea who attacked him. I'm afraid it was within minutes of ending your call though.' He reached over to give her hand a squeeze. 'You couldn't have predicted how the conversation would go.'

'I took a risk without thinking, and Jack almost paid for it with his life.'

Viv leaned forward and patted her on the shoulder. 'But he didn't.'

Eve would be eternally thankful for that.

'Jack says he wound up your conversation because he thought he'd heard someone in the woods, but he had a look and couldn't see anyone. He'd lowered his guard by the time the blow came.'

'And the killer messed up,' Eve said. 'Thank goodness.'

'Perhaps someone came along and put them off their stroke,' Sylvia said.

Robin nodded. 'That's one possibility.'

'Or the killer had decided he had to die,' Eve put in, 'but was having to force themselves to go through with it, because they liked him.'

'That's another,' Robin agreed.

'What did Jack say about the hammer and toolbelt in his garden?' It made Eve tense just thinking about it. She strongly suspected he'd hidden them to protect Angela, but even so, he'd surely be loath to admit it. It might help convince Palmer she was guilty.

'He says he's no idea how they got there. Greg's pretty sure he's lying, but the handle's been wiped, and they can't prove he touched it. And of course, we barged into his garden through the hedge, proving that anyone else could have too.'

'Did they ask him if he was Hattie's dad?' Viv put in.

Robin nodded. 'He says he's definitely not, and he's given a DNA sample to prove it, so I think we can take it he's telling the truth. She could still be Edward's though.' He turned to Eve. 'I like your theory about Steve Parks, but it's circumstantial. The police are going to ask Edward for a DNA sample now, discreetly. As Jo said, he did act as though he was fond of her. If they're not related, maybe they were lovers after all.'

Eve tried to see it, but wasn't convinced. 'I'm not sure he'd risk rocking the boat by having an affair. I think he loves his twins so much he was prepared to ignore Fifi's transgressions to preserve the status quo.'

Robin cocked his head. 'You could be right, but him speaking up for Hattie and celebrating with her still feels significant. And Susie Parks confirmed he and Posy Fifield were lovers. I just don't know if it has a bearing on the murders.'

Eve swallowed. 'We do have fresh information after the attack on poor Jack. It seems certain his would-be killer struck because of our conversation, so his words are crucial. He was promising me "full details", as you know, and he talked about having discovered what Duncan and Hattie were up to. He meant the scam with Tod, but presumably the killer assumed he was referring to something else. Something they're aware of and we're not. We need to work out what other secret scheme they were involved in when they died.'

Robin nodded. 'That makes sense. I'm afraid none of the key players – Fifi, Edward, Byron or Angela – has an alibi. By Angela's own admission, Cesca was in bed by half past seven. She could have sneaked out.'

'It's hard to imagine, though.' It was Sylvia who'd spoken. 'Don't worry, I'm not turning soft. But all the same, I saw her when she was nursing Jess. She and Jack formed a close bond. And Jack's very dear to Cesca.'

Daphne was nodding. 'Though, of course, if anything threatened Cesca's future, perhaps Angela might have been driven to the brink. And she's one person who could have failed because she was attacking someone she loved.'

Viv looked distressed and put her hands over her ears. 'Stop! You're meant to believe implicitly in everyone's innocence, Daphne, and Sylvia's meant to pooh-pooh your faith in human nature. I can't cope if you swap.'

Sylvia gave a cackle of laughter.

'Let's go through the suspects from the top,' Eve said. Surely the mounting evidence would help them make headway. 'We could take Angela first as we're already talking about her. It's true that Duncan tried her to the limit with his careless spending, neglect and the affair with Fifi, but it's like I said before, she'd decided on a response, and it involved driving a wedge between Duncan and Fifi and vandalising his projects, not murder. What's more, we now know that she could have got money without Duncan's life insurance, if she'd sold Byron's books. That explains her London plans. I don't think it's her, though I suspect Jack might have worried that it was and buried the murder weapon.'

Sylvia smiled. 'There you are, then. I think I was right to rule her out. Sorry, Robin. You're the expert, obviously.'

He took it in good part. 'I take both your points, but it's best to keep an open mind.'

'We could look at Fifi next,' Eve said. 'Assuming she's telling the truth, we now know that she'd discovered Duncan, Hattie and Tod had duped her, the night Duncan died. After that they had it out and she told him to leave.'

Simon put his wine glass down. 'She doesn't seem very likely either, then. She'd already taken action, just like Angela.'

Eve cut up another mouthful of fish. 'I agree. She'd have had time to cool off after their row. She could still have sat there brooding, but the idea that she'd sneak out later to kill him without taking her own weapon makes no sense.

'And if Fifi didn't kill Duncan, she automatically becomes less likely for Hattie. She must have hated her for her part in the deception, but to go out days later and kill in cold blood doesn't seem plausible.'

Robin nodded slowly. 'I see your logic, and Fifi's told the police what she told you now, so that all ties up. But again, we should keep an open mind.'

'True. Just to round off, I can't see Fifi's motive for Jack unless Jack knew she'd killed Hattie and/or Duncan.'

'What about Edward, then?' Viv asked.

'He knew Fifi had told Duncan he'd have to leave Kesham, so his torment was coming to an end. If Edward turns out to be Hattie's dad, I suppose he *could* have killed Duncan from jealousy. Hattie was so delighted for everyone to think she was his, and that could have hurt, on top of Duncan's affair with Fifi.' She glanced at her husband. 'But as you said before, Robin, it doesn't really seem credible when he could have just told everyone the truth.

'And once again, I don't see why he'd have killed Hattie or attacked Jack unless they knew he'd killed Duncan. His motive doesn't feel strong enough for any of them.'

'So we come to Byron.' Sylvia sipped her drink.

'I'm afraid he's my number-one suspect now. I was already convinced he'd fallen in love with Angela, but after the gift of such valuable books, his feelings seem worryingly intense. He's good at hiding them though. He always seems relaxed and charming. On top of his passion, I suspect he thinks he'd be a better father to Cesca than Duncan was. I could see him killing Duncan in a fit of frustration, to remove an obstacle, and I could imagine him being angry enough. Duncan really was treating Angela badly.'

Viv was nodding. 'His behaviour made *me* furious, and I'm not madly in love with her. And Byron would have had a motive for Hattie and Jack if they'd found him out.'

Eve nodded. 'Compounded by any attempt Hattie might have made to blackmail him.'

Daphne looked distressed. 'And he'd have struggled with the attack on Jack, of course, because they're friends.'

At that moment, there was an extra loud clap of thunder that set Gus howling. A chunk of soot fell down the chimney, landing in the hearth of the inglenook fireplace. It was closely followed by some moss, presumably from the chimney stack.

'Honestly!' said Jo, who was passing. 'Only had it swept in June. I knew that sweep wasn't giving it a proper go. Barnaby Ross should never have taken him on.'

A moment later, a strong gust of wind hurled rain against the windows and at the same time a second thing came down the chimney.

It was Hattie's missing folder.

37

Jo, as deadpan as ever, raised one eyebrow, picked up the sooty folder and placed it beside Eve.

'Sorry about the state of it,' she said shortly. 'Do you want a cloth?'

'Don't worry.' Eve was already opening its flap, the sharp smell of soot rising up. She was kicking herself. She knew the anatomy of a fireplace well enough, given the inglenook at Elizabeth's Cottage. At the bottom of the throat of the chimney, out of sight unless you were right beneath it, was a smoke shelf. The ledge was to deflect downdraughts and send smoke up through the flue. It was also meant to catch debris, but in weather like this, it had failed. It must have been where Hattie had tucked her folder for safekeeping. She'd have guessed it would be all right there until the fire was lit in the autumn. By that stage, Hattie had probably planned to be long gone.

Although the outside of the folder was damp and sooty, the documents inside were only lightly coated with dust.

The first paper she found was a positive DNA test result. It had no company name on it and didn't name the father or daughter either. Underneath were three more tests, all done officially by what looked like a reputable outfit. Consent forms were present for each, signed by Duncan Blake, Edward Tuppington-Hynd and Jack Farraway. All three were negative.

Everyone was craning to see what Eve was looking at. They were far enough away from other tables to keep their conversation private, but Eve lowered her voice anyway.

'It looks as though Hattie's dad was A. N. Other. My bet is still Steve Parks. But our key players clearly agreed to be tested. There are notes from Edward and Jack too.'

She turned Jack's round so the others could read it.

I'm afraid I can't be your father, Hattie. I never had an affair with your mother, but I'm happy to give a sample to set your mind at rest.

Yours faithfully,

Jack

He sounded formal but compassionate. He must have written it before he'd found out about the scam with Tod. She could see why he'd felt sympathetic enough to offer her a loan. He'd seen her anguish first-hand. And perhaps he'd got wind that Duncan might be her dad. If so, she might turn out to be a relation of Jess's. It would be all the more reason to support her.

Edward's note was different.

I can assure you, Hattie, that if you are mine I had no idea. Your mother and I were lovers briefly but I never knew she'd fallen pregnant.

'Fallen'. *Honestly.* Eve hated that expression. It made it sound like an illness that could happen to anyone and certainly nothing to do with the father.

If you are mine,

Edward had carried on,

then I'll be proud to have you as my daughter and keen to make it up to you. Either way, I'm deeply sorry for what you've been through, and I hope you find the answers you're looking for.

Eve was sure Hattie being his biological daughter would have made life difficult for him, but he'd clearly decided that was less important than doing the right thing. He was a dedicated dad to his twins, and it seemed he'd been ready to do the same for Hattie, but it hadn't been him either.

Nor Duncan.

Hattie had been steadfast in her search for the truth, and out for revenge once she'd got it, as indicated by the phone call Marjorie had overheard.

Eve spoke again in a whisper. 'I think this explains Edward's kindness towards Hattie and their apparent closeness. I guess he strongly suspected she was his, until they got the DNA results. It was probably during that waiting period that they celebrated the job she got here.' She glanced at the date on the results page. 'Of course, I saw them chatting later on too, after he'd have found out. He probably still felt sorry for her, just like Jack did initially, even though he wasn't her dad.'

'It doesn't seem likely that they had an affair, then,' Robin said.

'I agree. I don't think Hattie viewed Edward that way, and for his part, I believe Edward still loves Fifi. He's clearly happy to make a new start.' Eve thought of the touching scene she'd witnessed through the window of Kesham Hall. And then of all Edward had gone through when Duncan was on the scene.

The ridiculous, macho climb he'd instigated still puzzled Eve. Why had Duncan wound Edward up like that? Pure devilment was the easiest answer, but it didn't fit. Duncan had been goal-orientated. She couldn't see him wasting his energy on anything inessential. It had risked angering Fifi too, which would have been counterproductive.

'So Edward's looking even less likely than before,' Viv said, 'because Hattie wasn't his daughter?'

Eve nodded. 'I think that's right.'

At that moment, the pub door opened, letting in a blast of wet air that smelled of the sea, and Byron Acker walked in. He caught Eve's eye, raised his hand, then pushed back his hood and approached their table. Eve slid Hattie's folder onto her lap.

'Rotten night, isn't it? I couldn't face being at home alone. I keep thinking of what happened to Jack.' His eyes looked wide and bloodshot, though they might have been affected by the torrential rain. Eve couldn't help wondering if his emotion was down to guilt and astonishment at what he'd tried to do to a man who'd become a friend.

Eve bet his mind was on Angela too. She wondered if she'd returned his books yet. Byron certainly looked the lowest she'd seen him.

'It's nice to see you,' Eve said. 'But don't you normally go to the Pied Piper?'

He nodded. 'I went there first, but they're closed. A bloke I bumped into told me there's some kind of domestic problem between Susie and Steve Parks.' He shook his head. 'Everything seems upset at the moment.'

Eve wondered if Susie had challenged her husband and found he really was Hattie's dad. What must she feel about it? Byron was right. Everything was in turmoil.

'After that,' he went on, 'I just carried on walking. It felt good to have the wind and rain in my face. As though it could wash everything away. In the end I came here.'

He offered to buy them drinks, but Eve said she'd get them, so he joined her at the bar.

As they stood next to each other, waiting for Toby's attention, she turned to him. 'Everyone at Kesham must be so
shocked and frightened.'

He nodded, rain dripping off his floppy fringe. 'I feel very
isolated, sitting at home in Cotwin Place. I almost wondered
whether to book in here.' The Cross Keys did bed and breakfast.
Byron bit his lip. 'I'm worried about Angela and Cesca, alone in
White Cottage too. I was going to talk to Angela about it but in
the end... well, in the end I thought I should just send her a
note.'

Perhaps he knew she was pulling back. He shouldn't be
surprised – the gift of the books had probably felt overwhelming
when Angela found out how much they were worth. He'd done
the right thing by respecting her boundaries, but she could see
why he was concerned – assuming he was telling the truth. He
looked so forlorn that she couldn't help feeling sorry for him.
But she needed to be dispassionate. She didn't yet know if he
was an innocent who'd come on too strong, or a dangerous
obsessive who'd killed twice over. What she needed was
information.

'You've fallen in love with her, haven't you?' She was acting
on instinct. Risking him clamming up altogether.

He hung his head. 'Is it that obvious?'

'Not to everyone, I don't suppose. It's just that I've been
interviewing you all. I saw the books you gave to Angela in her
pantry.'

He put his hands to his face. 'I told Jack that I planned to
give them to her. Just to give her options. I wanted to see if he'd
tell me to butt out, but he didn't. He warned me not to do it
with any expectations, though. He said he didn't want to see me
or Angela hurt. But I think he saw what I saw: that whatever
happened, Angela and Cesca needed help. And I suppose I did
hope that one day, Angela might turn to me. As it is, I'm plan-

ning to move away once this business is resolved. It doesn't do to hang around when things haven't worked out.'

He sounded so selfless and genuine, but it was as Eve had thought before: it was quite something to give away such valuable books. It showed the depth of his feeling – a level of passion that could mean he was guilty. 'It was very kind of you. I'd never have dared get rid of them in your shoes, in case I ran into financial difficulties.'

Byron lowered his voice. 'I'm lucky. I've got other resources – family money – and even though my art doesn't pay' – he gave a rueful grin – 'my accountancy business is quite lucrative.'

Eve was on the fence. If he was seriously wealthy, that lessened the significance of passing on the books, but there was no doubting his love for Angela.

By the time Eve and the gang left the pub, Eve gathered from Toby that Byron had indeed booked to stay at the Cross Keys.

That suggested he really was nervous of being alone at Kesham. Eve went to bed, torn over what to think about Byron Acker.

38

On Saturday morning, Eve was taking a sustaining meal of toast, marmalade and English breakfast tea when her mobile rang.

It was Toby from the pub.

'*I thought you'd like to know that Byron Acker couldn't settle last night,*' he said in a hushed voice. '*In the end he ordered a taxi at around one – judging by the time Hetty started barking – but he came back to the pub again at two or thereabouts.*'

That was interesting. 'And Hetty barked both times? How's Jo's mood this morning?' She always said she needed her eight hours.

'*Volatile,*' Toby said succinctly. '*I served Byron at breakfast. He didn't say anything about where he'd gone, but I just bumped into Moira, and she's spoken to the taxi driver.*'

Of course she had.

'*Apparently, Byron got him to drive to the car park at Kesham, then walk with him to Angela's cottage to check everything was quiet. After that, he asked him to drive back here again.*'

'Thanks, Toby. That's very interesting.'

'*Happy to help!*' He hung up.

Eve relayed the information to Robin. 'It looks as though he was worrying for Angela so badly that he felt he had to check on her. That makes him look innocent, even if the dash to Kesham in the small hours looks a bit obsessive.'

Robin nodded. 'The plot thickens, just when it ought to be coming clear.'

Eve sighed. 'I guess we haven't looked hard enough in other directions.'

They sat at the kitchen table and went through the key players again.

'What would each of them kill over?' Robin asked.

Eve focused on them in turn. 'For Fifi, it's her reputation that comes to mind. The villagers looked down on her as a teenager and her father's affair must have been the talk of the town. I don't think the effect has ever worn off. And I guess she'd do it to protect her kids too. For Edward, it's the twins for sure. Then for Angela, I'd guess Cesca, and for Byron, Angela herself.'

Byron's devotion still made her uneasy. But why take a taxi to check on her if he was the killer?

She tried to make the thoughts add up to something but failed.

'And what about oddities? No matter how small.'

'It's a long while ago, but when Edward's kids were caught in that fire, Edward heard a noise outside. If he somehow worked out it was arson then he might kill in revenge. Except it wasn't.'

Robin nodded. 'The cause was ancient wiring – that's indisputable.'

'Agreed. The only other oddity I can think of is Duncan goading Edward into climbing the hall. I still don't get why he'd do something so showy that might have riled Fifi. He was reliant on her for his free lodgings.'

'Okay, good. That's worth bearing in mind. And what was driving each of the victims, just before they were attacked?'

Eve went through them again: 'Duncan was desperate to keep doing up bits of the Kesham estate. In Hattie's case, she wanted to find her biological father and make her name after a shaky start in life. And Jack was putting all his efforts into helping Cesca and Angela, as well as restoring Cotwin Place.' She felt there was something there – just on the very edge of her thoughts – but she couldn't grasp it.

'Don't push it,' Robin said. 'You need to relax your mind and let the key facts mesh.'

Eve nodded. 'True. I could talk to people again as well – revisit each of the key players in case something gives. I might try Fifi Tuppington-Hynd first. She still hasn't admitted to her affair with Duncan. If I can get her to open up, something might come out. I could ask her about Edward and Duncan's climbing exploits too. It all depends if I can get her alone.'

It felt safe visiting the hall. The maid seemed to be around most of the time, and the entire family were in and out, thanks to Edward's break from work and the school holidays. But Robin went with her to Kesham all the same. They wanted to be able to talk over her findings as soon as she'd finished. The sense of urgency felt even more acute after the attack on Jack. Eve debated about opening a call. On the one hand, it would allow Robin to get almost as good an idea of the interaction as she did, in real time, but on the other it felt deeply underhand when there was no argument for it on safety grounds. In the end, she promised to fill him in in detail, and felt more at ease with herself as she headed inside.

The maid showed Eve through to the formal sitting room, where Eve was in luck. Fifi was alone.

The French windows in the room were wide open and a

gentle breeze stirred some papers on the coffee table. Last night's storm had made everything feel fresher but the air was warming again.

Fifi frowned. 'Is everything all right?' Her voice was low. 'I told the police what I overheard Duncan say to Hattie and how it all played out.'

Eve nodded. 'Of course. I know. You told me you would.'

The strain of the situation was starting to tell. Fifi looked exhausted, though she sat bolt upright, her back straight. The Bengal cat was on her lap, but the beautiful creature had clearly picked up on its mistress's tension. Its tail was curled defensively around its body.

'So what's the trouble then?' Fifi said. 'I thought you'd have finished your research by now.'

Eve could only think of one way to get more out of Fifi, and that was to admit she knew about the affair. She spoke in a whisper. 'I'm afraid I haven't been quite honest with you. Please don't worry. I've no intention of including this in my obituary, but I know you were closer to Duncan than you've admitted. I saw the pair of you kissing in the woods. I didn't mean to. I was just looking out from the rooftop of Hideaway House.'

Tears came to Fifi's eyes. 'All that time when we talked, you knew.'

Eve nodded. 'I'm sorry.'

Fifi took a deep breath and there was a long pause. 'Well then, you can see why I was so especially angry with him and Hattie for using Tod to trick me.'

Eve nodded. 'I can. I'd have been devastated.'

For a moment, the tears were back, but then Fifi blew her nose and smiled weakly. 'I enjoyed telling him he'd have to leave, after all the effort he'd gone to. The look on his face was a picture. He still owned the estate properties, but I liked the idea of him having to bed down in the dust if he needed to stay on site. And with no water supply at the lodge, the place was a real white elephant.

'His behaviour made me realise what an idiot I'd been. I've got a loving husband, my beautiful childhood home, two wonderful boys...' She still sounded wistful when she mentioned them. 'This is going to sound crazy, but Edward's always seemed too perfect.' She heaved a great sigh. 'I felt I could never match up. But of course he's human, just like the rest of us.' She was whispering now. 'He's special too, though. He's forgiven me, even though he knew about the affair. I think things are going to be different in future. Better.'

'I'm so glad.'

At that moment, Edward came in with a tea tray. He greeted Eve, then leaned forward to lift the teapot and pour the drinks. As he did so, his sleeve rode up, revealing scars on his arm.

In a flash, Eve was back to thinking of the horrific fire and how terrifying it must have been. Thank goodness he'd managed to rescue his boys. It wasn't surprising that he'd achieved a god-like status in Fifi's eyes and made her feel inadequate.

As she had the thought, Fifi's Bengal cat let out an almighty yowl and leaped at Edward so he slopped the tea. Eve jumped out of her skin too.

She went to help him mop up the spillage, but Fifi got there first.

Eve kept the conversation neutral while Edward was present, but when he left them again, she made her next move.

'I'm sorry to keep bothering you,' she said, 'but there are certain bits of Duncan's character I'm still trying to understand. Did you know that he goaded Edward into climbing the outside of the hall? I was scared they'd fall.'

Fifi's hand went to her throat. 'Hattie Fifield put a note through our door about it.'

Eve remembered her, watching from a distance. 'She was warning you?'

Fifi nodded, bending to remove cat hairs from the rug. 'Her apparent concern made me livid, after the Tod business. She told me the children had been watching and claimed she was worried they might copy him.'

That only added to the mystery, as far as Eve was concerned. Why had Hattie been so keen to drop Edward in it when she had no reason to get revenge?

39

Eve rejoined Robin at a safe distance from the hall, and filled him in on everything so they could take stock.

'I've had a text from Greg too,' Robin said when she'd finished. 'It might not mean anything, but Byron Acker's put in an offer on Cotwin Place.'

The news made Eve pause. 'When did that happen? He told me last night that he was planning to move away, to put some distance between him and Angela.'

'This morning, according to the solicitor dealing with Duncan's estate.'

Had he been spinning her a line, to disguise his desperation to be near Angela? Maybe his taxi ride in the night was staged, to make him look innocent. He'd have heard Hetty barking, known word would get around.

For a moment, they were as silent as the woods around them, but then they moved on to dissect what Fifi had told Eve.

'I can't see Hattie caring about Edward setting a bad example to the boys,' Eve said, after they'd talked about the climbing. 'There has to be something else going on.'

'You could be right, though it's hard to imagine what.

Another thing that makes me wonder is Fifi's cat. What d'you think spooked it?' Robin asked.

'I'm not sure. Or if it's relevant, but it made me jump. I thought it was going to land on the tea tray.'

Robin had brought them a picnic and once they were off the estate, they made for the coast. It was the perfect day to sit amongst the sand dunes and eat, looking out to sea. The provisions included the most delicious rye bread with cheese and some succulent tomatoes, rounded off with Eve's favourite lemonade from Moira's store.

They reviewed everything they knew for the umpteenth time.

'So, we have Fifi being duped by Duncan. She discovered the truth, and told him to quit White Cottage,' Robin said.

'That's right. I originally guessed Duncan wanted to buy bits of the estate to get close to her, but I'm sure now that it was the other way round.' Various memories came back to her. 'Sylvia said Duncan moped around the estate after Fifi left. I assumed he was pining for her, but I think it was leaving the place that left him raw. I remember noting the manor he bought which burned down looked very much like Kesham. I don't think he ever forgot it, but it was only when Fifi moved here that he started his campaign to buy estate properties. On a practical level, using her to reduce his costs made it possible, but I wonder if he was driven by revenge and envy too. Perhaps he couldn't bear to see her sitting in a home he'd assumed would be his.

'Because in the cold light of day, it makes sense. Fifi was set to inherit and they were engaged, and her dad had offered him a job too. Everything probably seemed perfect, with Kesham at his feet, when suddenly the beguiling vision of the future was blown away. And it all happened at such speed. You can imagine his shock.'

Robin nodded. 'And when something's thrust upon you, it can make it very hard to accept.'

Eve thought of her ex-husband walking out. 'You're right. So it looks as though everything Duncan did after he came back was to make a future for himself at Kesham. Fifi was just a means to an end, being played so she'd sell off buildings cheaply and offer free accommodation. As we've said before, discovering all that must have been devastating, but I think she'd already started to see through him. When she got proof of the truth, she took action. She told me all about their row and everything rang true. And of course there were witnesses.

'It must have knocked the wind out of Duncan's sails. His hopes of buying the Warrener's Cottage would have been dead in the water. I'll bet he fantasised about buying the hall too, but even if his creative accounting had ever made that achievable, he'd have known it was no-go after the row with Fifi.'

For a second, Eve had that strange feeling again of wispy ideas floating past, not tangible enough to grasp. It made her feel panicky, as though she'd never knit them together. She took a deep breath and stopped pushing it, as Robin had advised earlier. Her mind went back to her visit to the hall.

'I noticed Edward's scars as he poured the tea, and it made me think of the house fire again. It's stupid, but I keep speculating about the noise he heard that night, despite the fire not being arson.'

Robin nodded. 'Duncan can't have been responsible, so neither of the Tuppington-Hynds can have killed him for that reason.'

Eve shook her head. 'I know. I don't know why it keeps bothering me.'

'It was a horrific event. What with the drama, the trauma and the bravery involved, it's not surprising.'

'I suppose not.' But Eve was sure it was more than that. Something she couldn't quite identify...

Then suddenly, it came to her. 'You're right about it being a dramatic and heroic story, but it's not just that. When I lived in London, I'd hear noises outside all the time. Especially on the street side of the house. Drunks returning home after a night at the pub, neighbours showing guests out, foxes knocking over the bins. It was normal.

'Something about the noise Edward heard must have put him on high alert. He was so anxious that he dashed outside without his keys and got locked out. And it must have been on the street side, or he'd have gone out the back way. But I know, I know. It wasn't arson.'

They carried on eating and chatting, and a while later, they were musing over a different aspect of her research. 'Tod's flat-mate said Hattie hadn't just come to London to hatch plans with Tod. She was researching her dad too. Of course, we're now all-but certain her father was Steve Parks, Suffolk born and bred. I suppose the research she did in London dated back to when she thought Edward or Duncan might be her dad.'

Robin frowned. 'Presumably.'

'Though it's odd in a way,' Eve went on, as she made a fuss of Gus for fetching the ball yet again, the salty smell of the sea hitting her as she looked up. 'Susie Parks had already told her that Edward and her mum had had a fling. And that all happened while he was visiting his parents in Suffolk. I wonder why she needed to dig for details in London. Perhaps Susie told her about Edward's heroics, and she wanted to know more. He wasn't rich like Fifi, but he was certainly dashing.' But it still seemed odd. Why go all that way when she hadn't yet confirmed that Edward was the right man?

'I'd forgotten about the money side of things,' Robin said. 'Is that why it's Fifi who owns the estate?'

'I guess so. Moira mentioned the previous owners split the property when they divorced. One of them took the east wing of the hall, the other the remainder and the wider estate. They both decided to sell up at once, and Moira said some investment of Fifi's had just matured, so she bought the larger chunk. Edward must have managed to take care of the rest on his City salary. I guess it pays well!'

'It must.'

They stared out to sea for a moment, and the facts floated in Eve's head, until suddenly, a whole new idea began to take shape. Eve went cold all over, despite the hot sun bouncing off the sand. 'Heck. Imagine if Duncan managed to get hold of Edward or Fifi's share.' They looked at each other. 'Robin, what if that's it? What if Duncan got something on one of them that meant he could force their hand? Get them to transfer their property without having to pay a penny?'

40

Robin was frowning in deep concentration at Eve's suggestion.

Eve was still thinking it through. 'The way the hall was divided into two separate dwellings would have made it a much easier target for acquisition by blackmail. Only one person to convince: lonely, isolated and desperate. Duncan could have found something one of them was hiding from the other.

'Fifi's accommodation plus the estate would be the grand prize in theory, but Edward feels like the easier target. It's pretty clear he'd do anything to preserve his relationship with Fifi and the boys. If Duncan knew something truly damning about him, that could have destroyed it. He could have forced Edward to move out of his section of the hall in exchange for his silence. Even if that led to divorce, Edward would probably go for it if the alternative was losing all access to the boys.' It would be a truly terrible position to be in.

'If you're right, then Duncan and Fifi would have been neighbours of the most intimate sort. The two dwellings might have their own front doors from when the hall was split, but all the same...'

Eve nodded. 'I'm guessing they've knocked bits through

since, but even with that reversed, it would be oppressive.' She had visions of Duncan making his presence felt, just as Tod had done.

'It can't have been an attempt to be with her?'

'Not after what he put her through and the way he used her. It would more likely be as a punishment. Imagine how she'd feel, living cheek-by-jowl with him, Angela and Cesca every day. The humiliation. The constant reminder of the way he'd fooled her. If the first part of Duncan's plan had worked, and he'd moved his family in, I could see her throwing in the towel and moving out. Perhaps Duncan would have made himself unpleasant to her prospective buyers, hoping she'd cave in and sell her portion to him at a rock-bottom price. She could probably afford to take the hit.'

Robin was frowning. 'What leverage might Duncan have had?'

Eve closed her eyes and willed an answer to appear, but it was like Robin said, if you forced it, it wouldn't come. Instead, she got up and paced, Gus following her footsteps, looking up at her anxiously.

'Something that's struck me throughout this investigation is the unhealthy partnership between Hattie and Duncan. She'd had a rough start, and he'd offered her a ticket to success. I imagine she'd have gone to some lengths to help him. What if whatever Duncan had on Edward came to him via her? It could have been something to do with her investigations in London. Duncan made a cryptic comment about Hattie when we met them at the lodge, do you remember? Something like, "Her research has been a godsend too. Understanding the past can make a vast difference to getting the result you want." And then he winked at her. I wondered at the time what he meant. And like I said, her going to London to research Edward seems odd, when Susie Parks had told her all she needed to know. Perhaps she was fishing for information which Duncan could use.'

Eve thought again of the fire. Of Edward exiting the front door because of a noise. Of him getting locked out. And then she revised all that she knew, and suddenly, everything fell into place. Bit by bit, the pieces fitted, and when she tested the whole, it all made sense.

She told Robin what she thought, but they agreed there was no way Palmer would accept Eve's theory. He'd think it was another one of her hare-brained ideas. Besides, Edward was a lord. Not someone to be trifled with. Instead, Eve and Robin went back to Kesham themselves.

Robin called Greg on the way to tell him their thoughts and he agreed to visit the hall himself, on a pretext. With any luck the French windows would still be open and he'd hear everything. The only drawback might be Fifi's presence. Ideally, they wanted to talk to Edward alone.

They were in luck when they rang the bell. Somewhere in the background, Eve could hear Fifi and the boys, but it was Edward who came. Perhaps the maid finally had some time off.

'We wondered if we could talk to you?' Eve said. 'In private if possible.' She heard a text come in on Robin's phone. It would be Greg hopefully, saying he was in position.

Edward nodded. He looked anxious and wrong-footed, which was good. It gave Eve the chance to lead the way, ensuring they went to the drawing room, where the windows were still open.

Once they'd sat down, Eve began.

'Over the course of my research for Duncan Blake's obituary I came across a lot of odd facts. I heard about the incredible rescue you performed when your London house caught fire.'

Edward flinched. He looked down at his hands.

'I also gradually concluded that Duncan could have been killed because he was a blackmailer. It became clear he hadn't really come to Kesham to reunite with Fifi.'

Edward's eyes were scared now.

'He'd come to get his hands on as much of the estate as possible, because long ago, when he and Fifi were engaged, he thought he'd end up living here. Instead, he found himself abandoned and homeless. I imagine he dreamed of his old stamping ground and the hall he might have occupied. When he realised this was where Fifi had ended up, living the dream, I expect he was angry, but determined too. He saw a chance to install his own family at Kesham.

'He'd seen how he could play on Fifi's feelings to get what he wanted. His classic end-justifies-the-means approach.' And of course, he'd told Angela he was doing everything for her and Cesca. It seemed he'd really meant it. It was so ironic.

'Duncan wasn't good with money,' Robin said, 'but he was willing to use any method available to get what he wanted. Blackmail was one in a long line of illegal workarounds that he indulged in.'

Eve thought of the woman who'd left the Built Heritage Trust all that money in her will, and the way Duncan had used Tod to diddle Fifi out of the true value of Hideaway House. 'We know you and Fifi each own part of the hall. If Duncan found some leverage over you, he could have forced you to transfer your portion to him. Or equally, if he found something on Fifi, but we guessed you were more likely. Apart from anything else, we know Hattie had been researching your life in London.' It was a slight exaggeration, but she needed to go in strong.

His eyes widened. She could see the picture she was building frightened him. He was very pale now.

'I kept coming back to the fire,' Eve said. 'We know without a doubt that you rescued your lovely boys and the bravery that must have involved. And we know it wasn't arson. But there were oddities. Why were you so anxious about a noise coming from outside? Sufficiently worried that you dashed into the front garden and got locked out.'

'I don't know what—' But Edward didn't finish his sentence. Eve guessed he hadn't the heart.

'And then there was what you did next, and the weather,' Eve went on, thinking of the news reports she'd read. 'Once you knew you were locked out, you went and sat in your shed for twenty minutes. Yet there was snow on the ground. It was below zero. You must have been freezing.'

Robin nodded. 'I'd have walked around. I realise you had your coat on, but all the same.'

'Ah yes, the coat,' Eve said. 'It's odd that you had the forethought to put it on, yet you didn't take your key. Even getting locked out was a little strange. I get that the door could have slammed shut if it was windy, but all the same...'

Edward's head was in his hands now.

'We wondered if you might have found adjusting to fatherhood tricky. We've heard people describe you as "wild" and "dashing" in your younger days, with hints of drinking and gambling. Hard to give up, I should think.' Eve waited until he was looking at her again. 'You didn't hear a noise, or get locked out and wait in the shed, did you?' Eve said at last. 'You left the boys at home alone when Fifi had trusted you to mind them. You had your key with you all along; you just broke down the door to make your lie believable.'

His tears fell and at last he nodded. Eve hoped Greg was managing to get all this.

'And Hattie, who was helping Duncan in return for what she hoped would be a big career break, found out. I imagine she heard the official version like me, and wondered if there was more to it. Once she'd investigated, I assume she came to the same conclusion as I have. I guess you didn't realise that the information came from her, though. It was Duncan who arrived to blackmail you. He wanted your bit of the hall, or he'd tell Fifi. He probably suggested she'd file for divorce if she knew.' More enlightenment came. 'I'll bet he goaded you into climbing the hall in front of the twins to make his threat more persuasive. Did he tell you Fifi was bound to demand sole custody of the boys because they weren't safe in your hands? Either back then, or now?'

Edward was nodding slowly. 'It felt horrible. Like I'd walked into a trap and heard the door slam shut.'

At last, Duncan challenging him to the climb and Hattie's note to Fifi with her fake concern about the twins made sense. Hattie had been doing Duncan's dirty work, priming Fifi to see Edward as an unsuitable dad.

'I've never forgiven myself for the night of the fire,' Edward went on. 'It feels unbelievable now, but when I left the boys alone, I convinced myself it was a minor thing. But when I got home and saw the place was on fire, it felt as though my heart was being ripped out.'

Once again, Eve felt sick at the mere thought. She couldn't imagine the terror. 'I'm surprised the lack of footprints to the shed didn't give you away.' But then she visualised the scene. 'Oh no, of course. I suppose the heat melted the snow.'

He nodded.

'Fifi's aware now, isn't she?' It had suddenly come to Eve. She'd said she'd finally realised that Edward was human, just like everyone else. Did she know he was a killer too?

Eve was convinced Fifi had created a distraction when she'd seen Eve looking at Edward's scars. She must have pulled at the cat's fur.

It seemed like an overreaction, but perhaps it was understandable if she was already on edge, terrified Eve might guess the truth. The scales had clearly fallen from her eyes as far as Duncan was concerned. She'd been looking forward to a brighter future with Edward at her side, but that wouldn't be possible. Not after two murders and the attack on Jack.

But Edward had taken a step back. 'What? No. Fifi's got no idea.'

Eve went cold all over. Because she was very sure Fifi did know. And if Edward hadn't told her... The hair on her scalp lifted. If Edward hadn't told her, then she must have overheard Duncan blackmailing him. It was the only possible explanation. Yet she'd hidden her knowledge from Edward, and panicked when she'd caught Eve staring at his scars – something that might get her focusing too closely on what had happened back then. She'd realised she'd made a mistake rekindling her affair with Duncan and known he'd been laughing at her. And she'd wanted to rebuild a life with Edward. But there was Duncan, ready to wreck things for the pair of them...

Edward was still talking. 'When Duncan died, it felt like a miracle. A second chance. I don't know who killed him. He had multiple enemies. But Hattie and Jack were intimately involved with him, so—'

Eve had to interrupt him, however unbearable it was to put him through such pain. 'Did it ever occur to you that Fifi could have killed Duncan?'

His mouth widened, almost as though she'd landed a physical blow. 'What? No! Of course not! As I said, she didn't even know.' But he wasn't meeting her eyes. The thought had lurked in the corner of his mind, Eve guessed, but he'd hoped against hope that he was wrong.

Robin slipped out of the French windows as he spoke, presumably to confer with Greg.

'I think she overheard Duncan blackmailing you.'

'But it was she who Duncan was threatening to tell. If she knew and decided to stand by me, she had no need to kill him!'

Eve wished that was enough to convince her. Perhaps she'd seen red. She'd already been furious with Duncan.

And now Eve understood the move with the cat. It spoke of a deep-seated terror at the secret she was keeping. She'd felt cornered.

Robin reappeared with Greg, who showed his warrant card.

'Lord Edward, please can you tell me where your wife is?'

Edward turned like a man in a daze and gestured behind him. 'Somewhere in the house.'

But when he, Greg, Robin and Eve looked, running ever more anxiously from room to room, there was no sign of her, or the boys.

41

Edward was wild with worry. 'But she'd never harm them,' he kept saying. 'I know she wouldn't.'

Eve hoped to goodness he was right. He must be, surely? But she had been jealous of their closeness with Edward. The pit of her stomach quivered.

Greg called for backup but time felt desperately short. They had the whole of the Kesham estate at their feet and no idea which way to turn.

Eve called Angela to explain what had happened and asked her to alert Byron to search too. She suggested they stick together, despite the awkwardness. She couldn't bear it if anything happened to them. But for her, Robin, Greg and Edward it felt more sensible to split up. They went off north, south, east and west, mobiles at the ready to call as required. Eve took Gus.

She was ploughing through the woods, passing Hideaway House, when she got a call from Edward. He was in tears. 'I've found the boys. They're fine. They were sitting by the lake, close to Cotwin Place. They said... they said that Fifi had hugged them and told them that she'd always loved them, and she always would.' He was sobbing so hard now that Eve could barely hear his words.

He put Byron on the line. 'Angela and I ran into Edward, so we teamed up.' His voice was grave. 'The boys say Fifi told them they must stay put and play until four o'clock. After that they could come home. She said she had to go back to the hall.'

Heck. Her wanting the kids out of the way sounded bad. Eve was worried Fifi had overheard their conversation with Edward and guessed they'd be out looking for her. She probably figured the hall might be empty. What might she do?

She thanked Byron and tore back the way she'd come, Gus dashing after her, a call to Robin connecting as she went. She gasped out the news and he promised to join her, and to update Greg too.

Eve's breathing was ragged as she fought to keep going up Kesham Hall's long drive. Her legs felt like jelly and poor Gus's eyes were wild.

The place looked deserted. If Fifi was there, she had to be inside. Eve signalled to Gus to wait on the lawn, then dashed indoors. She took off her shoes. Startling Fifi with an unexpected noise could be dangerous.

The house was eerily quiet. For a second, Eve wondered if Fifi could have lied to the boys about where she'd been going. Perhaps the entire search party was now homing in on the hall while Fifi went in a different direction.

But just as Eve was climbing a second flight of grand stairs, she heard a faint noise from higher still. A creak. And then the air shifted.

Eve swallowed. She was almost certain that Fifi had opened a window, somewhere very high up.

Eve followed the sound to the attic, where the servants must once have slept. At last, she found a dormer window that was open. *Heck*. Fifi had to be out there, at a dizzying height. Higher even than Edward and Duncan had reached.

Very cautiously, Eve peered out. Fifi was shifting along the pitched roof on her bottom, but now she got to her feet. She wobbled sickeningly as she stood, and Eve had to swallow down her nausea.

Below, Robin and Greg had appeared and Edward was starting up the driveway. Byron and Angela must be keeping the boys and Cesca at a safe distance. That was a mercy.

Robin and Greg were calling up, but it was hard to hear. They couldn't conduct a calm conversation from down there, but they were stuck. If they ran inside, she might jump before they reached her.

Eve turned her phone to silent and texted Robin.

I'm at roof level. Just inside. Fifi doesn't know I'm here.

His reply came a moment later.

Okay. Please don't do anything heroic. Wait a second.

Then he bellowed from down below, enunciating his words slowly. 'Fifi, we want you to stay calm. You're not alone. We know what Duncan was trying to do to you and Edward. Eve's up there with you and she's heard it all. She knows what Duncan was like. She gets it. Please just let her sit close by, in the window. Maybe you can talk. You're in complete control. She won't approach you.'

Eve felt sicker still. What if she said the wrong thing? Fifi's stance looked horribly unstable. But she had to try to make a difference. It would be horrific for the twins if she jumped.

'Hello, Fifi.' Eve's mouth was as dry as sandpaper. 'Please don't worry about me being here. It's like Robin said, you're in control. If you really want to jump, I can't stop you, but I do so hope you'll think again. I know your boys and Edward became inseparable after the fire, but they love you. You know that. They'd never want you to do this. And we understand why you killed Duncan. He treated you abominably.'

Fifi was crying. 'It was even worse than I told you.'

She shifted position and Eve hardly dared breathe. 'Perhaps you can tell me now, Fifi – it's important that people under-stand the sort of person he was.'

There was a long pause, but at last, she spoke. 'I tracked him down to the lodge, mid-evening, the night I killed him. He and Hattie were laughing so hard about me, they could hardly speak. They were incredulous that I'd believed Duncan was still in love with me. He said he loathed me. Part of the pleasure of being back at Kesham was the chance to rob me and cause me pain. He said he was enjoying it. The only disappointment was that I hadn't worked it out yet, so I was still happy. He said that was the last thing he wanted.'

'I'm so sorry, Fifi. It must have been terrible to hear that.'

She gulped. 'It was, but I'd never have killed him over it.'

'It was the blackmail that made you attack him, I guess? You overheard him talking to Edward much later, threatening to tell you the truth about the fire?'

'That's right.' Fifi's teeth were chattering. 'So I went to find him, and for the second time that night we argued.' She took a shuddering breath. 'I told him I was sticking by Edward. It was a shock to find out the truth, of course, but the fire was a long time ago and Edward's changed. I knew Duncan had goaded him into climbing the hall. It was all his doing, and he was poisonous. So I told him to stick his blackmail and go hang.'

'But that didn't work?'

She shook her head. 'He said he'd tell anyway. He said Edward would probably get the sack and no one would want to know us any more. I was furious but I didn't change tack – just kept telling him to do his worst. But then he asked how the twins would feel, knowing the father they adored had left them alone when they were toddlers. Had cared more about a drink and a game of cards than their safety.' She took another deep breath. 'I grabbed his hammer and hit him. It was like a reflex, done before I could think. I was so angry that I carried on. I was completely out of control.'

'You left the hammer by his body?'

She nodded. 'I wiped the handle with a hanky, then buried the hanky in the garden.'

Just as Eve was sure poor Jack had buried the weapon and the toolbelt, presumably imagining that Angela was guilty.

'Then a couple of days later,' Eve went on, 'you realised it was Hattie who'd worked out the truth about the fire, and she was intent on blackmailing you personally?'

Fifi nodded. 'She knew that Edward had been Duncan's victim, so she assumed he was the murderer. It wasn't logical, but I think she felt relatively safe, coming to me for money.'

No wonder Hattie had looked so scared, each time Edward accosted her after Duncan's murder. She'd told him she suspected Jack, and at the time, Eve had thought she was deflecting attention from herself. In reality, it was an act of self-preservation. If she could convince him she thought Jack was guilty, he wouldn't see her as a threat.

Yet that same sense of self-preservation seemed to have deserted her when she decided to blackmail Fifi. Why hadn't she been more guarded? Even if Fifi hadn't fought back, she might have told Edward what was going on.

But Hattie had been driven by desperation, Eve guessed: determined to find an alternative income source, just before she was revealed as a liar, her future career smashed to smithereens.

'Of course, I was the guilty one,' Fifi went on. 'I was almost blind with anger when I found out she'd not only helped Duncan to fool me, but also gathered dirt on Edward. And I couldn't let the truth come out. It would have destroyed the boys so I... I went and found another of Duncan's hammers and put paid to her too. She met me on the path to Long Stratford no problem when I said I had her first payment.'

Hattie had seemed so worldly-wise, but she'd had a blind spot. Eve suspected Duncan had trained her to despise Fifi as a pampered rich kid. They'd both underestimated her, with terrible consequences.

'And then I discovered that Jack knew about the fire and the blackmail too,' Fifi added. 'I heard him say he'd finally realised exactly what Duncan and Hattie were up to and he'd been wondering what to do with the information. I didn't want to kill him; he sounded as though he intended to use his knowledge for justice, not personal advantage. But that was even more terrifying. I didn't think he'd agree to stay quiet, even if I tried to pay him off. I was determined to do what needed to be done, but it was just so hard. I knew full well he didn't deserve it. I had a feeling I'd messed up, but I couldn't face hitting him again to make sure he was dead. I think I knew then that it would end up like this.' She gestured at the drop in front of her.

Eve didn't tell her Jack had been talking about Duncan and Hattie hiring Tod. It might tip the balance and convince her to jump. 'He's going to make a full recovery. You didn't do any lasting damage.' Not physically, anyway. 'And we all know you've been through an awful lot.'

'And I've *done* an awful lot. Things that can never be undone.'

'But one thing I can tell you is that jumping will make things more traumatic for the boys, not less. If you come down, you can explain to everyone what happened and why. And Edward will bring the twins to see you.' Eve had no way of knowing if that was true, though she thought it might be.

At last, very, very slowly, Fifi lowered herself to a crouching position.

'Can you manage?' Eve asked. 'Can I help you?'

But Fifi shook her head. 'I don't want to kill you too, even if only by accident.'

She shuffled very gingerly along the edge of the roof, until she was right outside the dormer window, and Eve stood back to let her in.

42

Greg Boles and DC Olivia Dawkins took Fifi away, and the minute they'd gone, Eve burst into tears. Nothing could ever excuse what Fifi had done. The fault was hers and the crimes were horrific. But the fact remained that if Duncan hadn't tried to blackmail Edward, he and Hattie would still be alive and poor Jack wouldn't have been left injured and traumatised. He'd gone about getting his own way with a breathtaking ruthlessness. If he'd lived, he'd be on criminal charges too.

Byron and Angela had managed to keep the twins and Cesca away from the hall as the most upsetting events played out. They'd carried on looking after them until Edward felt able to tell them what had happened. Fifi had begged him not to tell them about the fire. She was going to plead guilty, so none of it would come out at a trial. Eve wondered what he'd do. She had a hunch he'd admit it one day, but she very much hoped he wouldn't do it now. The twins had enough to cope with.

It was heartbreaking to think of them adjusting to the news about their mum, but there were expert counsellors who would help Edward manage the situation. He was going to resign from work, downsize to a cheaper home and make sure he was there for them.

The village, meanwhile, was rallying round. Moira had set up a rota of people who'd look in on the family, take them meals and so on. Eve noticed she appeared on the list at least once a day and guessed her crush on Edward was still in full swing.

'Blimey,' Viv said, when Eve told her. 'Poor, poor man.'

Meanwhile, Jack was out of hospital.

Eve had been to see him to apologise for the call which had brought on the attack. She still found it hard to fight tears when she thought of how kind he'd been. The day after she'd visited, *he'd* sent *her* a bunch of flowers. It was all wrong.

He, Eve and Viv were all trying to support Angela, who was grinding through the paperwork to repay Duncan's debts and sort out her move back to London. Eve had seen her and Cesca with Byron a couple of times, so they were clearly still friends.

Eve's worries that Byron was unhealthily obsessed by her had faded, as new facts emerged. It turned out that he was seriously rich and giving clearly came naturally to him. When she asked him about buying Cotwin Place, he eventually admitted, with many blushes, that he was giving it to Jack. He hoped the Built Heritage Trust might award him the grant they'd promised Duncan, so he could hire a team to finish the restoration. Either way, Jack would be 'back where he belonged', as Byron put it. And rather than following Angela to London, he was going to rent somewhere on the south coast. Reading between the lines, he wanted to give her plenty of space. But if she and Cesca decided to visit, Eve could tell how happy he'd be to see them.

Over in Long Stratford, the Pied Piper was still closed, and half their clientele were piling into the Cross Keys. Jo had spoken to Susie Parks and it was as Eve had thought: she'd put two and two together and challenged her husband over a possible affair with Posy Fifield. Steve had admitted Hattie could have been his. Eve wasn't sure where they'd go from there. It was all a long time ago, but Steve sleeping with Susie's best friend was a massive betrayal. Jo had lent Susie a shoulder to cry on and there was talk of Steve moving away, just as Fifi's dad had done. What a pair of rats.

The police had found Hattie's fingerprints on the Parks' son's car, next to where it had been keyed. Viv said it proved it was good not to wash your car too often.

Gradually, information on the criminal case against Fifi filtered through as well. The papers were full of it of course, especially with her being a lady. It turned out it had its disadvantages after all. Jo had lost patience with the hacks that filled the pub, though her husband Matt had managed to upsell them from beer to whisky, which had swollen the pub's coffers nicely.

Meanwhile, Fifi had told the police everything. Eve gathered from Greg that she knew she'd got it wrong about poor Jack now.

Eve was preoccupied with thoughts of her, Edward and the boys as she sat down to finalise the opening of Duncan's obituary.

Duncan Blake – restoration expert and television presenter

Duncan Blake, the charismatic presenter of documentaries such as *Living with the Past* and *Within These Walls*, has died aged forty-five. A woman has been arrested for his murder.

Duncan grew up on the Kesham estate in Suffolk, in a tiny damp cottage his father was entitled to, thanks to his job as stable hand there. The Landers family, who owned Kesham, were thought of as affable, but they likely had no conception of what life was like for the Blakes, who were living in poverty. Duncan's parents scrimped and saved but Duncan's mother was plagued by poor mental health and ultimately, when the marriage broke down, neither parent had the capacity to care for their son. It was then that Lionel Landers rose to the occasion. Duncan was already dating his daughter Josephine, and far from objecting, he saw Duncan's promise and invited him to live at Kesham. Meanwhile, Duncan and Josephine talked of marriage and living there for ever.

But then Duncan's life was turned upside down again.

A long-standing lover of Lionel's came to light, along with the three children she'd had by him. Instead of weathering the storm, Lionel sold the estate and arranged a move to California, hooking a highly paid job.

Josephine, rocked to her foundations by her father's lies, lost faith in love and Duncan. She ended their relationship and flew with her family to the United States.

In the end, she was right in her assessment of his character, but he only showed his true colours much later. Being abandoned at that stage through no fault of his own must have had a profound effect. Apart from anything else, it forced him away from idyllic Kesham. He met and married Angela, a woman he loved dearly, but his fixation on regaining what he'd lost interfered with the life they might have enjoyed together. He wanted to come home, to move to the estate and occupy the hall he'd once thought would be his. He didn't care what it cost, and that led to his downfall.

Eve sat there, staring at the words. She thought she knew now what Edward had meant by Duncan being able to compartmentalise. He'd had no problem conducting an affair with Fifi to get what he wanted for him, Angela and Cesca. In his head, he'd got them each in separate boxes and he was using one of them to benefit the other. Just as he was using the scam with Hattie to get free labour to benefit his family. But Eve saw it as an excuse he'd made to himself. What it really amounted to was arrogance and a lack of empathy. He hadn't been able to imagine how Angela would feel when she found out.

Robin entered the room, took one look at Eve and grabbed her hand. 'Not an easy one to write. I know nothing can change that, but I just bumped into Byron.'

Eve tried to focus on that. She was glad he'd been innocent, and Angela too. 'What did he have to say?'

Robin smiled. 'He wanted to thank you for ironing things out and "giving Angela and Cesca some sort of peace", as he put it.'

'Ah, that's kind. Palmer might have got there in the end.'

Robin raised an eyebrow. 'I doubt it. Anyway, Byron didn't just want to *say* thank you.'

Eve frowned. 'How do you mean?'

'He gave me this. Wouldn't take no for an answer.' Robin handed her an envelope. Inside was a booking for the most charming-looking boutique hotel just round the corner from Green Park in London, within walking distance of Shaftsbury Avenue. The location, close to the West End, was handy, since Byron had enclosed tickets to see a show too.

'Oh my word.'

Robin held up a hand. 'I have to confess, he checked the dates with me first. Swore me to secrecy. He insisted we must have a proper break after the one at Hideaway House didn't work out. He says if we go and enjoy ourselves, then he'll be happy. The hotel's dog friendly, and there's a sitter who'll look in on Gus if we go out without him.'

'As Viv would say, that Byron's a good egg. Can we really accept all this? It must have cost a packet.'

Robin smiled. 'He'd be terribly hurt if we didn't. I think we'll just have to grin and bear it.'

A LETTER FROM CLARE

Thank you so much for reading *Mystery at Hideaway House*. I do hope you had fun trying to solve the clues! If you'd like to keep up to date with all my latest releases, you can sign up at the following link. Your email address will never be shared, and you can unsubscribe at any time. You'll also receive an exclusive short story, 'Mystery at Monty's Teashop'. I hope you enjoy it!

www.bookouture.com/clare-chase

The idea for this book came to me after watching one of those TV shows where someone embarks on a major building project, absolutely determined to achieve their goal. Instead of looking at the standard reasons someone might do this, I played around with more sinister drivers, looking at why success might be so imperative, how low my character might stoop to achieve their goal and who they might anger in the process!

If you have time, I'd love it if you were able to write a review of *Mystery at Hideaway House*. Feedback is really valuable, and it also makes a huge difference in helping new readers discover my books. Alternatively, if you'd like to contact me personally, you can reach me via my website, Facebook page, Instagram or on Bluesky. It's always great to hear from readers.

Again, thank you so much for deciding to spend some time reading *Mystery at Hideaway House*. I'm looking forward to sharing my next book with you very soon.

With all best wishes,

Clare x

www.clarechase.com

 facebook.com/ClareChaseAuthor
bsky.app/profile/clarechase.bsky.social
instagram.com/clarechaseauthor

ACKNOWLEDGEMENTS

Very much love and thanks as ever to Charlie, George and Ros!

And I really can't overstate my gratitude to my fantastic editor Ruth Tross for her clever, incisive input, which is always invaluable. Big thanks too, to the entire Bookouture team who work on my novels. You can see what a phenomenal group effort it is by looking at the following page, where everyone involved is mentioned by name. They are the most fabulous, skilled and friendly group of professionals and it's an honour to work with both them and Ruth.

Love and thanks also to Mum and Dad, Phil and Jenny, David and Pat, Warty, Andrea, Jen, the Westfield gang, Margaret, Shelly, Mark, my Andrewes relations and a whole bunch of family and friends.

I'd also like to thank the lovely Bookouture authors and other writers for their friendship and support. And a hugely appreciative thank you to the generous book bloggers and reviewers who pass on their thoughts about my work, including some who have been with me right from the start. Their support is truly incredible, and it's also a joy when newcomers join in.

And finally, but crucially, thanks to you, the reader, for buying or borrowing this book!

PUBLISHING TEAM

Turning a manuscript into a book requires the efforts of many people. The publishing team at Bookouture would like to acknowledge everyone who contributed to this publication.

Audio
Alba Proko
Sinead O'Connor
Melissa Tran

Commercial
Lauren Morrissette
Hannah Richmond
Imogen Allport

Cover design
Tash Webber

Data and analysis
Mark Alder
Mohamed Bussuri

Editorial
Ruth Tross
Sinead O'Connor